INDECENT INVITATION

PIPER STONE

Copyright © 2021 by Stormy Night Publications and Piper Stone

All rights reserved. No part of this book may be reproduced or transmitted in any form or by any means, electronic or mechanical, including photocopying, recording, or by any information storage and retrieval system, without permission in writing from the publisher.

Published by Stormy Night Publications and Design, LLC.
www.StormyNightPublications.com

Stone, Piper
Indecent Invitation

Cover Design by Korey Mae Johnson
Images by Depositphotos/VitalikRadko

This book is intended for *adults only*. Spanking and other sexual activities represented in this book are fantasies only, intended for adults.

PROLOGUE

*Y*ou Are Cordially Invited...

Welcome to the world of Dark Overture.

You've been selected to participate in a special interview.

Candidates must be open minded, prepared to make significant changes in their lives.

If chosen, you will be well compensated, but you must agree to the terms of the deal made.

This once-in-a-lifetime offer will expire in twenty-four hours.

CHAPTER 1

ristol

"Miss Winters."

Trite. Dismissive.

Those were the two words to describe my new boss's attitude as I walked into his posh office, the beautiful texture of his Blood Heart wooden desk drawing my attention.

"Mr. Harrington. I've excited to become part of the firm."

I'd worked my ass off over the last few years, graduating top of my class from the University of Georgia. That hadn't come without sacrifices, my personal life taking a backseat to my studies. I'd finally landed a job with the most prestigious firm in Atlanta after several months of searching. The waitressing job at a greasy spoon had barely paid the bills. Obtaining a job at Harrington, Moorefield and Sutton seemed like a dream come true.

He adjusted the jacket of his high-dollar suit, taking a few seconds before giving me a hard, cold stare. "I'm afraid we're going to have to let you go."

The words were immediately shoved into a vacuum, a slight echo pounding in my ears. There wasn't a chance in hell that I'd heard him correctly. "I beg your pardon?"

His single curt nod of affirmation created a wave of shivers. "Certain... discrepancies have come to our attention."

Our. The word meaning the three partners who ran the firm with an iron fist. I'd heard all about their reputation before applying, but I'd been prepared to start at the bottom, slaving my way to an associate position. "I'm... sorry? I have no idea what you're talking about."

Mr. Harrington took a full minute to walk to his floor-to-ceiling window, staring out at the beautiful Atlanta skyline before answering. "You really should be more careful who you spend your personal time with. Sadly, Senator Langford is married, his wife a very good friend of mine."

Oh. My. God.

My entire world was crumbling before my eyes because of a three-week affair with a man who'd explicitly told me he wasn't married. Granted, I'd been the fool not to recognize him but as soon as I'd realized he had a family, I'd been the one to break it off. Besides, that had been three years earlier.

"That was a long time ago, a mistake I fixed as soon as I learned who and what he was." My words were stated with utter defiance. I couldn't believe that in this day and age I would lose a job over something that occurred on a normal basis with male colleagues.

"Unfortunately, discretion and high moral values are required within this company. You failed to meet those requirements. While I'll consider providing a recommendation, I suggest you take a significant amount of time to consider your wayward behavior." He turned to face me, a smug expression on his face.

"Wayward behavior? Are you seriously trying to insinuate that even a fine upstanding gentleman like yourself hasn't made mistakes? Oh, I'm sorry. You're not a gentleman." I'd unleashed my fury and while I'd been taught never to burn bridges, I refused to accept condemnation from a man I knew had two mistresses.

As he leaned over his desk, he smiled. "Ms. Winters. I suggest strongly that you learn that good behavior is a requirement within this industry. I'm certain you can find your way to the exit."

And there it was. I'd been ceremoniously dismissed.

Fuck the man.

Fuck the firm.

Fuck...

I'd not only burned a bridge. I'd torched it.

Now what the hell was I supposed to do?

* * *

"Rent overdue. Car insurance overdue. Electric ready to be cut off." I said the words out loud like they'd change anything. Furious as well as humiliated, I tossed the mail onto the kitchen table, kicking off and tossing my shoes against one of the cabinets with vehemence. I'd hoped it would make me feel better.

Nope.

Nothing could at this point.

Not even the bottle of wine I'd purchased on the way home. I studied the clock, realizing it was a little before eleven in the morning. As I placed the small box on the counter, the one holding my beloved pictures and a couple of trinkets I'd intended on putting on my desk, my new desk in my brand new office, I cringed. What in the hell had happened? How had my boss found out about an affair that had been kept in the shadows the entire time?

Huffing, I leaned against the counter, uncertain of what or if there was anything I could do. Had the great senator talked, confessing to his wife? Nothing was certain except for one thing.

I was finished in Atlanta. There wouldn't be a single firm that would hire me. Gossip traveled faster than water through pipes. As a bitter laugh erupted from my throat, I noticed an odd envelope buried in the stack of overdue bills.

Black in color.

Interesting. I walked closer, tentative for no other reason than to find out who sent a greeting card or anything else in a black envelope. When I picked it up, I realized the material was actual parchment, my address written in gold calligraphy with no return. Now my curiosity got the better of me. When I pulled the simple black note card into my hand, the writing the exact same, I shuddered.

An invitation.

INDECENT INVITATION

But not just any invitation. An offer for a job interview. What? I was stunned, laughing nervously as I turned it over. The location of the interview was on the back, including the time. And the appointment was for the next morning. Jesus. Dark Overture. I'd never heard of the company, although Atlanta was a huge city.

After ripping off my coat, I walked into the living room to my small desk, the invitation in hand as I opened my laptop. My hands were shaking as I popped up the internet, typing in the company's name. There was nothing but a landing page.

"For those with exemplary tastes, we carefully select the right match able to provide solutions to your needs. And your darkest desires."

While there was a phone number, there was no address, no indication of what the single quote was referencing. I sat back, turning the card over several times. There was no name of the company owner and no additional information I could glean. A laugh finally bubbled to the surface. There was no way I was going to a blind interview. None. This was obviously some kind of scheme.

I tossed the black card on my desk, shoving it out of my mind. So what if it was only eleven in the morning? A glass of wine sounded perfect after the shitty morning I'd had. After all, it wasn't every day that someone began their descent into full bankruptcy.

* * *

"You are out of your freaking mind," I whispered as I peered up at the skyscraper in front of me, the all glass building ominous in the shadows of the cloudy day. I hadn't given the invitation another thought for about an hour.

Then all I'd done was pace the floor, debating the odds that the invitation was real. After that, I'd tried to think about whether to move back home or throw my resume out to every other law firm in the city. Nothing seemed practical or realistic.

So here I was, standing in my best suit, red in color just because it made me feel powerful, wearing my tallest heels and an attitude. I almost snickered at the thought as I checked the four resumes that I'd brought with me, the papers carefully placed in my leather folder. I looked bold and professional, ready to take on the world. Maybe this would be my lucky day.

Taking careful yet calculated steps with my head held high, I walked into the building. Dark Overture was on the top floor. In fact, the company took up the entire top floor of a massive building. Okay, so they had to be legit. Right?

The elevator was empty, something I was grateful for. The silence allowed me to catch my breath, as well as release several audible whimpers. By the time the doors opened, I'd calmed my nerves.

Liar.

At least my little voice was wide awake.

The small marble foyer gave way to a set of etched glass doors, the entrance as grandiose as the invitation.

When I walked inside, I was impressed by the clean, modern interior, the beautiful artwork adorning the walls. The man behind the receptionist desk appeared well dressed, his smile genuine.

"You must be Bristol Winters. We've been expecting you. Allow me to see if Mr. Darke is ready to see you." Without waiting for any kind of response, he disappeared through a set of double doors, leaving me all alone in the oversized, posh reception area. While the most beautiful classical music filtered into the room through unseen speakers, I'd never felt so uncomfortable in my life. Mr. Darke had anticipated that I'd agree to the interview. Who was this man?

Fortunately, I didn't have to wait long, the handsome and very efficient receptionist returning. "Mr. Darke will see you now. Let me take you back."

Through a labyrinth of corridors, I was finally led to another set of double doors. He opened one, ushering me inside and immediately closing it behind me. I was stunned at both the opulence of the office as well as the incredible view outside the floor-to-ceiling windows. Standing in front of one of them was a tall, muscular man dressed in a charcoal gray suit.

He didn't flinch or move at all after the door was closed. I stood like a lost waif, scanning the contents of the office. The furnishings were beautiful, masculine, and very expensive. I was way out of my league.

"Bristol Winters. Recent graduate of the University of Georgia with a four point six average, receiving the highest honors as well as recommendations from several professors. You also received a glowing commendation from the law firm where you interned. You were selected to work at Harrington, Moorefield and Sutton over several more qualified applicants given their previous work experiences."

I shifted back and forth from foot to foot, his portrayal of my life leaving my mouth dry.

"Unfortunately, I just heard that you lost your illustrious position yesterday. Isn't that correct?"

"How did you find that out?" Now I was edgy.

"I do have my sources including very powerful and influential friends, Ms. Winters. Until recently, you were a waitress at Mac's Diner where you received on average two hundred and fifty dollars a week. You have no record, not even a parking ticket. You have several friends, although you are fastidious in maintaining an admirable work ethic. That includes eliminating dating to any degree other than a few social events you attended during the last few months. You have one hundred and nine dollars in your bank account. You have no savings. Your electric is about to be turned off and your rent is past due. Given you were recently fired, I would say your choices are bleak."

I was both in awe as well as incensed, bristling. The lengths that had been gone to were unimaginable. How the hell did he find out so many details? "I don't know who you are given your website provides zero information, but how dare you delve into my private life. Mine. I think I made a mistake in coming here." When I turned to go, I heard the man chuckle. My God. Whoever he was, he sure had balls.

When he turned around very slowly, I was taken aback instantly by his stunning good looks, the bluest eyes I'd ever seen, the kind that pierced right through to your soul. His tie brought out the shimmer in those eyes, his crisp white shirt starched and perfect.

Just like the man.

With his dark hair and commanding ways, I could tell he was a man of power.

"I will add feisty and highly intelligent to the list, which I suspected was the case. You are perfect."

"Perfect? For what?" I dared to walk closer, trying to keep my head held high. Meanwhile, I was shaking all over.

"As the invitation notated, this is an interview, Ms. Winters, or would you allow me to call you Bristol?"

"Who are you and what is this company?"

"Excellent. A woman who desires to get to the point. Another plus. Allow me to introduce myself. I'm Daniel Darke, owner of Dark Overture. The company was founded almost nine years ago to provide a coveted service to men and women who require not only privacy but special skills for life experiences or goals that they are trying to accomplish. As you might imagine, they are willing to pay handsomely for my due diligence, including mandated fees for the services of my employees."

As I tried to take in what he was telling me, I found myself moving closer. "What kind of *services* are you talking about?"

"I assure you they are discretionary in nature and entirely different for each client. While I am made aware of certain aspects, my clients are well aware that there are rules that must be followed at all times or the contract becomes null and void, their payments forfeited in their entirety."

"I'm not a prostitute, Mr. Darke."

He laughed, giving me a hard onceover. "That's not what this company is about, Ms. Winters, although what occurs between my employees and my clients is entirely private and yes, sometimes extremely personal. Again, rules must be followed. There are always consequences if they aren't. Are you interested in learning more?"

Consequences.

Wasn't that nothing more than a part of life in general? I should know.

While I wanted to have the courage to race out of his office, never looking back, I honestly had no other choice, at least nothing appealing. It certainly wouldn't hurt to find out more. Then I could walk out and never look back if necessary. "I'm listening."

"Very well. Take a seat, Ms. Winters. This will take about two hours of your time. May I say that very few people ever make it this far. I search through thousands of possible invitees before making a selection. I'm very particular. You should consider yourself lucky. Your beauty, your talents, and your skills are impressive and exactly what my client is looking for."

I'd never felt more like a piece of meat in my life.

"How did you find me?" I asked.

"I use various methods that I would not want to get into my competitors' hands."

His look was stern, just as dark as his name implied.

Still curious, I did as he commanded, easing into the luxurious leather chair opposite his desk. I remained nervous as a kitty cat.

"Before we get started, I will need you to sign a confidentiality agreement. The clients I serve prefer to remain anonymous. In addition, I will not allow anything that we discuss to be mentioned to the public. Those are my rules. I'm certain you can understand." As he shoved papers across the desk along with an expensive pen, I glared at him.

INDECENT INVITATION

Understand? What I understood was this was making me even more uncomfortable. I pulled the two pages into my hand, taking my time to read them over. There was nothing odd in the requirements, just a standard promise to keep every communication and experience private. After a full five minutes, during which Daniel Darke said nothing, I finally scribbled my name on the bottom. I had to be out of my mind, but my curiosity continued to increase.

"Perfect. Now, we get into a few of the specifics." He finally sat down behind his desk, although he continued to remain formidable.

"Who is this client?"

"I assure you that he is a reputable man, one of wealth and respect. I can tell you that he's from a very good family, his education top notch."

"What's the catch?"

"I assure you there is no catch." He picked up another set of papers, leaving them in front of him. "While my client has the autonomy to make the final selection, it is my belief that after your initial meeting, he will request continuing. You suit every one of his needs to perfection."

My God, the man was pouring it on thick. I wasn't certain whether to be giddy or insulted.

"And exactly what does that mean?"

Daniel smiled, the gesture far too provocative. "A good number of the details are between you and my client; however, I can tell you that you should be prepared for significant changes to your life."

"Changes that will require my flexibility."

His smile indicated I was still winning points. "Absolutely. As I mentioned, if selected, you will be well compensated."

"Meaning what, Mr. Darke? While I don't mind jumping through certain hoops, I do value truth in the reason behind my sudden change in behavior."

He hesitated for a few seconds as if debating whether or not to answer me. "My client is prepared to offer you one million dollars initially. Once your required task has been completed, you will be given another one million dollars. Does that suit your expectations?"

I was floored, my mouth suddenly dry. I found it difficult to breathe, my throat almost entirely closed off. "Are you kidding me?" This had to be a joke. No one offered that kind of money for a few dates.

That meant there was a hell of a lot more that would be asked of me. I wasn't certain I could stomach going through with it. But what if I could? The money would go a long way to providing a new life. I was shaken, trying to pull myself together. There had to be something wrong with his client.

"No, Ms. Winters. I am not in the habit of joking about money."

"What's wrong with him? There has to be something horribly amiss in order for him to go to such expensive lengths in securing a date."

Exhaling, he studied me for several seconds before answering. "Not only are my clients powerful as well as wealthy, they prefer no attachments. This isn't a date, Ms. Winters. This will entail several weeks of your life. As far as my client, he is… particular."

"Particular."

"Which is why I am convinced you are exactly what he requires. Is this something you are interested in?"

The man obviously was getting off on our conversation. I took my time before answering, weighing all the pros and cons that I could think of. A single meeting. "Why not, Mr. Darke? As you said, I have nothing to lose; however, this initial meeting will be a public location."

"Absolutely. That is one of the rules, Ms. Winters." He shoved another black envelope across his desk. "Inside you will find the details of your meeting with my client occurring this evening, including a recent photograph. Given my requirements for initial privacy, you will only know each other by first names. While my client was provided with a basic fact sheet regarding you, I suggest you refrain from providing too many additional details until the contract is signed. Do you understand?"

"Yes, that's crystal clear." The wealthy client had the advantage of knowing about some of my background while I'd been told nothing. The perks of the affluent.

"In addition, money will be wired to your account later this evening. Hopefully, that will cover any expenses you may incur as well as compensate you for your time. My personal and very private email is enclosed, which you will use only once, detailing your experience with the evening's event. Then you will have until noon tomorrow in order to finalize your decision. At that time, you will call me at the number provided inside this envelope with your decision. If you choose in the affirmative, then you will be provided with further instructions and requirements as well as the final contract. At no time will this offer be discussed with anyone. Do you understand me?"

While I'd already signed the confidentiality agreement, I had a feeling his words weren't a simple request.

They were a threat.

Whatever I'd gotten myself involved in, I had a terrible feeling that I wouldn't be able to get out of it.

"Yes, sir. I understand completely. And I'm certain you understand that as a practicing attorney, I will go over the contract with a fine-tooth comb?"

His expression didn't change to any degree, yet his eyes shifted in color, the light creating a dark shadow. "Very well, Ms. Winters. While both my client and I enjoy finding a woman of such vigor as well as power, you should realize early on that you will be required to follow the terms of the contract without question. If you break those terms, there will be consequences."

A cold shiver trickled down my spine, but I refused to allow Daniel Darke to realize he'd gotten under my skin. "I look forward to the challenge."

CHAPTER 2

Houston

"Your father is going to die."

The words continued to reverberate in my mind, the call in the middle of the night initiating a chain of events that I could no longer avoid. There'd been no explanation, no idea of the caller's identity. The number had been blocked, likely a burner phone that had been tossed seconds after providing the warning.

After the first thirty seconds, I'd laughed it off. When anyone calls you at two in the morning, they're usually blitzed out of their mind. While I certainly didn't advertise the fact that I was the son of a powerful man, it was also no secret. For all I knew, one of the other assholes at the brokerage firm made the call just to piss me off. Within days, I'd forgotten all about it.

Then my sister had left a message that couldn't be avoided. She was worried my father was heading for a breakdown or worse.

Ready to be carted off to prison.

Not that I gave a shit about his welfare, but I did give a damn about Ashley. She was far too young, perhaps blissfully innocent to the true ruthless nature of my father. Still, even that hadn't shifted my life's objectives or altered my way of life one damn bit.

Until the final call from my father's attorney.

Yeah, that had set things in motion. And here I was, honoring my father's demands that I return home or else.

Fuck him.

I could beat him at his game.

Ridiculous.

I'd reflected on the single word more than once since my meeting with the owner of Dark Overture. Sadly, I felt I had no choice but to use a firm who could provide exactly what I needed in the short term. I'd heard of Daniel Darke's ability to find the perfect candidate for every client's needs. While he required privacy for his company as well as others who requested his particular services, there was always someone willing to talk, risking the signed nondisclosure agreement. Daniel's reputation was interesting. The man was ruthless, calculating, and extremely successful.

That's why his payment terms were extraordinarily high.

Up to this point, the man seemed worth every penny.

If that changed, he'd feel my wrath quickly.

I sat in prime position inside the quiet corner bar, remaining in the darkness and able to see clearly the moment when his selection walked in through the door. While there was always a chance that the candidate wouldn't show, fear of the unknown crippling, Daniel had assured me that the woman selected not only suited my every desire but was tenacious, even bold. I chuckled at the thought as I peered down at the recent photograph taken of the prospective candidate. I'd read over her file, the limited information providing only what Daniel believed I should know.

Every time I glanced at her picture my cock twitched, my hunger sadistic and brutal. I was a man lucky enough to have any woman I desired, but none of them had ever satisfied me. Perhaps I was incapable of harboring anything but sexual feelings, no matter how beautiful the specimen. That's why the arrangement with Dark Overture was perfect.

No long-term obligations.

No emotional bullshit.

And absolutely zero possibility that there would be anything further.

Granted, the price tag was steep, but given my current state of wealth, I could certainly afford it. In doing so, my estate would continue to grow at a delicious pace. Enjoying the perks of an indecent proposal was merely a bonus.

I took a deep breath, drinking in the sensual atmosphere. The piano player was doing his best to provide the perfect backdrop to the setting, the music slightly on the gothic side, just as I'd demanded.

I swirled my drink, scanning the empty location, a smirk remaining on my face. When the door opened, I checked my watch. Bristol was right on time.

While the women who'd accompanied me to various black-tie events and concerts, dinner parties, and other required social events had been gorgeous, they'd never intrigued me like the woman walking through the door. There was something almost majestic about her from the way she held her head high, her long and dazzling red hair shimmering in the dim lighting to the manner in which she carried herself as she walked past the few tables. My cock was now pinched against my zipper, my balls tight as fuck. If I wasn't careful, I would lose absolute control with her, something that I loathed from any man for any reason.

I shoved her picture into my pocket, sitting back against my seat.

As she shifted her gaze from one side of the room to the other, I pulled my glass to my lips, licking the rim, my filthy thoughts shifting to imagining the taste of her pretty little pussy. When she finally shifted her gaze in my direction, she didn't express a single emotion whatsoever.

That only made me want to break down her defenses, peel away what appeared to be a haughty layer as if she believed herself to be better than the arrangement. My God, all I could do was envision her naked, her voluptuous body displayed and ready for my use. In her stunning violet dress, the material hugging every curve, I knew that any man who saw her would crave spending a single night in bed with her. She was my prize, my conquest and while she had no idea at this point, she would succumb to my every demand.

No matter how brutal or sadistic.

While she continued to advance toward my table, I could easily tell she was gathering intel about who and what she'd gotten herself involved in. Little did she know I was considered a monster in disguise, brutal and ruthless and not only in business.

Bristol now stood in front of the table, eyeing me as she would a predator, her eyes cutting right through me. I was going to enjoy the hell out of this.

"Houston?" she asked, her tone full of annoyance.

"Yes. Please sit down, Bristol," I directed, snapping my fingers at the bartender. "I've already taken the liberty of ordering you a drink."

She exhaled, the sound still managing to be contemptuous. "Let me guess. Mr. Darke scoured through my trash in order to find out the kind of alcohol I prefer."

I couldn't help but laugh. "I take it you don't approve of his methods?"

Bristol eyed me carefully before finally sitting down.

On her terms.

I could see that she would need harsh discipline from time to time. The thought only boosted my arousal.

"I don't appreciate being spied on. Would you?" she asked. As she raked her hand through her hair, several lurid thoughts shifted into the back of my mind.

"Mr. Darke is surprisingly resourceful."

"I don't like surprises, Houston. I'm a calculating woman, very organized and I prefer to be told the details of every deal I'm presented with."

"Then I believe this arrangement will be to your tastes." I couldn't take my eyes off her. Her complexion was utter perfection, her intense green eyes watching my every move. While I was unable to tell if she approved of the dangerous man sitting in front of her, that didn't matter in the least.

She was mine.

Mine for the taking.

Mine for the breaking.

I had no doubt she'd sign the contract.

The thought created a wave of electricity, pushing my longing to the limits.

Bristol glanced around the bar again as the bartender brought the drinks. When she glared at the glass of wine, my thoughts continued to remain dirty and demanding. "I find it interesting that the bar is completely empty on a Thursday night. Is this your doing?"

"Guilty as charged. I thought you'd prefer to have a conversation in private."

"Are you trying to impress me, Houston, because if you are, don't waste your time."

I knew enough about her hardships to realize that the offer was one of her extremely limited opportunities, although I refused to insult her to bringing that point to her attention. However, I didn't like to be pushed. "I think we need to get something straight, Bristol. I'm Dark Overture's client. You are the potential candidate for a life changing event."

"And what makes you think I need a life changing event?" Her glare was not only arrogant, it was laced with venom.

My God, I wanted to feel the woman writhing underneath my body, begging for me to fuck her. The vision was almost too intense to maintain my control. "You must be aware that Daniel provided me with a file with pertinent information on your current situation. I would assume your difficulties would make you very open to possibilities."

She huffed before taking a sip of her wine, shaking her head. "You're obviously the one in desperate need, Houston, or you wouldn't have spared no expense in making the arrangements for this first meeting. I think you're the one who is desperate for the possibilities as you call them."

While I'd insisted on a highly intelligent woman with a law background, a being who could hold her own when required, her attitude was starting to become irritating. Before I had the opportunity to answer, she leaned over the table.

"You have no idea what I need, Houston." Her arrogance continued.

"As you might have guessed, Bristol, I want for nothing in my life. I prefer the finer things and I don't mind paying for them. What I don't have time for are games of any kind. I have a very busy life."

"I'm exactly the same way. Unfortunately, I wasn't given much information about you other than being provided your first name and a picture. However, I was assured that every aspect regarding your life was investigated and that I had no reason to be concerned. I hope that's true."

I took my time answering. "Make no mistake, some of my colleagues would call me ruthless, some would use the term dangerous, but Mr. Darke performed his job as stated."

"All right. That's acceptable. However, I have a few questions before we continue. What do you do for a living?"

I hesitated but there was no reason not to provide her with an answer. "I'm a day trader."

She seemed almost amused. "A stockbroker. Fascinating."

"I do very well for both myself and my clients."

"Hmmm… Tell me, why would a man of your obvious… stature require the help of such a unique and expensive company? Not all women play the kind of games you mentioned. You rent out an entire bar, including a musician. That means you have the money to do whatever you want, including the ability to find a suitable girlfriend."

"Because I don't need any complications in my life. I'm certainly not looking for a girlfriend. I've had those, plenty of them. The relationships didn't end well. I prefer a business arrangement and nothing more. You will accompany me to various events during the course of the next few weeks. Then you can return to your meager life. Well, it will be different given the money you earned."

While she seemed to accept the answer on face value, her eyes held the same irritation as before. "Perhaps I can see why your relationships concluded on a bitter note. I'm curious what kind of woman you requested."

Chuckling, I was becoming more intrigued by her every minute. "One of absolute beauty and grace, a woman who could handle scintillating conversations as well as able to provide enjoyment by her company alone."

"So a Barbie doll is out of the question?"

"You have a mischievous streak, Bristol. I like that." I laughed, enjoying the way her eyes flashed.

"We all have different sides. Don't we?"

"I'm pretty straightforward. What you see is what you get."

Bristol was studying me again, dissecting every word, her eyes attempting to bore into my damn soul. "And you're not telling me the truth, Houston. You need more than just arm candy for a few events. That's not something you have to pay two million dollars for. The question is why are you lying to me? What do you have to hide?"

The fact she could see right through me was both intoxicating as well as infuriating. Perhaps Daniel had made the wrong choice. I pushed my drink away, doing my best to keep my anger in check. "Fine, Bristol. Have it your way. I am need of your expertise as well as your beauty."

"My expertise. I would assume that means given I'm an attorney is the expertise you're talking about."

"You would be correct." I sensed the connection between us, a combined desire that was carnal, savage in nature. However, if I accepted the selection, she would be forced to learn she had certain rules to follow. Breaking them would mean instant punishment. My heart thudded rapidly just thinking about it.

She shifted her glass back and forth, finally taking a sip. "At least you were truthful with me."

"I promise to be as honest as possible. I hope you will do the same."

"I'm generally always candid. That's a necessity in my line of work."

"Understood." An awkward moment of silence settled between us, but the electricity continued to build. "There is a business portion to our arrangement. I believe your understanding of contracts will be helpful."

"Helpful. That piques my interest but unless I know more, I won't be able to make a decision as to whether this is a right fit."

She was being just as cautious as I'd envisioned her being.

"As you might imagine, I only feel comfortable providing limited details until a deal has been struck. However, I will tell you that it involves certain obligations with my family."

"Then how are you going to explain me to your family? I doubt they will be very forthcoming to a girl you barely know."

Sighing, I tapped my fingers on the table, my patience wearing thin.

"You are very astute. My father is a formidable man. You will be required to act as my fiancée, a woman I've known for several months."

"I'm sorry. What did you say?"

I wasn't planning on telling her anything, but I could sense that she wouldn't budge until provided with some level of information. "You will portray my fiancée for a short duration before we exchange wedding vows. After that, you will be required to maintain the illusion of our marriage for a period of three months. At that point, there will be a suitable breakup then you can return to your life. As you were obviously told, you will be well compensated, and of course I will be required to handle any additional expenses including suitable attire. I assure you that you will find the arrangements more than acceptable."

"An arranged marriage?" Her eyes opening wide, she shook her head.

"Absolutely. They happen all the time."

"Not in this country."

"Don't be naïve, Bristol. It doesn't suit you. With what I am prepared to offer, I would think you'd have no issue pretending."

"Then you don't know a thing about me," she rebutted.

I remained quiet, studying her as I took a sip of my drink.

"Is this about impressing your family? That sounds a bit ridiculous," she continued.

"While I realize that might seem odd to you, there are certain necessities and responsibilities within my family, obligations that must be met. This is the best choice I could make."

"Then why do you need my expertise as an attorney?"

Her question was legitimate, driving ugly memories into the forefront of my mind. "I have my reasons, Bristol. That is a portion of the terms of our deal that I'll only expound on after you've signed the contract."

"A deal. Why do I feel like I'd be entering into a contract for some kind of illegal scheme?"

Patience had never been a virtue of mine. Tonight was no exception.

"You were correct in that Daniel not only spent significant time investigating your life, he did mine as well. I'm not a criminal,

Bristol. I am a businessman in need of services. Now, if you'd prefer to wallow in your recent termination, afraid to answer your phone because of bill collectors, then feel free to walk out. I assure you that there will be a replacement within a day."

While I wasn't certain what to expect in the way of a reaction, the fact she tossed her entire glass of wine in my face was surprising as fuck.

She jerked to her feet, standing over me as if she could easily dismiss not only my presence but the money without issue. "My God. I must have been a fool to think this… arrangement as you call it was on the up and up. This is nothing but crap. I don't need your deal, Houston whatever your name is, or your money. You see, I have integrity. The question is, do you? Don't bother. I already know the answer." As soon as she started to walk away from the table, the barbarian in me reacted instantly.

I grabbed her by the wrist, dragging her back to the table as I rose to my full height.

"Let go of me." She pummeled her fist against me, her dazzling eyes flaring with jolts of current.

"I don't think so." I was aching from being so aroused and a simple whiff of her exotic cologne was enough to make me drunk on desire. The animal attraction we shared was intense and the way her body molded against mine was breathtaking. Dragging her closer, I cupped her chin, tilting her face. "You are truly exquisite, Bristol." When I crushed my mouth over hers, she was shocked, pressing her palm against my jacket and remaining unmoving.

Then she did everything she could to get away, but the more she wiggled her hips, the hungrier I grew, the longing to take her off the charts. She tasted of wine and cinnamon, further enticing my senses.

Bristol continued to push hard against me as I thrust my tongue inside, exploring the dark recesses of her mouth. I was thrown by the effect she had over me. A stranger. A selection made by someone else.

But she'd awakened the man I'd buried deep inside.

Maybe Daniel Darke was worth every penny I'd spent.

A few seconds later, she stopped fighting, fisting my shirt, her tongue darting against mine. The kiss became even more passionate and a part of me wanted nothing more than to drag her into the bathroom for some privacy. I resisted the savage urge, sliding my hand over her shoulder, tangling my fingers in her long hair. Every cell was on fire, my heart skipping beats.

When I broke the kiss, still keeping her close, she took several shallow breaths.

"You're one feisty woman, Bristol. Be careful when you tangle with a beast."

"You're not a beast. You're a bastard," she half whispered.

"You're right."

After shoving her hands against me, managing to break free, she shook her head. "Have a good night, Houston. We will not see each other again."

"We're not finished with our conversation yet, Bristol."

"Yes, we are."

Another round of Neanderthal took over as I yanked her arm, pushing her over the edge of the table.

"What in the hell do you think you're doing?" she hissed, flailing her arms in a vain attempt to lash out at me.

I wrapped one hand around her long neck, using the other to rip her dress up to her waist. "Where I come from, women don't talk to men that way and they certainly don't toss wine in their face." I allowed drips of the red wine to fall across her back as I slipped two fingers under the thin elastic of her panties, snapping my wrist.

She gasped, undoubtedly from the sound as well as the force used.

"What… What are you doing?"

"I'm teaching you a lesson," I answered. "Bad behavior can't go unpunished." I could feel her entire body tense but the second I took a deep breath, a growl permeating the space around us much like the scent of her desire. I pulled her red lace thong to my face, drinking in her sweet essence. She was wet, just as hungry as I was and all I wanted to do was take her like the animal I truly was.

Perhaps that was exactly what was required to seal the deal.

I shoved her panties into my pocket then I brought my hand down across her bottom, every part of me shuddering. The adrenaline rush was unlike any I'd experienced before. Even my blood pressure was rising, my breath skipping as I peppered her beautiful rounded bottom with several brutal smacks, moving from one side to the other.

"Stop. Damn you, stop it," Bristol roared, almost managing to get out of my hold.

I leaned over, grinding my hips against her. "I suggest you learn how to be a good little girl. That's vital in order for our deal to work."

"Fuck the deal."

Every word out of her mouth dripped of sensuality. I continued the harsh punishment, my fingers tingling from both the sensational touch of skin against skin as well as the heat building in her bottom. Even in the limited lighting of the bar, I could clearly see a warm blush washing over her rounded cheeks. "Such nasty words for a lovely young woman. I can tell you've needed discipline in your life."

"To hell with you. Let me go or else."

"I don't like to be threatened, Bristol," I said under my breath before smacking her several additional times. Her scent was growing stronger, the fragrance making my mouth water. I was lightheaded, every muscle in my body tensing as the desire continued to increase. My focus was becoming blurry, but I was aware the bartender was doing everything in his power to keep his eyes averted. He'd failed more often than not.

"Trust me," she barely managed, "I'm making you a promise."

"We shall see." I fisted her hair, forcing her legs open even further, allowing me to see the glisten of her pussy lips. "You're very wet, Bristol. If I didn't know better, I'd think you enjoy being taken in hand."

"And you'd be a fool, not just an asshole." While she did everything to try to maintain control, I could tell she was failing rapidly, her breath becoming labored.

I was far too famished, the longing almost debilitating. I certainly hadn't planned on the evening turning out like this. I also hadn't figured that the candidate would be as rebellious as Bristol. Goddamn, I wanted the woman. She was actually the perfect fit whether she knew it or not. However, she would need to be tamed or the plan wouldn't work. At least I was the man to do it.

"Let. Me. Go." She used a significant amount of force, able to push up from the table, shifting until she managed to kick me in the thigh.

"That's going to cost you. I think I'll start your punishment all over again."

When a moan slipped past her lips, I entangled my fingers in her hair, yanking out the chair and pulling her down with me. The feel of her shifting back and forth across my lap was entirely too sinful. Spanking her in the middle of a bar fueling my sadistic side.

"What the hell is wrong with you?" she said in a fragmented voice. I could tell she was losing her will to fight.

"Absolutely nothing. The sooner you realize that the better. I simply handle a situation when necessary." I slid my fingers down the crack of her ass, using two and parting her swollen folds. I closed my eyes as her single whimper floated into my ears. The sound was lovelier than the musician tickling the ivory keys. "However, you are quite incorrigible."

She wiggled and tossed her head back and forth, muttering under her breath.

I couldn't help myself, dipping my fingers into her tight channel, fighting another disruptive growl as her pussy immediately slickened my fingers. As I pumped several times, adding a third finger and flexing them, she let out a series of scattered pants, her lovely body quivering.

"Very wet. Are you thinking about when I fuck you? And I assure you that I will fuck you."

"Fucking crazy. You're just fucking crazy."

I couldn't help but notice her words were now whispered.

When I slid my juice-covered fingers across my lips, the taste of her created an explosion of need that threatened to derail the rest of my common sense and humanity. After I began the spanking once again in earnest, concentrating on covering every inch of her bottom in order to provide a round of discipline she wouldn't forget, I was forced to realize that this girl could spell trouble in more than one way. She could manage to get under my skin, something I couldn't allow to happen.

At least for tonight, I was taking what belonged to me.

She lay limp across my lap, no longer fighting me. I rubbed her heated bottom, taking several deep breaths. The touch of her skin was scintillating, searing the tips of my fingers. The moment I draped her across the table, scooting the chair closer, she moaned.

"What are you doing?" she managed, her voice breathless.

"Feasting." I pushed her legs up and apart, inhaling and holding the amazing scent of her feminine wiles. Just the sight of her glistening pink pussy was enough to shove my cock against my zipper. It had been a hell of a long time since I'd had this kind of reaction to a woman. I planned on taking full advantage of it.

"No," she moaned, yet didn't try to get away. "Bastard."

"Something we've already agreed on." I dug my fingers into her thighs, lowering my head and darting the tip of my tongue across her clit.

She bucked up from the table, her chest rising and falling. "This is insane."

I didn't hesitate, sucking in her tender tissue, taking her clit into my mouth. Every sound she made further fueled my desire, every quiver of her body shooting jolts of electricity through me. When I thrust a single finger between her swollen folds, she pressed her hand over her mouth, turning her head toward the window.

After licking up and down her pussy several times, I blew a swath of hot air, chuckling in a dark and demonic tone. "Are you worried someone will see our filthy interlude?"

"You are... horrible."

"Or are you angry that you're enjoying the act of pure sin?" I plunged a second and third finger beside the first, thrusting hard and fast.

"I'm not... I would never enjoy this or you."

"Your body betrays you," I growled then buried my head into her wetness, lapping up her sweet cream. While there was a distinct possibility that I'd just voided a contract before it was signed, I refused to deny my desires.

Bristol's breathing became shallow, her entire body shaking. In the warm glow of the various candles, her skin shimmered.

"Oh... You are..." Unable to finish her sentence, she slipped her hand over her eyes, as if attempting to pretend this wasn't happening. That only made me want her even more.

I rolled my thumb around her clit, driving my other fingers as deep inside as possible. She was so wet, hot as Hades.

I'd decided that she was the perfect candidate, and nothing was going to stop me from getting what I wanted. The second I removed my fingers, she gasped. When I smacked her pretty little pussy lips several times, she couldn't stop a series of moans. I resumed my feast, driving both my tongue and fingers in a beautiful orchestration. There was no doubt I was bringing her close to an orgasm.

I refused to stop, licking and sucking as her body writhed. All I could think about was fucking her, shoving my cock deep inside.

"No. No…" She pushed up from the table, staring at me with glassy eyes and the second a climax rushed into her system, she bit down on her lower lip to keep from screaming.

The taste of her was sweet ambrosia, her juice filling my mouth, sliding down the back of my throat. I was crazed with need, flexing open my fingers as I pumped brutally. A single climax roared into a second, goosebumps popping along every inch of her body.

I took my time, savoring the taste as I studied her reaction, enjoying the way her lovely mouth twisted in frustration. After pressing my lips against the inside of her thigh, I eased back.

Only when she'd stopped shaking did I lower her legs, pushing away my chair. There was something about this woman that I craved. As I pulled her into a sitting position, I could see the spunk had already returned.

This time, she didn't bother lashing out. She merely got off the table, taking her time to adjust her dress.

Then she walked out the door.

* * *

"Would you care to explain to me what happened, Mr. Powers?"

I'd met with Daniel Darke on two occasions, both times the man appearing aloof, even arrogant. Today, he held an edge in his voice. He remained staring out his impressive looking window, his hands in his pockets. "I'm not certain what you mean." I eased one arm over the chair, crossing my legs. I'd enjoyed the evening, even though Bristol walking out of our meeting had pissed me off. What was even worse was that I'd thought about her a good portion of the night.

That wasn't like me.

Even her scent seemed to linger on my skin.

He exhaled in an exaggerated manner, shaking his head several times. "Perhaps I should clarify. Do you want to tell me what the fuck you thought you were doing?" He turned around to face me, his jaw clenched, his dark and angry eyes pinned on me.

"Getting to know your candidate."

When he slammed his hands on the desk, leaning over and cocking his head, only then did I feel the least bit uncomfortable. "With very few exceptions, the contract will give you the right to provide discipline as necessary. You'll also be able to wine and dine the candidate, fucking her as you choose fit. The possibility is spelled out to the letter in the contract. However, the terms of our deal were explicit for the initial meeting. You were to do nothing else than get to know her. That meant talking. Enjoying each other's company. That didn't mean ripping off her panties and spanking her in the middle of a public location. From the tone of the Bristol's email, I suspect that when the phone rings with her number attached that she's not going to accept the invitation."

"Then we find someone else." I was curious if she told Mr. Darke everything.

His glare became icier, disbelieving my attitude. "You are a spoiled man, Mr. Powers. I know the reputation of your family pretty well. I have no doubt you were taught that money has the ability to buy everything that you want."

"That's where you're wrong, Daniel. My father taught me that everything and everyone has a price, even if it's not literal money. You just need to find out their weaknesses."

"And what weakness does Bristol have in your opinion, Mr. Powers?"

"While she portrays being in control, even pushing everyone's buttons when she has the opportunity, she enjoys a dominating man. Discipline will be very good for her." My mouth watered at the thought.

I was surprised when he laughed, genuinely amused at my statement. That pissed me off.

"I guess we shall see, Mr. Powers. However, if she rejects the offer, which she has every right to do, then I assure you that my work with other clients will take precedence. I fast-forwarded your request based on your current situation, but I don't appreciate, nor will I tolerate anyone going against my rules. When I find the time to return to your search, you will be required to pay the finder's fee all over again."

No wonder the man was considered brutal and difficult to deal with. While I had significant funds available, the thought of losing a cool two hundred and fifty thousand dollars certainly didn't interest me.

"I stand by what I said. She was intrigued last night, our chemistry off the charts."

"I certainly hope that you're right. From what I could tell, Bristol was the perfect candidate. It would be a shame to lose her over your indiscretions."

Indiscretions.

I'd heard the accusation my entire life and I was sick to death of being told about them.

"What else did Bristol tell you?" I asked casually.

He shook his head. "What did you do to her?"

"Nothing that she didn't want. Or crave."

"You should be very careful, Mr. Powers."

I gave him a hard look. "I assure you that Bristol will take the deal."

"Your arrogance is going to keep you a very lonely man. You can go, Mr. Powers. I'll let you know her decision."

"While I've appreciated your capabilities, Daniel, I am not the kind of man to be told no. You need to keep in mind that Bristol already belongs to me. I suggest you find a way to make that happen. Given what you know about my family, you must realize just how powerful and influential we are. I would hate for your business to suffer. Even worse, I would hate for a man of your stature to come into harm's way."

I rose from the chair, taking long strides toward the door.

"I hope that isn't a threat, Mr. Powers."

I suddenly remembered my conversation with Bristol. "No, Mr. Darke. It's a promise. And I always keep them."

CHAPTER 3

ristol

"Fucking asshole." I glared at the clock on the kitchen wall as I paced then fisted my hands, pretending I was in a boxing match. Envisioning his face helped ease the pain.

And the continued ache.

Why the hell had I remained awake almost all night, my body aching for Houston's touch? I'd been sick with embarrassment at what had happened, furious with myself for going through with the bizarre date. Now I had a decision to make. I shuddered when my jeans shifted across my bruised bottom. The asshole had spanked me! He was nothing but a nasty, rude brute.

He'd been so damn dominating, refusing to take no for an answer.

And he'd spread my legs wide open, bringing me to not one but two orgasms. A cold shiver trickled down my spine from the thought. I'd actually enjoyed it. No, I couldn't have. I'd been in shock. That's all.

"Let me get this straight, girlfriend. You were honored with a one of a kind invitation for a job that will ultimately pay you two million dollars. For that money, all you have to do is marry a gorgeous hunk of a man for three months, a wealthy and powerful man who you are obviously attracted to. Or you can wallow in self-pity, trying to find a job that doesn't leave you smelling like bacon and pork butt. Did I miss anything?" Reggie looked down at Houston's picture, shaking his head. "Mmmm… Hmmm… Girl, if you don't want to marry the stunning ice cream sundae with whipped cream and a cherry kind of dreamboat, I sure will."

I gave Reggie a hard glare. He'd become my best friend almost the day I'd arrived in Atlanta, his free spirit and love of life always able to bring me out of my doldrums. Nothing was going to work today. "Very funny but he's not your type. And what he did to me was humiliating. That wasn't fair."

"Pity, honey. Whew." Reggie jumped off the counter, swaggering closer then giving me a wag of his finger. "Tsk. Tsk, sunshine. You do have a mouth on you, girl. My guess is that Houston the Hunk was giving you a dose of your own medicine."

"By spanking me in the middle of a bar?" I refused to further humiliate myself by telling him about being eaten on top of a table in the middle of a bar on a corner street where thousands of people walked by every day. My God. I was mortified.

Then why is your pussy clenching?

I rubbed my eyes, hating the fact Houston had managed to coerce my body into betraying me.

Reggie chuckled. "Look, so his methods are dominating. What's not to like? You only have to put up with him for three months. That's like taking a vacation. My guess is Mr. Stockbroker has a deliciously gorgeous condo."

"I don't think we're staying in Atlanta. That's just a guess."

"Hmmm… I wonder where Mommy and Daddy are from? I will admit the mystery is almost as juicy as the fake marriage."

"I don't know, Reggie. Something about this seems off." I glared at the clock again, Reggie following my gaze. I had ten minutes to decide.

"Well, you could always come and live with me."

I rolled my eyes. "While I adore every inch of you, I refuse to live in your condo, even as nice as it is. You have far too many boyfriends. I think I'd just get in the way."

"Sugar, you never know," he said, laughing then his expression turned more serious. "I couldn't find much on Dark Overture, but they are a legitimate corporation if that makes you feel any better. You're an attorney. You can look over the contract then decide. No matter what this Daniel Darke says, only put your name on the dotted line if everything is on the up and up. Demand the one million dollars be placed in your account pronto."

"Yeah, I know. I will." What the hell was I thinking? Was I really going forward?

"All right. Tell me about Mr. Sexy."

Sighing, I thought about walking into the bar. I'd been shocked that Houston had rented out the entire space in order to meet me. Although my guess was that the man was grandstanding and nothing more. However, even the darkness in the bar couldn't hide his good looks. Shaggy, dark blond hair hitting just below his shirt collar, broad shoulders, and a muscular body his exquisite suit was unable to hide. His eyes were piercing, and while I wasn't entirely certain of the color, I'd managed to see the gold flecks around his irises. And his voice was what wet dreams were made of.

"He has the most engaging eyes, soulful yet there's something dark within them, as if he's hiding some great mystery or tragedy. He's commanding, the kind of guy that when he walks into a room, everybody stops talking."

"That powerful, huh?"

I wanted to pop Reggie for continuing to tease me, but I was lost in the vision of Houston. "Yes, he's that powerful. He has this distinct swagger about him, as if nothing could ever bother him. And the way he kisses is just..." I sighed, realizing that Reggie's eyes were open wide.

"You didn't tell me you kissed him."

"Well, actually, he kissed me. He wasn't taking no for an answer."

"Sounds like a match made in heaven."

"Try in hell. I don't know. I just have this feeling about him that's unsettling."

Reggie winked. "That's called lust, girl. Unbridled lust. I'm surprised you didn't go home with him."

"Shut your mouth. I'm not that kind of girl."

"By the way, is this Mr. Darke just as yummy?" Reggie asked, chuckling under his breath.

I smacked him in the chest. "You're a terrible man."

"And you love me."

"That I do."

He grinned then snapped his fingers. "Wait a minute. Didn't you tell me that money was wired into your bank account, compensation for your time?"

"You're right. I forgot all about that."

"Why don't you take a look, girlfriend? If this company is legit, then my guess is you were paid well. Maybe a couple thousand dollars. Who knows?"

I wrinkled my nose but headed for my laptop. "I think that's a little steep for just meeting with the guy." Hell, at this point I'd settle for a couple hundred dollars. At least that would mean I could make my rent payment.

When I sat down at the computer, I was nervous and I had no idea why. As I pulled up my bank account, Reggie crowded behind me. He'd been protective of me, acting like the big brother every time we went out to a bar. He was the one who gasped when I pulled up the recent deposit history.

"Five thousand dollars? Are you shitting me? How do I get on this invitation list?" Reggie exclaimed, the sound bouncing in my ears.

I swallowed hard, staring at the screen. "I don't believe it."

"Well, believe it, girl. I think you should have your answer right there. This Dark Overture and Mr. Sexy want you bad, girl."

After closing my eyes briefly, I brushed my fingers across my lips. The kiss had been incredible, the electricity surging between us unbelievable. His husky, deep baritone alone had created a wet spot in my panties.

"Ugh. I don't know." I hated making this kind of decision.

"Go with your gut. Ask that inner voice you have this question. Could you see yourself as Houston's wife even for a short period of time?"

While a part of me wanted to run far away from the deal, my inner voice was nagging at me. "Yes. I could. I might have to punch him in the gut a few times, but he'll get the point."

"There you go. Good girl. Now, make the call before you chicken out."

"You're pushy, Reggie."

"Somebody's gotta be, honey child."

He trailed behind me as I walked back to the kitchen, grabbing my phone. As I dialed the number, my stomach did flips. "Mr. Darke? This is Bristol Winters. I've made a decision."

"I'm glad to hear that, Bristol. And what would that be?"

"Go ahead and send the contract. I will accept your invitation."

"Excellent. I'll email you an advance copy. Then we'll go over the remaining details in my office in the morning. Is nine all right?"

"That's perfect."

"I will see you then. Welcome to the Dark Overture family."

When I hung up the phone, I almost threw up. "Ugh. What did I just do?"

* * *

"You do understand that you are to follow all the rules as stated in the terms of the contract?" Daniel Darke's tone held no inflection yet he studied me with his dark, ominous eyes.

"Yes, I'm aware of the terms."

"Including the possibility of punishment for breaking those rules."

I took a few seconds before answering. Since I'd already been privy to Houston's type of punishment, while I hated it, I could certainly endure a few spankings if necessary. "Yes, I understand."

You must follow Mr. Powers' directions at all times.

You must remain in character while in public.

You must refrain from discussing the terms of the contract with anyone.

Once the assignment has been concluded, you will never disclose the arrangement made.

The rules that had been laid out were succinct and to the point.

"Then I think we have almost everything we need," he said, giving me a nod of approval.

I took a deep breath after I'd pushed the contract toward Daniel. I still had dozens of reservations, but I was confident that I could endure the three months pretending to be married to someone like Houston. "What now?"

Daniel smiled as he leaned over the desk. "Now, we simply need a medical evaluation. Then you will have a few days to prepare for departure."

"Medical evaluation? Since I know you've checked everything else about me, I'm certain you have those details as well." For some crazy reason, I folded my arms over my chest, as if that could keep me from experiencing yet another moment of embarrassment.

"While there are aspects of your life that I could obtain legally, your medical records aren't one of them. As you can imagine, my client wants to ensure that you are free of any issues."

"You mean issues with my sexuality? Or is Houston worried that I'll get pregnant, thereby altering the terms of our contract? If that's the case, I can provide proof that I'm taking birth control."

His smile was likely meant to be comforting. In truth, it pissed me off. "On page eight, section C of the contract you just signed, a medical exam was detailed. You agreed to the terms, Ms. Winters. I assure you that the findings will be kept confidential, unless, of course, a problem is detected. This won't take long."

"Does that mean you have a doctor on staff?" When he didn't answer, I was floored. "My God, you do." I was repulsed, but the fact I'd skimmed over the paragraph meant I only had myself to blame. I yanked the contract into my hand, flipping the pages. The majority of the few sentences didn't cause any heartache.

Except for one.

"He's going to be in the room?" I was appalled, my mind shifting into an ugly blur. My God. This was getting to be a sick and demented situation.

"Standard procedure. I assure you that Mr. Powers will not be allowed to touch you in any inappropriate manner," Daniel said casually. My God, the man acted as if this was no big deal. It was a huge deal to me.

"But he can watch."

"As stated per the contract."

I wanted to call out 'bullshit' but it was a blip in time in order to move forward. I'd been through more humiliating experiences. Right? "Fine. Let's just get this over with."

Everything about the man was perfunctory as he led me out of his office to a private elevator. He remained quiet as I was taken to the floor below. When the doors opened, a cold wave skittered through my arms and legs. The corridor was bleak, the walls completely white without any adornment. I felt like I was in a horror movie, the subject being forced to endure experiments.

As he led me down the hallway, my high heels clipping against the cold, hard tile, I found it difficult to breathe. I'd allowed myself to be tossed in a surreal world where money really was capable of buying anything.

Including a fake wife.

I heard the sound of a door opening and sucked in my breath. The sight of a nice-looking woman wearing a doctor's coat, her smile far too pleasant for the situation, left me feeling sick inside.

"Mr. Darke. This must be Bristol," she said, holding open the door.

"You will be in good hands, Ms. Winters. Once you are finished, Dr. Banfield will show you out. Unless a situation arises, you will have the allotted time to make your arrangements. As I mentioned, I've given you my private number only to be used in case of an emergency."

"I understand." My statement was bland and without emotion.

"Excellent. Mr. Powers has already made arrangements for your initial payment. When your assignment has been completed, I'll ensure the second payment is wired to your account. Good luck, Ms. Winters."

I closed my eyes briefly before watching him walk down the hall, the sound of his shoes hitting the floor sending a series of vibrations into my stomach.

"Right this way, Bristol." After the doctor led me into a small room, she immediately moved toward a computer. "I just need to confirm your identity. Will you provide your full name and social security number?"

I did as I was asked, struggling to keep my nerves under control.

"Perfect. Follow me." Dr. Banfield opened another door, leading me into a standard examining room, yet this one had no pleasantries of any kind. There were no pictures on the walls, soft lighting, or colorful paint. There was a single cabinet, a partition positioned in the corner, and a hard, steel table complete with stirrups. There was also one chair in the opposite corner of the room. The chair where Houston would sit as he observed my moments of shame.

I realized I'd issued an audible hiss after the doctor eyed me carefully. When she smiled again, I wanted to wipe it off her face with my fist.

"I assure you, Bristol, nothing odd is going to happen. I'm going to check your vitals, take a blood test, and do a pelvic exam. That's it. It shouldn't take more than a few minutes. You can go behind the curtain and undress. Make certain and remove everything."

I remained mortified but found myself walking behind the partition, taking several deep breaths before removing my shoes. I was completely numb by the time I managed to remove my dress, fighting with the single hook in an effort to hang it off the floor. When I was completely naked, I was shivering uncontrollably. How in the hell was I supposed to get through this? I managed to grab the gown, the thin frock reminiscent of the one used in my regular doctor's office.

After taking several deep breaths, I walked out. I hadn't heard the door open but there he was, Houston Powers in all his glory. He'd already taken up residence in the chair, his long legs crossed and his face pensive. At least he wasn't gloating, or I would find something sharp to stick him with.

"Right this way, Bristol. You can sit on the table while I take your blood pressure and listen to your heart." Dr. Banfield's demeanor remained pleasant as she guided me to the table, the same plastic smile on her face.

I refused to look at him as she did as she'd told me, taking my blood minutes afterwards. At least I was covered, although the short, skimpy gown did little to hide anything.

"All right. Now, I need to take your temperature. You'll need to bend over the table for me."

It took a few seconds for her words to filter into my mind. "A rectal thermometer?"

"That's all I will use. It's far more accurate."

"Wait a minute."

She patted me on the arm. "All standard procedure, Bristol. There is no need to worry."

I hated the fact tears had formed in my eyes. This was by far the worst, most humiliating experience that I'd ever gone through in my life. But I did as I was told, trying to keep the two-million-dollar prize in my mind. When I leaned over the table, she immediately lifted my gown, exposing my naked bottom.

"Spread your cheeks for me. That will make it easier."

There was nothing I could do but suck in my breath, a wave of heated embarrassment washing over me as I did as I was told. The second she inserted the slender tube, my muscles tightened around it.

"Just relax. This will take a couple of minutes."

I was sick inside, the embarrassment of being treated this way almost overwhelming. To think the bastard was watching me was disgusting. Every part of me shivered as I tried my best to count the seconds, barely able to take shallow breaths.

"There you go," Dr. Banfield said. "You did well."

The couple of minutes were excruciating but finally it was over.

"From what I can tell, you are very healthy. Just maintain that position. I'm going to check your rectal reflexes."

"Are you…" *Out of your mind?* The thought was one I wanted to spew, but decided it wasn't in my best interest. I closed my eyes, fisting my hands. There was nothing more horrifying than the feeling of being invaded in such a personal manner as she slipped a finger into my bottom.

"She's very tight, Mr. Powers. Something for you to keep in mind," Dr. Banfield stated. "Otherwise, perfect."

"I'll definitely keep that in mind, Doctor," Houston said, and I could swear there was amusement in his tone.

"Can we get this over with?" I barked, blinking in order to keep ugly tears from falling.

"Of course. Go ahead and return to the table. Just lie back and place your legs in the stirrups."

I just wanted this over with, yet the entire situation was almost too much to bear. When I was in position, at least the doctor had the decency to block a portion of Houston's view. That didn't make the embarrassment any less or the realization that I'd sold off a portion of my body as well as my soul any less damaging to my psyche. When she inserted the speculum, it was all I could do to keep from whimpering like a whiny girl.

After a few seconds, I dared to shift my gaze in his direction. There was absolutely no expression on the man's face. Just the same hard, cold eyes I'd seen during our initial meeting. This was nothing but business to him. I was just the woman to try to help him get whatever he was searching for.

"I think we're done. You did very well." While I heard the doctor's words, they seemed in a vacuum that was very far away.

When the three months were over, I would never see the bastard again. Money or no money, he would never own even a tiny portion of me.

CHAPTER 4

ristol

The next few days went by in a blur. Between signing the contract then the wretched exam, the event almost scaring me to death, then attempting to move what little mattered to me into storage, I'd barely had any time to sleep. The thought of moving to San Diego, even for a few months, was both exciting as well as terrifying. I'd seen little of Houston, but at least I'd learned his last name. Houston Powers. I'd also learned just how wealthy his family truly was and to say I was just a little bit intimidated was an understatement.

Houston's father, William Powers, had been involved in Silicon Valley early on, serving in several capacities from president and CEO of one of the largest chip manufacturers to being on the board of directors of Google, where he continued to serve. From every scrap of information that I'd been able to find, the family's wealth was listed in the top one hundred on the Fortune 500 list. William also owned two companies outright, both of which were considered worth several million dollars.

I was definitely in way over my head.

Their wealth wasn't the most disturbing fact. There'd been a solid six accusations made of not only unscrupulous activities, but deadly ones, claims made that two enemies of the Powers family had disappeared. While no formal charges had been filed, the information remained in the back of my mind.

Now I stood waiting at the door to my empty apartment, two suitcases positioned next to the wall. My future husband was on his way to take us both to the airport. I felt more like being dragged to the dentist's office kicking and screaming than flying to my new temporary home. An arranged marriage. I thought they'd been outlawed or something.

When I noticed a Mercedes pulling up, I almost locked the door and pitched the entire idea. Sadly, the contract I'd signed was ironclad. There was no way out unless the rules were broken, and those were very few but meant to keep me safe.

What they didn't do was protect me from performing my marital duties. I closed my eyes briefly, struggling to catch my breath. I had to be an excellent actress, pretending that the sun and moon rose and set over the man. That wasn't going to be easy. At least he was excellent eye candy. The thought gave me a smile.

When I heard the rap on the door, for some reason I thought he was just going to come inside. I smoothed down my dress, hoping this was appropriate to begin our fake life together. I'd used some of the money to purchase a new wardrobe, although I had been given limited information on what was expected of me in the way of attire. Somehow, I figured hot pants and a tube top wasn't the best choice.

I was still chuckling as I opened the door. The sight of the man standing in front of me gave me butterflies all over again. I'd expected to see him wearing a suit. His faded but deliciously tight blue jeans and a cobalt blue polo shirt highlighted his magnificent physique. Dreamy. That was the term that came to mind.

He lifted his sunglasses, whistling as he glanced down the length of me. "You look fantastic, Bristol. Are you ready to go?"

"Would it matter if I said no?" Just seeing him again created a wave of nausea as well as excitement.

"A deal is a deal."

Fuck the deal. The words remained on the tip of my tongue.

After raising a single eyebrow, he took both my suitcases into his hands as I retrieved my purse. I took one last look at the small but comfortable apartment. I had a funny feeling I wasn't coming back to Atlanta, although I certainly wasn't going to stay married to him. I was surprised he even opened the door for me.

"I'm not an ogre, Bristol. Believe it or not, I have certain manners," he said with a hint of disdain before closing the door.

I didn't know him at all. I'd been given a basic script to learn.

Where we met and when.

The first date—a lavish party.

Our first kiss. Yeah, that was easy.

The moment he asked me to marry him—over a champagne dinner.

His favorite color—green.

His favorite food—hamburgers on the grill.

His favorite drink—bourbon, neat.

I knew a lot about him but nothing that really mattered, although I had no intention of getting close to him.

With the engine still running, he hesitated, staring out the windshield. "This doesn't have to be a chore, Bristol. We might even have some fun." His statement was almost bitter, the acrid tone he used just as disturbing as the man.

"When are you going to tell me about what you need from me, and I don't mean carnal activities?"

He laughed, the throaty sound sending a shower of vibrations dancing to my toes. I shivered, biting back a moan that threatened to give away I was attracted to the man.

"We will discuss more when we get to the hotel. I don't want to talk about it on the plane."

"Oh, we're not taking a Learjet?"

"I have money, Bristol, but not that kind of wealth. You're a real brat, aren't you?"

"Card-carrying member." But his family certainly had that kind of money. Had he been cut off or refused to play by his family's rules?

"Hhhmmm… I guess it's something I'm going to have to deal with."

The harsh look I gave him only forced Houston to smile. Still, he hesitated. What was he waiting for?

"I have something for you, Bristol." When he pulled a small box out of his pocket, everything that I was doing hit me square in my stomach, the butterflies almost crippling. "You're going to need this. It should fit. You need to wear it at all times. Is that understood?" When he opened the box, I sighed.

Any other girl would have squealed from delight, the huge diamond sparkling in the sunlight. I was sickened at the thought, reminding myself that this was just a lucrative job and nothing more. The money would allow me to settle anywhere else in the country.

Hopefully, I wasn't shut out of every law firm.

He didn't bother putting it on my finger. This wasn't about romance. I took the ring, the weight of it surprising. When I placed the thick gold band on my finger, I sighed all over again. Of course the ring was a perfect fit.

"What I will tell you on the plane is about my parents."

"I think I'm up to speed."

Shaking his head, he shifted the gear into drive. "I should have guessed you'd be thorough in your private investigation of my family. Just keep in mind that looks and reports on paper can be deceiving. My father is a shark, a man with no love for anyone, including his family. I'm surprised my stepmother tolerated being married to him all these years."

His admittance wasn't just a bit odd but very sad. I could only imagine what his family life had been like.

"And one more thing, Bristol. You will obey my every command, no matter what I demand, no matter how dark or kinky you think my request might be. I'm a formidable man and I refuse to accept any level of disobedience. If you remain defiant, I will have no issue disciplining you as necessary. And I assure you that my methods can be as brutal as the incident necessitates. Is this understood?"

The words swirled in my mind as I shuddered. My throat closed off, my breathing ragged and difficult. But I managed to mutter the words he was looking for.

No, the ones he was demanding.

"Yes. Sir."

He snorted, taking one last long gaze before driving away.

The deal I'd made wasn't just indecent.

It was dangerous.

By the time we checked in, we had only a few minutes to board the plane. When he pointed toward a seat, I shouldn't have been surprised. "First class?"

"Only the best for my wife to be."

"You can cut the crap when we're alone, Houston. I know what's required of me. I assure you that I'll be the best little actress you've ever seen in your life."

"And you're going to have to be. Both my father and my brother are untrusting. They could easily see through this charade and if they do, then my life will turn to shit."

"What does that mean?"

He sighed, a blank look crossing his face. Then he turned his head, his magnificent blue eyes mesmerizing.

"It means that I won't be eligible for my inheritance, which includes a significant portion of my father's companies."

"This is all about your inheritance?"

"Not entirely. This is also about that integrity you were talking about. It would seem someone is out to get my father, ruining the family's wealth in the process. I don't intend to allow that to happen."

"I thought you and your father didn't get along."

"Blood is thicker than water, Bristol. That's something you should keep in mind."

I certainly planned on it. While Houston's voice remained steady, it was easy to see how troubled he was about returning to his hometown. Secrets. I knew every family had them, but I had the distinct feeling that his had turned him into the cold, demanding man he was.

"Let's just get the party started," I said through gritted teeth.

After fastening his seatbelt, he leaned over, insisting on fastening mine. I glared at him, my chest heaving as I did everything I could not to spew off some horrible statement.

Remember, you made a deal. Then you can enjoy the rest of your life.

The inner voice wasn't helping at this point. The man was insufferable.

"Relax, Bristol. This isn't going to hurt a bit." His words were far too close to the ones the doctor had said. Even the smirk on his face reminded me of the disgusting occurrence.

"Champagne?" the flight attendant asked, peering over us with a huge smile on her face.

"Why not?" Houston said casually. "This is a celebration after all. I'm taking my fiancée to meet my parents. I think drinks are in order."

"Congratulations!" Her smile was far too bright, her eyes remaining entirely on Houston's face.

And his body.

"I'll open one of our best bottles for you."

"Perfect," he said, chuckling as she walked away.

"I don't think you need to lay it on so thick at this point in time." I couldn't stand looking at him any longer.

I wasn't surprised when he leaned over, whispering in my ear. What did shock me was the way my body reacted, the jolts of current stifling my breath.

"You have no idea how many enemies my family has or where they might be. We maintain our relationship no matter where we are. Is that clear?"

His hot breath tingled every inch of me as it cascaded across my skin. "Enemies. From what I've learned, your father is into computer chips. What kind of enemies could your family possibly have?"

He laughed in a low-slung way. "I never said my family was entirely on the up and up, Bristol. I have told you that my father is a ruthless man. He will do what it takes to get what he wants, including crossing that fine line between good and evil. I assure you that there are dozens of people, if not more, who would enjoy not only watching but participating in his demise. I refuse to allow that to happen. It's as simple as that. Now, behave like a good little girl or I'll be forced to take matters into my hands earlier than I expected."

Hissing, I refused to look in his direction even when the attendant delivered the glasses of bubbly.

"Enjoy. We will be taking off in a few minutes, so I'll need your glasses by then." The flight attendant's perky voice had already become grating.

"Here's to a beautiful venture together."

I finally shot him a look, hesitating before I allowed our glasses to touch.

"I can see I'm going to have my work cut out for me." Sighing, he swirled the liquid in his glass before consuming half the flute.

"You really are a bastard. I don't know why I'm surprised."

"What I am is a consummate businessman who made an arrangement that I thought would be beneficial for both parties."

"Then at least you've done something right."

He growled, the sound reverberating through every cell and muscle all over again. "At least we agree on something, my beautiful bride to be. Sit back and enjoy the trip. We'll be there before you know it."

I'd been lucky enough in my life to enjoy accommodations in a lovely hotel once or twice. Even my parents had spared no expense for a trip to Disney World when I was ten or eleven, but the vision of the interior of the hotel was utterly gorgeous, the lobby encased in floral details and marble, beautiful works of art adorning almost every wall. There were people everywhere, a musician providing island tunes.

Perhaps for the dozens of couples walking through, this was a premier and very romantic establishment to rekindle a romance.

For the couple strolling toward check-in, this was nothing but the first of many pretend moments.

I'd never been to California and the sights from the airplane window as we'd flown into the airport had been incredible.

The afternoon sun had provided a perfect backdrop with a blue-skied, cloudless day.

Houston checked his watch as the bellman led us to the elevator. "We have two hours before we'll need to leave for dinner. That should give us enough time to get acquainted."

"We already are." I fingered the ring he'd placed on my hand, trying my best to keep my mouth shut. I hadn't been able to get his comment regarding enemies out of my mind. He'd promised me additional information, a short but effective soliloquy on what he was attempting to do. Without it, dinner would be abominable.

"Here you are, the penthouse suite." As the bellman led us inside, I was no longer surprised at the lengths Houston had gone to impress me.

Or maybe this was exactly what he'd become accustomed to his entire life.

Either way, the opulence was overwhelming.

"Here you go. If you will, make certain we aren't disturbed." Houston seemed jovial as he handed the man a hundred-dollar bill.

I simply rolled my eyes. He thought he could buy anyone.

"Yes, sir. I'll take care of it for you." The bellman's face was lit up, nodding to both of us before walking out, Houston trailing behind him.

I bristled when he locked the door then swaggered toward me.

"What do you think?"

"We're staying at the hotel the entire time?" I put my purse down on one of the tables. The room looked like a fabulous den in someone's estate complete with a full bar and entertainment center. The view from the sweeping set of doors was incredible, the ocean maybe fifty yards away.

"Only for tonight. I purchased a house for us. That seemed more appropriate."

I laughed, his statement catching me off guard. "Does that mean you're planning on staying here after our deal has been concluded?"

"We shall see. If things go according to my plans, then yes. If not, I'll sell the place. It means nothing to me."

"At a significant loss."

"Perhaps you'd like to purchase it?" He grinned as he walked closer, purposely bumping into me then heading toward the doors, unlocking then swinging them open. "You will fall in love with the ocean. I'm going to venture a guess that you'll also adore my selection of houses. If you're a very good girl, you'll even have the opportunity to furnish it."

"Let me guess. You purchased the house sight unseen."

"I found a real estate agent that suited my needs. If it's not to your tastes, we can purchase another one."

"My God. Money means nothing to you."

"Money is the means to an end and nothing more. It can sully a person easily."

Sighing, I shook my head. "Something you should know about intimately."

He remained inside, not reacting when I walked directly past him and onto the balcony. The light breeze as well as the scent of the ocean was incredible. I knew he was watching me like a hawk. The electricity we shared sparked even though we were several feet apart. I hated my body's reaction, the way my throat felt parched and my nipples scraped against the thin lace of my bra. I clung to the thick iron rails, studying the rolling waves, still so uncomfortable in both the arrangement as well as my surroundings.

While I'd taken a small portion of the original five thousand dollars and purchased several new pieces of clothing, I knew in my gut that the attire wasn't good enough. I also realized I'd be judged on that fact, as well as everything else about myself.

I didn't need to hear his approach. His all male scent merely infiltrated my nostrils. Woodsy yet exotic, it threw me into a place of longing. When he placed his hands next to mine, crowding my space, the heat of his body all consuming, I sucked in my breath.

"What happened at your job?" he asked. The question threw me. "From what I can tell, you are more than highly qualified for the position and the firm is quite reputable."

"What does it matter?"

He inhaled, remaining quiet for a few seconds. "Because that was the motivation for allowing you to accept an indecent business proposal."

"Let's just say that we all make mistakes. Hopefully we learn from them. I allowed my guard to fall and was betrayed."

"Betrayal is something I understand very well. Perhaps the money will lead you to a better life."

"Perhaps."

Another moment of silence settled between us. There was such an edge to our caustic relationship, making everything we did that much more awkward.

"I will enjoy showing you off, my beautiful fiancée."

"Like a trophy."

His laugh was guttural and when he nuzzled against the side of my neck, I did everything I could to pull away from him. "You are more of a feast for the eyes."

I hated the fact I was trembling. "I don't know what you want me to say."

"Thank you would be appropriate."

"Then thank you."

He growled then nipped my earlobe, grinding his hips back and forth. The feel of his hard cock forced my throat to tighten.

"You are going to be a handful, aren't you?" he murmured.

"I'm exactly like you, Houston. What you see is what you get."

"Then I'm definitely going to need to break you."

"That's not going to happen. Not now. Not ever." I stiffened, trying to shove him away with my body.

He pushed me forcefully against the railing. "You will do as I say."

"Damn you."

When he placed his hand over mine, forcing our fingers to intertwine, I managed to elbow him in the stomach. "That wasn't nice, little girl."

"I'm not your little girl."

There was no hesitation. He backed away, able to yank me from the railing. "I think we need to get to know each other better."

"Meaning what?"

"Meaning," he said, grinning, "I'm going to fuck you."

The words shouldn't have stunned me, but they did. I couldn't react fast enough, Houston pulling me toward the room. He didn't bother closing the door. He simply shoved me against one of the walls, crushing my body against it.

"Let me go, Houston. Not now."

"Now is the perfect time. You'll need that beautiful glow when you meet the family. Besides, I've been looking forward to this since you opened your door. I'm a lucky man to be able to feast on something so irresistible."

When he captured my mouth, I remained stiff, unyielding. He had me at a disadvantage, unable to move at all, yet I did my best to slide my hands between us, pressing my palms against his chest. He shifted his hips again, making certain I knew exactly what his plans were for me.

I moaned into the kiss, wiggling until I almost managed to break it. He was having none of it, yanking first one arm then the other over my head. Bucking, I continued to fight, refusing to give into him in any manner.

Houston was much stronger, able to keep me in control while using his tongue to press apart my lips. The moment he swept his tongue inside, an overwhelming sense of suffocation crowded into my mind. I was suddenly frightened, although in the back of my mind I knew he wouldn't spoil the deal.

Or would he?

He was far more egotistical and reckless than I'd originally thought, a man who either had no conscience or didn't care about anyone but himself. He certainly didn't give a shit about his family. Why would I think he'd treat me as anything other than his servant?

I wanted to hate him, to use the anger embroiling every inch of me to remain at a distance in my mind if nothing else. But there was such an enigmatic pull between us, sparks that had lingered for hours after our last engagement. This was going to be no different. The taste of champagne and whatever breath mint he'd eaten fused with a bitter kind of sweetness that I couldn't recognize.

He growled into the kiss as it became more passionate. I continued to yank against his hold, determined to get away from him. Obviously frustrated, he slammed my hands against the wall, the amount of force enough the picture only a few feet away rattled.

Even though he dominated my tongue, I wouldn't engage, trying to numb myself in order to keep from complying. He broke the kiss, laughing softly before nipping my lower lip.

"A little hellion. I like that about you, Bristol, but I will grow tired of the game at some point." He shifted my arm, able to grab both wrists with a single massive hand. I hadn't realized how powerful he was, his sculpted muscles giving him a solid advantage.

I wasn't going anywhere.

"I won't," I rebutted, the whisper little more than garbled sounds.

"I guess you're going to need serious discipline." He chuckled again before dragging his tongue across my jaw.

I couldn't stop quivering as he brushed his hand against the side of my breast. The sensations were dazzling. Still, I wanted to scream at my own body for betraying me. "I hate you." The words seemed ridiculous to spout off, as if they mattered on any level.

"Then hate me. That doesn't change a thing. Besides, I can tell you're wet and hot, hungry to have my cock thrust inside that tight little channel of yours."

"No. Not in the least."

He rubbed his face against mine, the shadow of his two-day stubble prickling my senses. When he continued his exploration, taking his time and crawling his fingers down my side, curling the material of my dress in his hand, there was no stopping a ragged whimper from escaping my mouth.

"Why don't we find out?" he murmured, the tone so husky and sensuous.

I struggled again, rocking as much as the space would allow, but it was to no avail. He simply kicked my legs apart, rubbing his hand between them. I'd already known I was wet, my damp panties now giving me away. He rubbed harder, managing to shove the material between my swollen folds.

"Very nice and extremely wet, Bristol."

"No." The single word was not only futile, it was stupid. The sensations increased, every inch of my skin covered in goosebumps. Even my scattered breathing gave me away.

He slipped his fingers under the elastic, rolling the tip of one around my clit.

"Oh." I closed my eyes as embers burning inside of me caught fire, embroiling every nerve ending. How could this horrible man have such a tremendous effect on me?

"Yes, very wet." Houston dipped his fingers inside, pumping as much as the tight confines of our coupled bodies would allow.

I realized I could no longer feel my legs, the tingling sensations rolling up and down my body even more electrified.

He continued drilling into me for at least twenty seconds before pulling his hand completely free. "I think you need to accept how wet you are. Open your mouth."

"No."

"Do it or I'll be forced to drag you over my knee."

"You wouldn't dare."

He cocked his head, giving me a stern look all while keeping a smile on his face. "Do you really want to try my patience, Bristol? If you think you hate me now, I assure you that you will despise me after doing so. Open. Your. Mouth."

I had no recourse, no possibility of getting away from him. I did as I was told, parting my lips as I glared at him with all the venom I could muster. When he slipped his slickened fingers inside my mouth, I was ready to snap my jaw shut.

"Be careful, little girl. I wouldn't suggest biting me or you won't be able to sit for a week. Suck. I want you to know that I'm not lying to you."

There was such atrocious audacity in the man. This wasn't just about arrogance. His attitude had everything to do with entitlement and good fortune.

And still, I opened my mouth, trying not to gag when he shoved his fingers inside. Even the scent of my feminine wiles disgusted me but there was no denying how wet I was. He enjoyed every second of the humiliating action, his eyes twinkling as he pumped his fingers in brutally.

"Now you know just how delicious you taste." He changed his smile to a smirk. When he was finished, he took a deep breath then wiped his fingers across my cheek. I was shocked when he took a step away from me, freeing my hands.

I rubbed my wrists, keeping my glare pinned on him.

"Remove your clothes." He said the words matter-of-factly, as if he was ordering coffee or a plate of food.

"No."

"You need to learn some respect, Bristol, which you will give me at all times. I expect you to call me sir."

"In front of your parents?"

"When we're alone. Now, I don't think you'd like that lovely dress to be shredded. Undress or that's exactly what's going to happen."

I shot a look out the wide-open door, the closest building only appearing yards away, even though I knew it was much further.

He shook his head. "I assure you that at this moment I have no intention of showing off your gorgeous body. Perhaps that will come in time. You have five seconds to comply or I will follow through with my decision to undress you myself."

There was no winning with this man. There was also no sign of returned respect or even a hint of romance. He was playing into the game he'd prepared and paid for. I refused to allow my embarrassment to get the better of me, even smiling as I pulled the dress over my head, tossing it to the floor.

His smirk turned into an expression of lust, his upper lip curling. "Panties and bra. I need you completely naked when I fuck you."

Swallowing, I reached behind me, fumbling before I was able to open the clasp, pulling the straps of my bra forward. I could swear the man was drooling as he watched my every action. After tossing my bra, I bit back a moan given how aroused my nipples were, the slight breeze floating into the room tickling the hard points. I gave him a huge smile as I shimmied my panties over my hips. I could portray the part, pretending like I didn't give a shit what he was trying to do, which was to break down my defenses.

"Come to me," he said with even more allure in his tone.

I inched closer, trying to keep my breathing even.

He cocked his head, taking a deep breath and holding it. When he exhaled, he blew the hot air across my jaw and neck. "Your scent is like sunshine and musk, a dangerous combination."

Why did the man have to be so good looking, his angular jaw and piercing eyes keeping the fire burning deep within? My trepidation and anxiety about the entire situation took over. I slammed my hands against his chest, catching him off guard, the force just enough to shove him against the back of the couch.

I wasted no time, although I had no idea what I was going to do. Perhaps I'd underestimated the power of his carved muscles. Within two seconds, he'd snagged my wrist, yanking me around to face him then easily tossing me over his shoulder.

"What are you doing?" I snapped.

"Exactly what I told you I was going to do." He took long strides, moving into another room.

I struggled to see where he was taking me, half expecting he'd arranged for a cage of some kind. When he tossed me onto the bed, I scrambled to my knees, almost making it off the other side.

I hadn't expected his laugh, the husky sound bouncing off my ears, sending another shower of electrified quivers pulsing from my fingers to my toes. I also hadn't expected his roughness but as he yanked me backwards, dragging me across the expensive, soft comforter of the king-sized bed, I knew that this was just the beginning of what could be a nightmare.

He wasn't just powerful or ruthless.

He was dangerous.

He fisted my hair, dragging me backward as I remained on my knees. "My God, woman, you test me, but I've never wanted anyone like I've hungered for you." He kept his firm hold as he slipped his hand down my neck, feathering his fingers across my chest. His touch awakened every nerve, my heart racing.

I wanted nothing more than to scream that there was no way I could want him, but I was aching inside from a desire that confused me. He was as dynamic as he was infuriating, not nearly as one-sided as I'd believed him to be. Whether or not there was any goodness in the man didn't matter.

At least for now.

Stars imploded in front of my eyes as he pinched my nipple between his thumb and forefinger, twisting until I cried out. I realized I'd lolled my head backward, taking gasping breaths as the combination of pain and pleasure became a powerful aphrodisiac. I continued struggling for air and when he released his hold on my hair, cupping and squeezing my other breast, I fell into the darkness of lust.

Unbridled.

Filthy.

Sinful.

He flicked his fingers across my other nipple, the ache increasing.

For once I wanted to let go, to refuse being the good girl that I'd tried to be the majority of my life. For once I longed to feel the kind of passion that other women gushed over, a roar of need and hunger meshing together, two people who couldn't get enough of each other.

Only this wasn't about heart-stopping romance.

This was about something much darker.

"You will learn to obey me. For that alone, I'll give you the kind of ecstasy you've never experienced before. If you don't, your punishment will be a swift reminder." His words were like sweet music, his promises ones I'd knew he'd keep. "Stay right where you are."

They also weren't a request, but the kind of command that should send trickles of fear into anyone. Only I was further embroiled in the heated moment, our combined scents of desire crashing together.

As I heard the sound of his belt buckle and zipper, I dragged my tongue across my lips, still quivering, my pussy aching even more. While I couldn't understand my body's reaction, I shoved aside the anger and disdain.

Immediately, I was reminded this wasn't about romance. I felt the pressure of the tip of his cock as he slid it up and down my pussy. I clawed the bedding, yanking part of it as I arched my back.

He smacked my bottom several times, the sound of his ragged breathing matching my anguished moans. But his desire was too great to play some kind of a game. When he pushed the tip past my swollen folds, lights of various colors flashed in front of my eyes.

"Oh. Oh…"

"Does that feel good, Bristol? Is that what you wanted, to have my cock inside?"

"You're so…"

He chuckled. "Say it. Say all the bad words and call me all the names you want to. You're not going to hurt my feelings." He thrust the entire remainder of his shaft inside.

The ache was immediate, my body convulsing from the pressure as well as flashes of immediate bliss. "Bastard," I managed.

"More. I want to hear more." He pulled all the way out, plunging into me again.

And again.

"Asshole," I continued.

He growled, the sound like an animal consuming his prey. "Keep going."

"Son of a bitch. Prick." I was breathless as he pounded into me again, the force rocking my body forward. I did everything I could to push back, with several growls of my own.

"More. I love it when you talk dirty to me, Bristol." He smacked my bottom several more times, chuckling darkly after every strike.

Houston wanted me to feel the combination of agony and ecstasy, pushing me to the limits. "Madman."

"More."

"Brute. Barbarian."

He tangled his fingers in my hair, yanking me partially off the comforter as he pummeled into me. We were nothing but wild animals, my pussy muscles stretching to accept the thick invasion and I was ready to scream, more. More. More! He sensed my growing excitement, jutting his hips forward as he thrust harder and faster.

I could no longer think clearly, my breath skipping and my mind foggy. He had a way about him that was irresistible, even though hate still coursed through me.

"Imagine when I fuck that tight little ass of yours. Or when I shove my cock down your long and lovely throat."

Closing my eyes, I could feel a climax approaching. Just when I was ready to let go, he dragged me off the bed, pushing and turning me until I was against the bedroom wall. He wasted no time, his eyes dilated as he lifted me into the air.

I was shocked at his strength as he held me aloft, his chest heaving, his eyes dilated. I'd never seen a man so expressively hungry, his need consuming him. I wrapped my legs around his waist, holding my breath as he yanked me down, filling my pussy all over again with his thick cock.

The throbbing sensations were even more intense, our combined electricity exploding like bottle rockets. He yanked my arms over my head, rolling his hips forward as he continued fucking me. Every sound he made was savage, every hard drive of his cock stealing my breath.

"I want to see your eyes when I make you come," he whispered, his nostrils flaring, his mouth twisting.

Together we rocked, the building heat combustible. The scent of him embroiled every one of my senses, his testosterone intoxicating. There was no light or other sound, no sense of being. Just the incredible round of sex.

As a climax started to build, I struggled against him, my body bucking hard.

"That's it. Come for me. I want you to come so hard, baby."

Baby.

The word was so foreign coming from his mouth. "Asshole," I whispered, although I couldn't keep a slight smile off my face.

"Always. Come. Come now!"

There was no way of holding back just to be spiteful. I tilted my head as the stars continued floating in front of my eyes, trying not to scream like a crazed animal. But the pleasure was so intense, the single orgasm shifting into a second or maybe the first one never stopped.

"You're gorgeous when you come," he whispered, the sound strangled. He continued to pump with vigor, slamming me hard against the wall.

I gasped for air, tossing my head back and forth, a string of moans pushing up from my throat. I knew he was close to coming. My pussy clenched and released as the orgasm continued. When his body tensed, I clamped down, pulling his cock in even deeper.

Houston's eyes closed and as he threw his head back and roared, filling me with his seed, I couldn't stop shaking.

An indecent invitation.

A deal I hadn't been able to refuse.

A dominating and savage man.

My thoughts shifted to the note I'd received in the mail.

This wasn't just dark and depraved.

This was… intoxicating.

CHAPTER 5

Houston

Some people embraced every family member no matter how good or bad, how caustic the relationship might be. I'd chosen to walk away instead of enduring the agony of criticism and constant arguments, preferring to try to forge a life of my own on my terms. Little had I known that the lure of significant wealth and influence would draw me back into the family fold.

I hadn't spoken with my father since I'd left almost five years before. Not only had I wanted nothing to do with his tyranny and overbearing methods of fatherhood, I'd loathed his vile and disruptive decisions with regard to his personal companies. He'd acquired dozens of enemies over the years, mostly due to his unscrupulous activities. Given my father's easy acceptance of my arrival, I could read between the lines.

He was fearful he was losing his grip on the industry that had made him worth hundreds of millions. Maybe that's why someone had already planned his demise.

I would never forget the last words my father shouted as I'd walked out of his house, the final confrontation also the last straw.

"You will never make anything of yourself without my help. You are nothing to me, boy, and you never were... Don't come crawling back to me. You will never be welcome in my house again."

They'd been words to live and die by and I'd fully intended on remaining the black sheep of the family, wearing the title like a badge of honor. Sadly, my sister's nagging calls had pushed me into falling into the same trap that always seemed to happen.

Succumbing to the will of my father.

His wishes.

His demands.

Next, I'd received the call from the family attorney on a late Friday night after I'd had one shit of a week. That had pushed me over the edge.

"Your father is going to die."

When I'd called, I'd expected the pompous man who'd become wealthy off my father to share some scathing story, not the bullshit he'd relayed.

The trust fund that had been established when I'd been born, the initial cash funded with my mother's money, wouldn't be released. Of course that had been directed by my father. At first, I'd laughed, even hanging up on the old coot. When he'd persisted, along with subsequent calls from my sister begging me to reconsider coming home, I'd finally listened to the details.

And they'd curdled my blood.

The thirty-five million dollars would go to my brother unless I completed certain tasks.

One: return to San Diego and establish residence.

Two: work alongside my brother in preparation of him taking over the great empire, as my father liked to call his regime.

And three: marry a suitable candidate in order to keep me grounded.

The bastard of a man my father had turned into had actually used the word candidate as an insult. He'd known since my early days of adulthood that I loathed the concept of marriage, had never planned on settling down and raising a family. Some excellent psychiatrist would tell me that I was pushing back against a difficult childhood and the best thing for me to do was get married.

That was freaking bullshit.

I'd left without looking back and I'd enjoyed almost every minute of freedom building my own goddamn empire. I'd also amassed a fortune of my own, enough to enjoy a good living. With a gorgeous skyscraper condominium and two expensive cars, I'd been living large.

Returning had less to do with the money than the principle and the fact my brother wasn't going to get a red cent of what I deserved. He was a fucking bastard.

Then there was the mysterious call in the middle of the night. There was a more substantial reason for my father's sudden push for my return.

The last straw had been a phone call from my father. While he'd been conceited as normal, he'd almost sounded eager to see me again. As if I'd bought his lines of bullshit.

No, I could read between the lines. He was panicked. What the hell did he want me to do?

I took a deep breath as I twisted my hand around the rental car's steering wheel. Tomorrow, I'd purchase something bright and shiny just to piss my father off. Sadly, tonight I'd committed to being on my best behavior. I snickered at the thought.

"Where are we going?" Bristol asked. She'd been quiet since our encounter.

I looked over, enjoying her exotic perfume as it wafted into my nostrils. Everything about her was surprising and few women ever astounded me. I also couldn't seem to keep my hands off her. While she belonged to me for at least three months, I certainly hadn't planned on hungering to the degree I was.

"A prim and proper club my father belongs to. I suspect my brother does as well."

"Do I need to know anything personal about your family? If so, how am I going to fake that unless you provide details?"

I laughed. "Because my entire family knows how much I hate my father, loathe my brother, tolerate my stepbrother, and feel sorry for my stepmother. The only person I do really care about is my sister, Ashley. She didn't deserve to be born in such a fucked-up family."

She twisted her head in my direction, narrowing her eyes. Up to this point, I'd told her nothing about them or just how deep my hatred for them went. However, it was time she understood that I wasn't merely a playboy looking for cash.

"Wow. I'm glad you finally told me something."

Sighing, I shot a look into the rearview mirror, my instinct telling me it wasn't beneath my father to have us followed. "Don't all families have dirty little secrets, Bristol?"

"No, not all of them."

"I will agree to disagree. All you need to know is that my father is truly a merciless beast. I am here because of demands made in order to obtain access to my trust fund. While I know what you're thinking, I couldn't care less about the money. I have very personal reasons why I don't want anyone else to get their hands on it."

"That's something you're not going to tell me, is it?" she asked.

"I will."

"And my involvement?"

After giving her another glance, I could clearly see the smirk on her face. Actually, I didn't blame her. I could only imagine what she was thinking.

"As I mentioned before, I will be happy to share more of the reason why you were selected, but only after this blasphemous dinner. I prefer to have your unbiased opinion on my various family members."

"A blended family you can't stand. This should be interesting."

I snickered as I made a turn. Twilight had settled in, the full moon highlighting a vast number of twinkling stars. I'd never really cared about paying any attention to the scenery around me. I'd grown used to the insides of ancient buildings positioned in pristine but very secluded locations during my days in boarding school. Then there'd been the boardrooms I'd frequented during the time I'd worked for my father. There was no working with the man. He didn't appreciate team members or partners.

At least until my brother, Chase, had stepped up to the plate, announcing that he wanted to follow in the footsteps of my father. Even in Atlanta, my chosen career had prevented me from truly enjoying the outdoors. Perhaps it was time to make a change.

"My mother died when I was a child. Within three months of her death, my father had brand new arm candy. They were married less than three weeks later. If you're asking if I'm close to Charity, I am not. In fact, she never had a motherly bone in her body, although she'd brought an unwanted spawn into the fold. I feel sorry for the two of them. That's all."

"And this hatred for your brother?"

I could see the giant rounded orb of the club just over the horizon. A lump formed in my throat. I'd loathed the place, the pomp and circumstance of the upper echelon of society sickening on every level. I'd never fit in, not that I'd ever wanted to. "Chase is a tool. He's five years older and always treated me as if I was the unwanted child. We've never been close, less in the years before I left. However, you will likely find him charming. Be careful of him, Bristol. He's like a scorpion, his sting deadly."

"Here I thought my family had issues," she half whispered.

I laughed softly as I made the turn into the long, winding driveway, the tree-lined aggregate just as I'd remembered. Every acre of landscaping was perfectly manicured, the garden staff ensuring that every flower bloomed and every shrub was trimmed to exactly the same height. I'd often wondered if whips and chains were used to keep them working in the brutal sun.

"As I said before and wholeheartedly believe, every family has secrets, but not every family is born out of evil."

I could feel her heated gaze and all I could do was smile. As I pulled up to the grand entrance, a servant in a white coat immediately popped out of a glorified hut, scrambling in my direction. Almost certainly he was judged on his performance and timing, scrutinized for his demeanor and if he'd been able to handle the multiple insults I'd heard given over the years. Sadly, the position had one of the highest turnovers, drunken fools stumbling out of the club insisting they could drive.

After shifting the gear into park, I turned my full attention toward her. "Make no mistake, Bristol, my family will be searching for any sign of a ruse. While I believe in your abilities, I need to reaffirm that you belong to me as stated in this contract. As of now, you are a happy fiancée eager to start a new life with the man you love. Anything less won't be tolerated. Do we have an understanding?"

She gave me one of her sweetest smiles, batting her eyelashes on purpose. "Of course, darling. I am your dutiful servant."

Between her words and the inflection of her voice, my cock was immediately pushed to full attention. I would much prefer to devour her in the lobby of the affluent establishment than endure sitting through food and wine. My sadistic needs would be fulfilled later. One taste of her wasn't enough.

I grabbed her jaw, digging my fingers into her skin. "I am being serious. If you act out in any fashion, I'll be forced to punish you."

Jerking away, she gave me a scowl. "I'll keep that in mind. Sir."

I climbed out of the car, adjusting my jacket. I'd purposely chosen black for the color, a crisp white shirt and scarlet tie as accents. I'd changed significantly in the five years, time spent in the gym well worth the effort. After closing the door, I took a few seconds to drink in the atmosphere before walking around to the passenger door.

"Will you be staying for dinner, sir?" the attendant asked.

"Unfortunately, yes. If you will, make certain the car is easily available for a quick getaway. You will be handsomely rewarded."

His eyes opened wide then he grinned. "You got it, sir. I mean, yes, sir."

I took her hand, easing her out of the vehicle. In all probability, my father had sent a lookout to watch my arrival. His curt text confirming I was in town established his mood for the night.

Surly.

Nothing had changed.

"What is your sister's name?"

"Ashley. You will find her... let's just say entirely different than the rest of the family."

"If you were close, why didn't she come and visit you?"

"Because she was forbidden to and I assure you that she has been well versed in following my father's rules."

"Jesus," she said under her breath.

I led her inside and almost instantly we were approached by the same man I'd always called a gatekeeper. He'd aged, his eyes just as lifeless as I'd remembered. The club sucked the life out of everyone who worked there.

"Sir. Do you have an invitation to be here? This is an exclusive club. Members only." He barely gave Bristol a single glance. As per the rules, women were not allowed to frequent the club alone, nor did their requests have any viable meaning, unless authorized by their male counterpart.

"How quickly you forgot me, Roger." I waited, tilting my head as he searched my eyes.

When he smiled, the expression genuine, I gave him a respectful nod.

"Oh, my goodness, sir. I am so sorry I didn't recognize you. Welcome back!"

"Roger, you can call me Houston. Unlike the rest of my family, I actually don't bite kind people."

He seemed embarrassed, his face reddening. "You know the protocol, sir. Your father is patiently waiting for your arrival."

Of course, I'd decided to be fashionably late on purpose. "I think you mean he's fuming around the collar."

Roger laughed then immediately stopped the noise. "Let me take you to your party. I do hope you enjoy your evening."

"Let's just hope there aren't any fireworks, Roger. I'm not certain the great city of San Diego could take it." I offered my arm to Bristol, giving her a wink. Why not have fun with this? It was just the beginning of a ridiculous but profitable adventure.

While she accepted like a dutiful bride to be, I could see the look of apprehension in her eyes. She didn't like this any more than I did.

Roger led us through the sparsely seated smaller dining room, a private room located at the very end. While the club had been redecorated, it still had the same stodgy, conservative feel that I'd grown used to. At least a good portion of the members appeared younger than I remembered. Perhaps the old codgers had finally died off.

May they rot in hell.

"Here we are, sir. The private dining room." When he backed away, he finally acknowledged Bristol, giving her a slight smile.

"Well, here we go, darling. Keep your guard up and you'll do just fine," I whispered in her ear, nuzzling against her neck if for no other reason than to hope we'd already been seen.

"Is drinking allowed?" she asked.

"Absolutely. You'll find it's a necessity around my family. Just make certain you keep your faculties. My father is a wolf after all. He will enjoy making you his prey."

"I thought that's what you were."

A real smile crossed my face as I walked her inside. Almost immediately, my father noticed our arrival, but he kept his seat, not bothering to notify the others. In his eyes was the same contemptuous look that he'd given me the day I left. I could see the old bitterness remained. What a shame.

The table was full, although there weren't any unexpected guests, unless I could consider my stepbrother, Riley, to fall into that category. He'd also changed, turning from nothing more than a boy to a hulking man. I had no information on him, nor did I care what his life had turned into. He'd been nothing more than a baby when he'd arrived, yet he'd never been accepted by anyone but my sister.

Perhaps Ashley was the only decent member of our family.

My beloved sister noticed us next, shrieking as she tossed her napkin, almost turning over her chair in order to race in our direction.

"Oh, my God. Houston! I thought you'd never get here." She flung her arms around my neck, half laughing and half crying. "I've missed you so, dear brother."

I rubbed my hands down her back, taking the time to stare every other family member in the eyes. Chase was smug as usual, Charity obviously on her fourth or fifth cocktail, and Riley curious, his eyes flashing.

"I've missed you too, sis. Allow me to introduce the love of my life. Bristol Winters, this is Ashley Powers."

True to form, Ashley studied Bristol from head to toe. Then she burst into a bright smile and wrapped her arms around Bristol in the same loving way she'd done with me.

"Welcome to the family. For a woman to be able to snag my brother's cold heart, you must be very special. I hope you'll allow me to be involved in your wedding plans."

Bristol laughed genuinely, her body language tense. Then she relaxed, her bright smile exactly as I needed. "I don't know about special. I think I kicked your brother's ass to get him to love me."

"Oh, God! She's a pistol. I'm going to love spending time with you. Come on and meet Daddy." She took Bristol by the hand, dragging her toward the table. "What do you have planned for the wedding?"

"We've only talked about a few details," Bristol said, sneaking a glance in my direction. "I'd be glad for some help."

"Fabulous! I know all the best caterers and I guess you're going to need a dress."

"I need everything. Your darling brother sprang the trip on me as a surprise. I feel like a lost puppy."

"Then you have the right girl to help you," Ashley almost purred, clapping her hands together.

I took my time, keeping a smirk on my face as I walked closer, unfastening my jacket then shoving my hands into my pockets. The rest of the family needed to come to me.

"Son. About damn time you made it. I know your freaking flight was on time," dearest Daddy barked without getting up from the table.

"Well, my beautiful bride was eager to… relax, Pops. And I do love indulging her." I shifted my gaze in Chase's direction, daring him to rise to his feet, surprised when he did.

He moved around the table, taking his damn sweet time. This was nothing but a line being drawn in the sand or perhaps the preparation of a shootout at the Powers Corral. Either way, it was clear to see he was furious at my decision to return.

"Brother. I'm surprised to see you. I understand that you're a stockbroker." Chase stated the words as if the career was demeaning, below our family.

"Yes, a demanding and lucrative position. I found the time. Hell, I felt it was important. Besides, I'm making changes in my life."

"You must be Bristol." There was utter disdain in his tone.

"Yes, and you must be Chase. I'm sorry to say, I've heard almost nothing about you." There was a bite in her tone, as if the woman was already feeling the need to be protective of me. While I found that fascinating, I pressed my hand against her back as a reminder to be the lovely little sparrow for the evening.

Chase gave his usual smile, shaking her extended hand. "And you are a complete surprise. I must say, my brother's tastes have improved."

"Can we just enjoy an evening together," Ashley dared to say. "Pathetic."

"I'd watch your mouth, sister. You're coming dangerously close to making a fool of yourself." Chase's bitter words caused my sister to retreat into a shell.

"I told you that you shouldn't have dumped your fiancée," I heard my father hiss to Chase. Suddenly, my brother's anger was directed toward our father. Another ugly secret in the family. I should be used to them by now. I snickered at the thought.

"Leave Bridge out of this," Chase snapped, his jaw clenching.

I was actually surprised when Riley jumped up from his seat, his expression one of disgust directed toward the rest of the family. He made a wide berth around my father's chair before advancing. "Don't let the bullshit scare you off, Bristol. We're always contentious." There was something entirely different about him than before, as if he'd grown a backbone. Well, he certainly had to, or he'd be swept under the coattails of Chase and my father.

"Don't worry," she said, holding her own.

"He's right. Let's sit so we can get this over with. I have more important things to do." I guided Bristol to her seat, smiling at my father in spite. I immediately motioned for the waiter, ordering drinks for both of us. At least Bristol didn't contest, but I could tell she was fuming. Hell, I didn't blame her in the least. This was just the farce I knew it would be.

"Why don't you tell us where you met my brother, Bristol? I'm certain it will be enlightening to hear." Chase eased into his seat, immediately pushing the chair away as he grabbed his drink.

And so the charade began in earnest.

While I wasn't necessarily surprised that Bristol was able to provide such a stunning performance, appearing giddy from her adoration of me, I wasn't certain her acting skills would be enough to pass the first test.

There was a moment of utter silence after she finished speaking, my father and Chase exchanging glances while my stepmother held her usual nasty glare.

"To the two lovebirds," my father said, lifting his glass. "May you find all the happiness you seek."

Ashley suppressed a giggle, which I could tell was difficult for her.

"What are your plans for the wedding?" Charity asked. "I'm certain we could obtain a reservation at this glorious club." She lifted her glass as she shifted her gaze in my direction, her eyes glassy.

"As Bristol said, we haven't made any formal plans. I was thinking maybe an outside wedding and reception." I didn't give a crap about the wedding, but it certainly wasn't going to be held in the horrific setting of the club.

"That is just like something you'd say, brother," Chase snarked.

"I think an outdoor wedding would be fabulous." Bristol kept her smile but damn if the woman didn't have an icy stare.

"As long as it's appropriate for the Powers family, the correct guests invited, then I don't give a shit. I do hope your relationship can last." My father's booming voice didn't just indicate disapproval. He was already challenging both of us as to the validity of our special union.

"Don't worry, Pops. I'm certain it will be the elegant affair that befits such a glorious family." My counter was repaid by another hard, cold glare from my father. All I could do was smile.

And so the fucking evening progressed, the conversation growing edgier by the minute. While Bristol was able to maintain her calm and collected manner the majority of the time, she'd thrown enough barbs of her own to both titillate as well as infuriate me.

"I think I need to freshen up," Bristol stated.

When she shoved her chair away from the table, quickly walking away, I took a deep breath.

"You're going to need to teach her some manners, boy," my father said, swirling his damn cognac as he smirked at me. "She needs harsh discipline in order for your marriage to work. I think that will help create a harmonious environment in the household."

"Is that how you handle Charity, Pops? By issuing strict rules?"

"Don't you dare talk to me that way, boy. I am your father." When he pounded on the table, I'd had enough, jerking to my feet. "You could do well learning from my actions. They've served me for a hell of a long time. Not that you ever listened to my advice over the years."

My God. The man had gotten worse over the years.

"She's mine to do with as I please."

Ashley placed her hand on my forearm, whispering under her breath, "Don't."

Sighing, I walked away, milling through the other dining room toward the restrooms, waiting until she opened the bathroom door. I caught her by the arm, dragging her into the shadows of the hallway. "What do you think you're doing?"

"Defending myself. You neglected to tell me that my choice in careers was going to become fodder during dinner."

"I warned you that my father will try anything to get under your skin and he succeeded."

She shook her head. "You know what sickens me? You're just like him whether you want to admit it or not."

I pushed her against the wall, planting my hands on either side of her. "Don't push me tonight, Bristol. I'm in no mood. Behave for a little while longer then we'll get the hell out of here. Can you do that?" As I lowered my head, she pressed her palms against me.

"Yes," she said through clenched teeth. Perhaps I was far too much like my father, a brutal, unforgiving man. All I could think about was dragging her into the bathroom and fucking her. What did that make me?

"My father is a harsh taskmaster and always has been."

"I gathered that from his ridiculous statement."

Her defiance was admirable but challenging the darkness inside of me. "My father believes that punishment is good for the soul. His father was exactly the same way."

Her eyes opened wide. "That's… horrible."

"That's the way of my family." I dropped my head even more until our lips were almost touching. "Don't force me to follow through with the tradition."

"If I've learned one thing about you, it's that you do exactly what you want to do."

"That may be so, but it's necessary to remain on neutral ground. That requires your compliance."

"As I said, you should have provided more warnings."

A slight growl erupted from my throat. Unable to resist her, I captured her mouth and wrapped my hand around her throat, keeping her in position. The taste of her was even sweeter than before, her brazen attitude and refusal to play the game in its entirely a tremendous turn-on. There was no pushback as I slipped my tongue inside, enjoying the simple moment of domination. My cock ached like a son of a bitch, my blood pressure rising. She had no way of knowing what she did to me.

She crushed her fingers around my shirt, tugging as the moment of passion exploded. Our connection continued to be strained but even more enigmatic than before. When I finally broke the kiss, keeping my hand caressing her lovely throat, I nipped her lower lip. "Just be a good girl for tonight."

"I'll see what I can do."

As I pulled her by the hand, returning to the table, I could see a glint in my father's eyes. He was such a freaking bastard.

The banter turned relatively normal for a period of time, at least getting us through the main course. After the plates had been removed, I needed fresh air, the innuendoes and biting comments restarting with vigor. I also wanted to see if Chase would follow, providing any information that coerced me into finding out more about what the hell was going on.

"Listen to me very carefully. Don't make a scene. I need a few more minutes then we leave." While I kept my voice low, I made certain she heard every word. My anger was already riled, my patience worn thin. I was no longer certain I cared whether we passed the test. I'd already risen to my feet, my drink in my hand.

"Why yes, sir," Bristol snipped as she glanced up at me. "Just don't be gone too long. I still find it difficult to hold my tongue."

Snorting, I squeezed her shoulder before walking around the table, heading for the set of open doors leading to the private deck. As I moved toward the railing, I inhaled, enjoying the various scents of the club's grill as well as the ocean water. There was a peacefulness to the serene setting, the myriad colorful lights surrounding the walkway leading to the shore twinkling in the light breeze.

As I leaned over the railing, swirling my drink, several memories from the past crept into my mind including the first time I'd been brought to the club. I'd been eighteen, my father insisting that I was ready to take a man's place at the table, the visit nothing to do with a family gathering. He'd wanted me to see firsthand as he destroyed one of his competitors, the once powerful man my father considered an enemy begging my father for reconsideration.

My father had enjoyed every moment, including threatening the man's family. I would never forget the gleam in my father's eyes, the laughter that burst from his mouth the moment the broken man walked out of the private room, shivering from the realization that his livelihood and his private life had both been destroyed.

Then my father had gloated, ordering me a scotch as if the legal drinking age didn't matter. There wasn't a single person in the club who didn't cater to him as if he was a god. To me, he was a monster, a man who had no conscience or humanity.

That was the day I no longer worshipped the man who ruled his family with an iron fist. I'd rebelled against everything the great William Powers commanded, turning into nothing but a delinquent. All the years of boarding school hadn't prepared me for his ruthlessness or his punishment for rebelling against him.

I'd learned the hard way what challenging someone so powerful could mean. I lifted my glass, shaking my head. While he no longer had any level of control over me, that didn't mean his influences weren't toxic. After all, Bristol had been very astute.

I'd become far too much like him.

I heard footsteps behind me and bristled, refusing to turn around.

"She's lovely."

The sound of Riley's voice surprised me. "She's perfect in every way."

"Did you warn her?"

Huffing, I shot him a look as he flanked my side, remaining a solid two feet away, his eyes locked on the shoreline.

"About our caustic family? To a degree. She can make up her own mind after tonight. I can tell she's not a happy camper."

"How could she be, Houston? My God, the gall of that man never ceases to amaze me." I was surprised to hear Riley talk with any discord regarding the old man. He'd been the quiet kid, the one who remained studious, staying in his room. He also hadn't been required to attend boarding school. That had always pissed me off.

"Well, she needs to learn to turn it off."

A smile crossed his face. "That can be difficult given his oppressive nature."

I had nothing to say at that point. A moment of tension slipped between us.

"I'm surprised you returned," he said quietly.

"It's all about the trust fund." I was curious if he'd received the same middle of the night phone call, although I had no intentions of mentioning it to anyone at this point.

"Ah, that surprises me even more. I heard you were doing well."

"What little bird told you that?"

Riley shifted his gaze in my direction. "You know how Ashley is. She did her best to keep up with you and your illustrious career. I say kudos to you for getting the hell away from here."

"You could do the same."

"You've seen my mother. She's not well. I couldn't leave her here by herself."

I knew the real reason Charity remained married to the bastard. The prenup she'd been forced to sign detailed her years of marriage. She wasn't eligible for the big prize just yet. That wouldn't happen for at least a couple of additional years. "But you deserve to live your life the way you want to."

He laughed. "Your father has a way of squelching happiness and ingenuity."

I'd always found it interesting that Riley had never used terms of endearment for my father. Granted, he'd been treated like an unwanted creature, his existence barely tolerated. What I'd learned through months of investigation was that somehow Riley had been coerced into working at the great empire, handling every aspect of the new accounts brought in. "I'm certain with the money you're making you're getting by."

His face hardened. "I did what I had to do in your absence, Houston. I know we've never gotten along, but I'm not the wet behind the ears kid you remember."

"No, I can tell you're not." What I was keeping close to my vest is that I suspected Chase was planning some kind of coup, his longing for power and authority moving to an entirely different level than before. If he succeeded, my gut told me my trust would be placed in jeopardy. What role Riley played I wasn't certain. But I would find out. Until then, the family gatherings would be kept to a minimum.

"I heard you bought a house."

I couldn't help but laugh. "News travels fast. Perhaps it's past time to take what belongs to me."

He seemed antsy, even glancing over his shoulder. "Be careful, Houston. There are things happening within the company that are changing the course of the future for all of us."

"Would you care to elaborate?" Before he had a chance to answer, my attention was captured by the sound of a loud voice. When I turned toward the club, I was able to catch sight of Bristol in some kind of confrontation with Chase.

"Jesus. He's at it again. No wonder he refused to bring his girlfriend to the great party." Riley polished off his drink, laughing softly.

I didn't like the sight or the sound of what was going on. The second I crossed the threshold, the sight of Bristol slapping Chase in the face was the last straw. My father would never allow her behavior to go unpunished. I could either succumb to his demands or get us the hell out of there.

As I stormed inside, I noticed the smug look on Chase's face. He'd provoked her on purpose, trying to break her resolve. And goddamn it, she'd allowed that to happen.

I took her hand, ignoring the grin on my father's face. "We're getting out of here. Then we're going to have a talk."

CHAPTER 6

ristol

Talk.

There'd been nothing but silence since leaving the club. Now, I certainly understood much better why Houston had required someone to portray his fiancée. The entire situation was ridiculous, one a normal human being couldn't tolerate. Had he really grown up in that kind of household? If he had, no wonder he was so dark, almost soulless.

At least he hadn't lied to me about his family, especially his father. The man was an older carbon copy of Houston, but harsher, more brutal. Chase was entirely a different story. His words bothered the hell out of me, his hatred for Houston evident.

"You have no idea what you're getting in the middle of, Bristol. My brother is nothing but a cold, calculating man who will enjoy destroying you. I suggest you get out now."

The statement had seemed offhanded, a true warning. Whatever was going on, I doubted Houston was the only victim.

I brushed my fingers across my lips, trying to hold onto the kiss, although I wasn't certain why. If he had told me the level of compliance that was expected, I would never have signed the contract.

Or was that just another lie I was trying to tell myself?

Three months. You can handle this for three months.

At this point, I wasn't certain.

After he parked the car, he took my hand, intertwining our fingers and taking long strides into the garage elevator. He crowded me against the steel wall, tilting his head. "You defied me."

"I felt I needed to." My words were little more than a whisper, my nerves kicking in.

"Do I need to remind you about the terms of the contract?"

I almost laughed. "No, you don't. Do I need to remind you that information is helpful?"

He took a deep breath, his expression ice cold. "Did Chase hurt you in any way?"

My breath catching in my throat, I shook my head. "No. He was just so… condescending, trying to put me in my place." I shuddered given the words Chase had used, uncertain of how to deal with his implied accusations.

"I'm onto you, Bristol. There's nothing that happens with regard to my family that I won't find out about."

While he'd refused to elaborate, the secrets Houston and I were keeping were a ticking timebomb. The last thing I wanted to do was drive my fake fiancé into a bout of anger. For now, I'd keep Chase's comments to myself.

"That's to be expected. You could have walked away."

"That's not my nature."

He took a deep breath, holding it as the elevator continued to rise. There was something even darker about the look in his eyes, possessive as well as hungry. Everything about his demeanor had been entirely different. He hadn't just been on edge. He'd been in a quiet yet bitter fight. There was a hell of a lot more going on than he'd allowed me to learn.

"For every action there are consequences."

"Meaning what?" I knew challenging him wasn't in my best interest, but the night had been draining.

"I'm going to have to punish you."

"You're kidding." My stomach was suddenly nauseous, my heart hammering to the point the sound echoed in the tinny space. The same tingling I'd felt before shifted down to my toes, my mouth completely dry.

"I don't kid about the rules, Bristol. I thought you realized that." His look was stern.

"You are just like your father." The entire dinner had been arduous at best, although Ashley had tried to make everything better. I couldn't imagine being a daughter in their household, let alone a real fiancée.

There was a flash in his eyes, a distinct emotion that I couldn't read, but I knew he hated being compared.

"In some ways his beliefs and traditions make sense. You were told to do one thing, pretend you were a happy woman, not to pick a fight with my brother. He was spurring you on and you missed it."

"No, I got it. I just refused to allow that to happen. What is the bad blood between the two of you about?"

"That is a story for a full bottle of wine. Perhaps tomorrow night when we're in our new home." He snickered after making the statement.

Our. The word seemed outrageous for him to say. "Fine. In order for me to continue with this charade, I'll need more from you. That is also part of the contract."

Houston fingered my chin, rolling the tip back and forth aimlessly. "You will continue to be challenged. I'll be happy to provide as much information as you need, at least within limits."

"You don't trust anyone, do you?"

He chuckled. "Trust is something that must be earned, but you're right, I haven't bothered to try since…"

I could tell he wasn't going to deem it either appropriate or necessary for me to know.

The ping of the elevator provided an entire round of shivers. He didn't bother taking me by the hand this time. He expected me to follow like a good little girl. I was the one who closed the door behind us, locking it then remaining pressed against the wood.

He headed immediately toward the bedroom, leaving me aching inside. The night had been more difficult than I'd imagined. My acting skills weren't good enough to pretend I was a demure woman. How was I going to handle going through a bogus wedding? I kicked off my shoes, placing them ever so carefully by one of the tables. I'd never felt so inadequate in my entire life.

Dozens of thoughts raced through my mind as I walked out onto the balcony, the slight chill in the air instantly giving me goosebumps. I held my arms as the breeze whipped through my long strands. I was three thousand miles from the city I'd hoped to call my home. What would happen if I left now? Would Mr. Darke or Houston go after me for the money? The real question was all about if I cared or not. Sadly, there was a tiny part of me that wanted to get to know my fake fiancé a little better. Was I just a glutton for punishment? Maybe.

Or maybe he'd touched me in a way that had awakened my senses.

I could sense his presence without him needing to utter a word. As he'd done before, he was watching me.

"I want to put this behind us so we can start fresh tomorrow," he said so very quietly.

"Fine." Was he really going to go through with punishing me?

"Go into the bedroom and remove your clothes. Place both pillows in the center of the bed then lie across them."

I shifted my head, barely able to catch a hint of him standing in the doorway. "All right. I mean, yes, sir."

His sigh was exaggerated. "You need to understand that the choices I've been forced to make were all influenced by my father's requirements. While I didn't understand them in the least when I was younger, I'm starting to realize that there is a necessity for rules in order to flourish. Whether that's in business or in relationships. Maybe you are right that I'm exactly like my father. However, I refuse to succumb to his depths of tyranny."

While I couldn't understand what he was getting at, it seemed important for him to tell me. "I'm sorry if I embarrassed you but I'm not used to being treated like I'm not important enough to be in your life. I feel very sorry for what you had to endure. Only you can change the course of your life." I turned around to face him, a part of me wanting to provide some kind of comfort, which was absolutely insane. A man like him couldn't understand compassion to any degree.

"You are very wise, Bristol. Please get in position and wait for my arrival." When he walked away, I could swear he'd fallen into a shattered moment of sadness.

Then again, I could be very wrong.

Still chilled, I padded into the bedroom, turning on a single light by the bed. There were no blinds in the damn room, no way to cover the oversized window. I turned my back before removing my clothes, neatly folding them over one of my suitcases. If only I could go back a week then things would be different.

I'd made all kinds of assurances to myself that pretending would be easy, that two million dollars was a once in a lifetime opportunity. Maybe I wasn't as strong as I'd believed I was, capable of handling a lie this significant. I also wasn't certain I could tolerate the kind of man Houston truly was. He was so cold and indifferent. It didn't matter that he had his reasons. There was nothing redeemable about the man.

The cold chill shifting down my spine had nothing to do with the air temperature. By the time I positioned the pillows as he'd commanded, my entire body was shivering. When I eased across the fluffy mound, tears instantly formed in my eyes, but I refused to allow them to fall. I wasn't going to show any sign of weakness, more for myself than for the brute of a man.

I folded my arms, resting my head and staring out into the night. There were hundreds of lights on in the other buildings, the exteriors brightly lit with tropical colors of lime green and fuchsia. While the club itself had been old world, stodgy in a way that had surprised me, the hotel was a stark contrast. I could only imagine what kind of house Houston had purchased. Was it modern or traditional? A beach house or maybe located in the city limits?

Oh, what the hell did it matter? I certainly wasn't going to feel at home.

I heard nothing coming from the other room. No music. No television. He wasn't making a call or pacing the floor. The quiet was unnerving. After a few minutes, I grew antsy, doing my best to stay in position, even though my patience was waning. Huffing, I closed my eyes, trying to will away the situation.

Finally, I sensed his approach, the scent of his exotic cologne giving him away. When he walked into the room, he'd already removed his jacket and tie, unbuttoning his shirt. He stood in the doorway, studying me as he took his time rolling up his sleeves. The look on his face was stern, but instead of the cold bleakness of his eyes, they were shimmering.

The thought of punishing me made him excited. What did that say about the man?

When he was finished with the task, he walked closer, crouching down by the side of the bed. I wanted to demand to know what he was waiting for, but I kept my mouth shut, preferring to keep some level of humility.

"I'm going to repeat this one more time, Bristol. I do understand this is a difficult situation for you. In fact, I realize I'm asking a lot; however, you will soon learn why following my rules is important."

"Why can't you tell me now?"

"Because you haven't held up to your end of the bargain as of yet."

"That's not fair," I commented, hating the whiny sound to my voice.

"Perhaps not, but very little in life is fair. I hope at some point we can learn to trust each other. In the meantime, you will give me your respect at all times."

"Respect is earned."

Sighing, he glanced out the window. "I used to think it was. Now, I realize that money and power are the only things that can require absolute respect from anyone."

"And you have both."

"Not as much as I hope to have." He stood, towering over me as he slowly unfastened his belt.

A rush of insecurity made my mouth dry, my heart race. From where he stood, I couldn't take my eyes off the action. He was taking his time, his eyes never shifting, barely blinking. The bastard wanted the anticipation to continue increasing in order to reaffirm that he was the one in charge.

I hated the way a trickle of apprehension and a hint of fear washed into me. I'd never been spanked as a child. I'd never experienced the anguish of having a leather strap cracked across my bottom. I certainly had never wandered into a BDSM club or desired to enter into a dominating relationship. That was for heroines in books and strangers on street corners, not for a practicing attorney who preferred staying at home versus clubbing it.

While the thought was ridiculous, almost making me laugh, it helped to ease the growing anxiety.

"I know you won't believe me, but I don't like having to discipline you," he said in his soft, velvety tone, the one that tickled my arousal.

"No, I don't believe you. Isn't this what you were brought up to do?"

He cocked his head but didn't answer, merely tugged on the thick strap until it started sliding from the confines of his beltloops. I couldn't take my eyes off his hands as he performed the task. They were strong hands, his fingers muscular. They were the kind of hands that were supposed to caress a woman's back seconds after tossing a football.

Somehow, I suspected he'd done neither in his life.

When the belt was finally free, I couldn't stop shivering. I bit my lower lip, my throat threatening to close. There was a chance I was going to hyperventilate from the sickening feeling of expectancy.

Houston rolled the strap between his fingers before folding one end against the other. Every damn move he made was so slow that a scream formed in my throat, angry words to get it over with. When he finally moved behind me, I shuddered, trying to push my mind in a place of peace.

A pearlescent beach with turquoise blue waters.

A beautiful mountain cabin after a fresh snowfall.

A rainstorm in the middle of a lush green forest.

An appointment with a dentist.

"I think thirty will be appropriate for tonight. You need to stay in position."

I could see a hint of his reflection in the window, his powerful figure looming over me like a predator prepared to catch his prey.

When he tapped my bottom, I jumped.

"Do you understand, Bristol?" He tugged my legs apart, brushing his fingers along the inside of my leg.

"Yes." Respect. The word flew into my mind. "Yes, sir." I was more vulnerable than ever, my buttocks several inches in the air, my pussy lips exposed. I clamped my hands around the bedding, my breathing now so shallow I was lightheaded.

"Better."

I closed my eyes, burying my face as I waited. It seemed like forever before I heard the first whooshing sound in the air. When he brought the belt down, I was jarred more from the blunt thud directly across my bottom than the sting that immediately formed. As air was pushed out of my lungs, a cry escaping my mouth, I balled my hands around the comforter, yanking with all my might. I didn't have time to register any pain before he delivered two more in rapid succession. The sound seemed exaggerated, pain blossoming from the tops of my thighs.

While my body registered the anguish, my mind hadn't processed it until he smacked me with two more. A wail erupted from my mouth that was certainly heard in other rooms. Gasping for air, I kicked out my legs, squirming and wiggling from side to side.

He leaned over, planting his hands on either side of me. "If you can't remain silent, I will need to gag you."

Gag me? Men did that sort of thing?

"I... I can. I mean, I will." My voice was unrecognizable, quivering to the point I wasn't entirely certain he could understand me.

"All right. We'll try again, but you need to remain in position." He had the nerve to rub his hand across my heated ass cheeks, caressing as if what he was doing was benefitting me. Fuck him.

I smashed my face into the comforter, counting numbers in another crazy effort to get my mind off the horrible experience.

Then the cracking sound reverberated in my ears and I couldn't hold back a cry. He stopped before the leather sliced against my bottom, exhaling as if disgusted with me.

"Once when we're in our house, there will be no need to limit your expression of pain or pleasure; for tonight, that will be necessary."

Every word out of his mouth was perfunctory. I glanced over my shoulder as he walked toward my clothes. What was he doing? When he returned, he moved to the other side of the bed, peering down.

"Open your mouth for me, Bristol."

I lifted my head, realizing that he had my panties in his hand. Jesus. Swallowing, I almost promised that I'd be a good girl and very quiet, but I refused to do that. When I opened my mouth, I gave him a hateful glare.

He was so damn smug, as if far superior to me. I really did hate the man.

After he shoved the ball of lace into my mouth, he shook his head. "You're going to fight me every step of the way during this venture. While I find that irresistible, my patience is already wearing thin."

The taste of my earlier arousal was disgusting, turning the butterflies in my stomach into a churning mass.

He returned to the other side of the bed, wasting no time in starting again.

My first muffled cry was ridiculous, but the realization of everything that had happened during the last few days came crashing down. Tears slipped past my lashes, burning hot tears that pushed me into emotional overload. I wanted nothing more than to curl in a ball under the covers, pretending that with the dawn of tomorrow came another year in my life.

I also hated the realization that tingles had arisen all throughout my body. When he smacked me two more times, I was forced to face the fact that I was fully aroused, my nipples aching to the point of actual pain. This was crazy. I couldn't believe that a spanking would turn me on.

But as the scent of my pussy juice trickling down my legs floated all the way to my nostrils, there was no doubt. This wasn't just my body's betrayal. This was absolute tyranny. The thought was ridiculous, pushing my mind into a surreal state as another volley of brutal smacks was given.

Everything became a blur, agony and ecstasy mixing together, my heart hammering in my chest. I was lost to the crazy rhythm of the spanking as heat continued to build on my skin. I tried to maintain position, but when he smacked my upper thighs, I tumbled off the pillows, a strangled moan slipping past my panties.

I expected some kind of savage action, but he gingerly pulled me back onto the pillow, taking his time to caress my skin all over again.

"You're doing very well."

Why was his tone actually soothing? That was crazy.

I couldn't keep my face planted on the comforter any longer. When the next strike hit me, I arched my back, knowing in the back of my mind that there would be a stain from my slickened pussy on the bedding after the horrible round of punishment was over. Stars floated in front of my eyes, the pain still biting, but as my pussy clenched and released, all I could concentrate on was the embarrassment coursing through me.

Nothing could have prepared me for my reaction, not even the few trials that I'd experienced during my limited career. I was drained, helpless, and excited. The combination was ridiculous but unable to be denied.

I lost count of how many he'd given me.

But he spanked me long and hard for the next minute or two, maybe three. There was no way of telling. I simply knew I'd have difficulty sitting for an extended period of time.

"Five more then we're done." His voice seemed to float above me, infiltrating my senses much like his scent had roared into my system, creating the feeling of being intoxicated.

I expected him to start again but instead, he slipped his fingers down the crack of my ass, teasing me with the tip of one, fingering my pussy lips until I was panting from desire.

"You're wet. I think you actually like this."

Who the hell was he kidding? I couldn't stand him or what he was doing, especially the way my body responded to every stroke. I realized I was shaking my head, yet my body was bucking backward, trying to pull his finger in even deeper.

He chuckled as he thrust it inside, pumping several times then pulling out completely. "Very wet. You make me crave you, woman." There was something enticing about the way he growled, the slow and guttural sound as it permeated the room.

I was breathless, my hunger increasing. When he smacked my bottom again, the heat now blistering, I fell into a place of sheer euphoria, confused yet longing to be touched.

Fondled.

Fucked.

My emotions continued on the rollercoaster as he brought the belt down again.

And again.

When it was finally over, I knew he'd tossed the strap onto the dresser. I was also aware of the sound of him releasing his cock.

I bristled, uncertain of what to expect. When he dragged me to the edge of the bed, yanking the pillows out from underneath me, I twisted my body in an effort to look at him. He was like some crazed man, his hunger all consuming.

When he walked closer, gripping my hips, I couldn't keep a series of whimpers and moans from trying to escape around the gag.

"I'm going to fuck that tight pussy of yours. Then I'm going to claim your ass."

No. No!

Fuck me in the ass? That had never happened in my life. It was never something I'd wanted to try. Just hearing the words make me feel filthy, but I couldn't deny the round of excitement.

I was no longer stunned by anything he did. When he pressed the tip of his shaft just past my swollen folds, I was unable to take my eyes off our combined reflection. There was something entirely animalistic about the way he was fucking me, taking me from behind as if against my will.

Only I found it difficult to resist him. I was now wet all over, heat building as the fire in my belly continued to expand.

When he slipped into my tight channel, holding his stance for a few seconds, I couldn't stop shaking. "Damn, you're so wet. So freaking tight." His voice was barely a whisper, but I heard his robust guttural sound when he thrust the rest of his cock inside.

The force was significant, and I was pushed against the comforter, immediately scrambling to push up, arching my back as he pulled out. Then he slammed into me again, the hard pounding echoing in my ears. As he repeated the move, his heavy breathing became growls, his fingers digging into me.

A beautiful moment of rapture washed over me, my pulse skyrocketing as every cell was set aflame. He was so rough, taking exactly what he wanted, using me in whatever way he wanted. I could feel I was close to coming, the tingles in my body prickling every inch of skin. Every sound muffled, I met every savage thrust with one of my own. We were in a perfect rhythm together and as the climax rushed up from my toes, I threw my head back with a silent scream.

"That's it. Come for me. That feels so damn good." He continued plunging as the single orgasm shifted into a beautiful wave. I was stunned at the euphoria, no longer able to feel my arms or legs.

Seconds later, he slowed down, still sliding in and out as he rubbed up and down the length of my back. When he rolled his hand down my bottom, I cringed even as my pussy continued to clamp and release. He pressed his thumb between my ass cheeks, pushing into my darkened hole. "Are you ready for me to fuck that tight ass of yours?"

"Mmm…" I undulated my hips, trying to crawl forward but he tugged me back several inches, patting my bruised bottom before sliding the tip of his cock to my puckered hole.

"Does that mean you're a virgin, Bristol? I can tell that you are. We'll take it nice and slow."

I continued to watch our reflection as he pushed his cockhead just inside. Then I almost panicked, smacking my hands against the bedding as he thrust in another inch. Within seconds, another wave of pain coursed through me, my muscles aching. His cock was huge, wide and long and I blinked several times as the wave of anguish continued.

"Breathe for me. That's it." He slid in an inch at a time, holding me in place as I clawed at the comforter, making horrible noises over the panties. This was even more humiliating.

Revolting.

Horrible.

I threw my head back as he thrust the last few inches inside. I'd experienced nothing like this before, a combination of anguish and ecstasy that rolled into every cell and muscle. I was blinded from the intensity, the fire swarming through my aching limbs. I was unable to focus on the blurry reflection, nor did I care. I finally closed my eyes, no longer fighting him, in fact moving in time to his hard thrusts.

"So tight. So damn tight." His words were muffled at best, his husky growls fueling the fire and electricity we shared. For all the hatred I felt for this man, there was no denying our chemistry.

I had no idea how long he continued, his breathless sounds becoming more ragged. But as he pounded into me in rapid motions, his grip even firmer, I hung my head. The sound of his strangled roar as he filled me with his seed was just as sinful as the act itself.

Houston wasn't a man to be liked or respected.

He certainly had no capacity for love.

Yet I remained drawn to him for some inexplicable reason, like a moth to a flame.

He was nothing but the devil in disguise.

And soon, he would be my husband.

CHAPTER 7

ouston

The power of money.

I'd learned early in my life that money could buy almost anything, including feigned happiness. I'd also realized at a young age that there were thousands of people living a life of pretense and pretend, the concept of keeping up with the Jones taking on an entirely different level.

Of deceit.

Of carefully crafted tales.

Of polished smiles.

All in an effort to become top dog.

It didn't matter the circumstances, the game often played used untold rules, often fueled by deals made behind closed doors or in dark and smoky bars where the players asserted their control. My brother had been especially good at molding himself into a carbon copy of my father. In some ways, Chase was even more ruthless than the great William Powers. Chase's ability to sniff out weakness was well known, his enjoyment of destroying his enemy's reputations, families, and livelihoods.

In my early days, his actions had been revolting.

However, I was no longer the younger brother who'd refused to fall into my father's footsteps. My time spent entirely on my own had given me a new appreciation of the need for full control over every situation.

That's why I wanted nothing other than blood.

My brother's blood to be exact.

At this point, I didn't give a shit what happened to him. I snickered at the thought as I stood on the balcony, admiring the view of the ocean. What I'd also realized only in the last few days was that I'd become nothing but an animal in expensive clothing. Perhaps I'd suppressed the majority of my true nature for a good portion of the five years I'd been away. Although I'd been merciless in my handling of stocks, I'd also parlayed limited funds for my clients as well as myself into a portfolio of true wealth.

Sighing, I shoved my hands into my pockets, the plan I'd enacted morphing between my eyes both disturbing as well as exciting. I certainly hadn't planned on Daniel finding a single woman who challenged me the way Bristol continued to do. I also had made a commitment to myself that I wouldn't give a flying fuck about the girl. As long as she followed my rules, played the game well, then I'd mostly leave her alone.

Unfortunately, I'd already realized that my cravings for her were bordering on sadistic in nature. We had a connection between us that defied the odds. I was honestly surprised she hadn't walked out the night before, catching an early morning flight back to her life.

But she'd remained.

I'd even felt her presence during the middle of the night, as if she'd been searching for me in the darkness. Sleep hadn't come easily; the two hours or so I'd managed had been fraught with dreams. She'd stood over me, watching me slumber as if trying to figure out the monster she'd made a deal with.

Today was the official start of the little game I'd set in motion.

"What are we doing for our great nuptials?"

Her voice held the same rebellion as the night before. I could clearly see her discipline did little to calm the fire. I shifted around to face her, my cock instantly stiffening at the sight of her. She'd selected a tropical dress, the flowing material unable to hide her voluptuous body. Even standing in bare feet, she held an air of elegance as well as defiance.

"It's entirely up to you. I'm certain Ashley has it all planned out by now."

Bristol laughed as she leaned against the doorway, taking a deep breath. "I guess you expect me to wear a frilly white dress. Isn't that what your family requires?"

I couldn't help but laugh. "I think you're already aware I couldn't care less about what my family thinks."

"Then I'm not going to suffer in a long train and white veil. That would seem too much of a farce. Forget the church wedding as well. I don't want to perform some kind of blasphemy in front of God."

"I didn't know you were religious."

"Does it matter?"

"No, not in the least. My family has always pretended, but that was only for appearances' sake. As you likely gathered, that's the way of things."

"So sad."

I walked closer, drinking in her perfume. "Don't feel sorry for us, Bristol. I don't know of a single family that hasn't endured tough times and tragedies."

"I'm sorry about what happened to your mother."

Her statement cut me like a knife, her tone of compassion pushing a lump into my throat. "There's no great drama with regard to the story, other than why she married my father in the first place."

"Still, I'm sorry about your loss."

"As I said, don't feel sorry for me. What is the saying? We make our beds and are forced to lie in them? So be it. I'm rich and soon I'll be powerful. That's the only thing that's important in my life. Are you ready to go?"

She stared at me with those huge green eyes of hers. My balls tightened from the sight alone. "Of course money is the only thing that matters to you. Why should I expect anything different? I'm packed and ready to go." She backed away, shaking her head, her eyes remaining locked on mine.

Sighing, I snarled when I heard the sound of my phone. When I pulled it from my pocket, all I could do was smile. The game was on. "Pops. You're calling earlier than normal. What can I do for you?"

"After that little display last night, I think we need to talk. My office in one hour."

"Not going to happen. We take possession of the new house this morning. It's high noon or nothing else."

I could tell my challenge pissed him off, his huffing and puffing his usual reaction when anyone dared to go against him.

"Fine. Don't bring her with you."

"She has a name. You will give Bristol respect. Period."

"Fine," he hissed. "This meeting is private. She's not your… possession yet."

When he ended the call I laughed, more gleeful than I should be. Yes, my plan was working. Soon, my father would crumble, but not because of my illustrious brother. Soon, the great William Powers would succumb to me.

Watching Bristol's reaction was like enjoying the moment a flower opened from sunlight and water, petals wafting in a light breeze. While I had no doubt that she loathed me on every level, she couldn't hide her glee at seeing the house I'd purchased. Yes, it had been sight unseen. I had no desire to maintain the house for longer than necessary. However, I had some insane kind of satisfaction in watching her ever changing expression.

"This is gorgeous," she whispered as she turned in a full circle in the kitchen, running her hand over the pristine appliances and granite counters. As she flitted from one area to another, I followed her, keeping my distance and allowing myself a few moments to enjoy.

"What are we going to do for furniture?" she asked after a few minutes while she unlocked one set of doors leading to the trio of decks.

"I meant what I said. That's entirely up to you. Money is no object. Ashley will be here shortly to escort you to several suitable locations. Select what you want."

"I thought I wasn't worthy."

I shook my head. "It's up to you. Furnish the house entirely in beanbags if you want."

She narrowed her eyes and gave me an odd look before taking a deep breath. The sound of the ocean splashing against the shoreline seemed to fascinate her. Maybe she'd never been to a beach before. The thought gnawed at me for some insane reason. I'd taken advantage of where I'd grown up, caring little about the ocean other than an occasional day spent with buddies, surfing the waves without a care in the world. "Be careful what you ask for."

"I will remind you that our wedding is in less than a week. You will also need to concentrate on the details."

There was no response to my statement. In fact, she ignored me, heading toward the stairs. I followed behind her, barely glancing at the various rooms as she headed toward the end of the hall, throwing open the double doors. I could hear her slight exclamation before I walked into the room.

I had to admit, the real estate agent had earned her commission. While the space was bare, the oversized windows and attention to detail with regard to the woodworking was more than just suitable.

She shook her head several times then moved into the bathroom. "My God. This is larger than a good portion of my apartment."

I didn't bother following her. I certainly didn't see us taking a shower together. "I have a meeting with my father this afternoon. Perhaps we can make plans to go out to dinner later."

There was no answer at first. When she walked out of the bathroom, she purposely searched my eyes. "That will be fine. Obviously, it's your choice."

While the electricity we'd shared the night before remained between us, it continued to surge through me. Just the thought of the way my belt sounded as it connected with her porcelain skin created the kind of need that was difficult to shove aside. Fucking her had been nothing but icing on the cake. Did that make me a bad man? Absolutely.

"As I mentioned before, this doesn't need to be contentious," I said as I tugged my wallet from my pocket, selecting a credit card.

"Then don't make it that way."

When I inched toward her, she tensed as if I was going to inflict punishment for her frank words. "Take this."

She glanced down at the card, smirking afterwards, refusing to accept. "I assume it has the necessary limit for my needs."

The woman was pulling out all the stops to push me over some imaginary edge. I closed the distance, using the edge of the card and skimming it down her cheek. She shuddered from my actions, her body quivering. For a few seconds I contemplated chucking the appointment with my father. I certainly wasn't going to play by his rules and my hunger was even more significant on such a gorgeous morning.

"I assure you, beautiful brat, that I have enough funds to keep you happy." The second I brushed the card across her glossy lips, she pulled away, snatching it from my hand.

"Of course you do. I'll try and find furniture that's suitable to your family's illustrious requirements."

Unable to help myself, I cupped her chin, tugging her forward. Her single moan was telling. She was just as aroused as the night before, but her longing was tempered by her fear of my actions. I lowered my head, rubbing my lip against hers then pulling away. "I'm not my father, Bristol. You choose whatever will make your stay more comfortable."

She pressed her palm against my chest, allowing her fingers to toy with my shirt. "I hope you aren't your father, Houston, but not for the reason you think."

"Please do tell me why."

Lifting her head, she narrowed her eyes. "Because he's so unhappy, mostly with himself. That's not only sad but disheartening."

"Maybe that's all I deserve."

"I don't buy that, but it would seem you want to believe it."

As I shifted my other hand down the length of her curls, pressing my fingers against the small of her back, pulling her even closer, she pushed against me. She was such a fighter, a woman refusing to succumb to anyone.

That made me want her even more.

That also would make breaking her that much more enjoyable.

I captured her mouth, darting my tongue inside. I wanted nothing more than to devour her, her struggle in my hold only fueling the rapidly increasing blaze. As my cock pressed against my pants, the pain becoming agonizing, all I could think about was stripping away her lovely dress, fucking her like some wild animal against the counter in the bathroom.

The sound of the doorbell was the only reason I didn't.

Bristol managed to push hard enough that she shoved me away, breaking my hold entirely. Although she rubbed her fingers across her lips as if she'd enjoyed my near taking of her, she shook her head, her eyes expressing the venom she obviously felt.

Chuckling, I winked at her. "That must be Ashley. She's early."

She flew past me as if I was planning on keeping her locked in the house. At least she'd accepted the credit card.

By the time I made it down the stairs, Ashley was already squealing from the sight of the house.

"This is fantastic! And a clean palette. I have so many ideas."

I shifted my gaze from my sister toward the feisty woman I'd soon be exchanging vows with. At least she appeared comfortable around Ashley.

"You did good, brother." Ashley's grin was infectious, at least for Bristol.

"I do have my moments. Take good care of my bride while I go to Pops' office." I took purposeful steps toward Bristol, gripping her arm. I expected her reaction to be to pull away. Instead, she threw her arms around me, shifting her body back and forth. The friction she created as her body rubbed against my trousers was far too seductive.

"I'm going to miss you," she purred.

"I don't think you will at all," I countered. "Just don't buy out all the stores." I laughed, the sound something I didn't recognize.

Happiness.

I was faking a relationship but for a few precious seconds everything felt normal.

As if I'd know what that meant.

Bristol backed away, holding the credit card in front of her face, swaying back and forth like the bad girl I knew her to be. "Now I have the card."

Ashley laughed with her, obviously delighted she'd have a chance to show my sister the town.

I kept my smile as I walked to the door.

"Be careful. I think our dear father is on the warpath," Ashley warned.

As if that was anything different than usual.

* * *

On the warpath.

I actually enjoyed the thought.

My father's office was in the same location it had been for years, the midlevel building maintaining a prime view of the ocean from his suite of offices. While he'd never shown interest in the water for any recreational purposes, the view was a requirement in his mind, only the best. He was nothing but a bully, including using his office as a pretentious method of showing off his power.

The lobby was bustling, dozens of people coming and going. I'd stopped to grab a cup of coffee on the way and took my sweet time heading for the elevator. Maybe I was the one pressing every button available. I kept my smirk as I waited for the 'bing' of the elevator, walking onto the floor and taking a deep breath. While I'd been given no indication of the reason for the visit, I could only imagine it was his real opportunity to grill me about my sudden marriage as well as my arrival in town. Or perhaps he was making good on a single promise he'd made five years ago before tossing me out of his office.

A portion of the business.

Which I'd wanted nothing to do with then. Now? It was an easier method of determining whether Ashley's concerns were well founded.

However, I was prepared for whatever he had to sling in my direction. I'd had a lifetime to prepare for a moment just like this.

As I would have expected, the office was also busy, the employees barely acknowledging me as I walked in, heading directly for my father's office. While it was only a few minutes past noon, I knew my tardiness would only further fuel his anger.

What I wasn't prepared for, although I should have suspected, was the sight of my brother standing over my father. My brother wore a wry grin while my father's face was beet red.

"Fuck you. I'm not going to listen to this any longer," my father exclaimed before slamming down the office phone with enough force he toppled several items onto the floor. "God damn that asshole."

Trouble in paradise?

"Get rid of him, Dad. You don't need the crap," Chase stated, although amusement remained on his face.

Only when I slammed the door closed behind me did they seem to notice my arrival.

The look shared between the two of them would ordinarily piss me off. Perhaps I was in a good mood from indulging the night before or the anticipation of angry banter. Either way, I was easily able to keep a smile on my face.

"Trouble, gentlemen?" I asked casually.

"Nothing we can't handle or that needs your interference," Chase was quick to snap.

My father glanced at his watch, his expression a mixture of disdain and something even more unexpected. Amusement.

"Did your lovely bride to be keep you awake last night?" His question seemed out of character. There was a second look shared. He completely ignored the fact I'd overheard a part of the conversation.

"We enjoyed our evening together, that is after we left the festivities." I glared at Chase, still preferring to wipe the smug look off his face. While it was only noon, I headed for my father's bar, selecting his finest whiskey.

"Drinking so early is out of character for you," Chase said in a condescending tone of voice.

"I'm on vacation. Soon to be married to the love of my life." I kept my glass raised as I turned to face them, leaning against the bar.

"Yes, which is an interesting scenario," my father said.

"For what reason?"

"Your timing as always is impeccable."

My brother's offhanded comment was loaded with a point. "Ah, yes. The release of my trust fund. I must admit that I scheduled the trip to commemorate the occurrence, something Bristol is in full agreement with."

"I'm certain she is," Pops huffed. He moved around his desk, heading toward the bar, giving me a heated look before reaching around me for a glass.

I took my time giving him space then moved toward the windows. "A stunning view as always."

"Do you really think we're going to buy this shit?" Chase challenged.

"And what shit is that, brother? That I could manage to find someone to love me for who and what I am?" I could see where this was going.

"Enough!" my father bellowed. "Just accept the fact your brother has found a mate. While we might not consider her suitable, that no longer matters. Houston has always done whatever the hell he wanted to with his life, including his decision to crawl back into the family business."

Suitable? I knew he was tossing out bullshit to see if I'd take the bait. I had to admit, it was difficult not to. "Well, it's good to see that nothing has changed in the family resolution. Tell me, Chase, have you found a woman who could tolerate your idiocy?"

"Fuck you, Houston," Chase hissed.

"I said enough! This meeting is about business and nothing more." After preparing his drink, Pops walked back to his desk, huffing as he sat down. He'd aged significantly in my years of absence, his complexion sallow and his breathing labored. His good fortune and libations had caught up with him.

"Business. Then let's get to it." I remained standing, further challenging my brother as he retreated to one of the chairs in front of my father's desk.

"Yes, he has a fabulous wedding to plan." Chase's normal demeanor had returned, hiding any notion that my words had angered him.

"All right. That's better." Pops pulled out two folders from his desk, sliding one toward Chase and other to the edge of the desk. "Given your agreement to work in the business, I've developed new contracts for both of you."

"What does that mean?" Chase asked, darting his eyes toward the folder but making no move to retrieve it.

"It means that your brother is going to play an equal role in the corporation." It would seem my father was enjoying ruffling Chase's feathers. That I hadn't expected on any level.

From what snooping I'd done after Ashley's first frantic phone call, I'd gathered enough intel to believe Chase was attempting to undermine the corporation. While I had no solid proof as of yet, my brother was a grandstander, likely to leave forgotten clues that would be his path to destruction. While I didn't necessarily care about the corporation as a whole, I certainly didn't want it taken apart piece by piece, another investor able to get his or her hands on the family fortune.

What I hadn't realized was just how troublesome the thought really was. Seeing Chase today made the nagging that much worse. While I'd never considered myself a decent man on any level, hating my father more like a sporting event, there was a small part of me that didn't want to see him crushed because of family greed.

I was determined to find out what Chase was up to. This would be the perfect way, even though I continued to have zero desire to work with the corporation. What the hell did I know about computer chips? I mused over the request, at least coming to terms with the fact I certainly had an affinity for making money. I could parlay my father's offer into a very lucrative moment.

"That's bullshit, Dad. We talked about this. Houston is only here for the money. Isn't that right?" Chase's glare was just as I'd expected. Hateful. Full of the need for revenge.

"What about Riley?" I asked with no inflection in my tone whatsoever. I knew my father never had any intention of allowing someone who wasn't considered his true family into the fold.

He laughed. "Riley has no work ethic and he's not my blood."

"I'm certain Charity would beg to differ."

My father pointed his finger at me, his face red as a beet. "Don't you dare question my decisions. Riley means nothing to me and never has. I threw him a bone. He should be happy for the crumbs. They'll still make him a rich man. At least as long as he obeys my commands."

"That's tragic, Pops. Riley is a grown man. He can make his own decisions." I wasn't as much coming to Riley's defense as I was trying to find out more of what the hell was going on.

"Don't fuck with me, boy. Riley is old news. I'm offering you a deal of a lifetime. Either you want to be involved or you don't. If you decide against my offer, then I want nothing to do with you any longer."

"As if you ever had anything to do with me." The anger that I'd held inside rushed to the surface. I closed the distance, shaking my head. "Don't threaten me, Pops. You won't like what happens if you do."

My father reared back then as I'd seen so many times in business scenarios when he was pushed against the wall. He smiled. The expression was one of calculation as well as hatred. I couldn't care less. "Fine. Sign the contract or don't."

Chase huffed, squirming around both of us and heading for the door. "I won't take this sitting down, Dad. I will challenge your decision in court if necessary." When he left the room, slamming the door behind him, all I could do was grin. I certainly didn't mind getting under my brother's skin.

However, this sudden change of heart was an interesting switch.

"Why don't we cut the bullshit, Pops. What do you want?"

After taking a deep breath, my father walked toward the window, swirling his drink as he peered out at the vibrant setting below. "I know you won't believe this, son, but you were always my favorite."

I almost burst into laughter. Who the hell was he kidding? I did my best to keep my mouth shut. I wanted to see where this was going. My father always had an angle to everything he did. "As I said. Cut the bullshit. There's a reason you want me here and I doubt it has anything to do with the trust fund, which is peanuts in comparison to your stock value, let alone the assets you own."

He took a gulp, finishing almost half the glass before speaking. "I know you weren't a happy child. Hell, I wouldn't have been either. After your mother died, I guess I felt business was the only thing that mattered to me. When Charity came along, well, I admit I couldn't resist her gorgeous body and the way she clung onto my every word. But blood is thicker than water. You are the star of the family, the person I trust the most to take my vision of the company into the future."

I rolled my eyes, doing everything I could to keep the anger out of my tone. "What about Chase? He's certainly capable and just as conniving as you are. He'll make good on his threat to take whatever you offer me straight to court. I don't think you want that kind of publicity."

Sighing, he tipped his head in my direction. I could swear there was sadness in his eyes. "Perhaps you're right, but that doesn't mean I approve of his methods. Let him challenge. Honestly, I don't give a shit. He's a shark, even more so than I've been. However, I'll stick to my guns on this one to my dying breath."

Dying breath. Who was he kidding?

Now there was no way to keep the laughter from my voice, although my thoughts drifted to the odd middle of the night phone call. Why did I have a feeling I was stuck in the middle of some game? "Whatever you say, Pops. What is the point of this little heart to heart? Just to piss Chase off as much as you've done to me my entire life?"

"Always straight and to the point. That's another trait I respect about you. The point is that I want you on my team. I was hoping you'd come to your senses a couple years ago. I have tremendous plans for the future, but I'm getting older. I'm not as aggressive as I once was and this business is all about dog eat dog, the survival of the fittest. There are dozens of hotshot kids out there trying to make inroads into the world of computers. You wouldn't believe the technology that's being developed, and I like to think I've had a hand in providing the most robust systems in the world. Did you know that I just signed a defense contract with the United States Marines for one of our new designs?"

The look he gave me was full of pride, something that I'd also rarely seen. "That's great, Pops."

"Yes, but there are two companies fighting my patents, even accusing that certain technology was stolen. As you might imagine, that's already affected our stocks. It's bullshit, but I've had a suspicion that someone is selling highly classified information to the highest bidder. I need someone who has my back and that would be you, son."

"The call you just had? Did it have something to do with these accusations?"

He rubbed his jaw, his chest heaving. "A small contract. They're pulling out. They mean nothing in the scope of things, but I feel a domino effect coming on."

Jesus Christ.

It would appear that Ashley's concerns were spot on. I thought about his request as well as Chase's reaction. The man wasn't telling me everything. I had to wonder if he ever would. Then again, would I give a shit? "I'll need to read over the contract, Pops. That is the prudent thing to do."

He laughed, the sound reeking of bitterness and perhaps a touch of admiration. "I would expect nothing less of you, son. You are by far the most intelligent child I produced."

Produced. I was nothing but his spawn, and perhaps one that could continue to allow him to live the lifestyle he enjoyed. "Well, I guess I'll take that as a compliment. I'll get back to you when I'm ready."

"Try not to take too long, Houston. There are deadlines that need to be met. I don't feel I have to say this, but I will. If you perform well over the next few months, you will become VP of the entire corporation and eventually all of this will belong to you. Imagine the possibilities."

Yeah, I could imagine all right.

There were so many oddities about the meeting, not just the fact he suddenly wanted me to take over the company. What the hell was he hiding from me?

I placed my drink on the bar. "You'll have my answer in forty-eight hours."

"Good enough." A shadow fell across my father's face, his eyes glassing over. "This was never the way I thought things would go. Selling off assets. Losing respect."

"Selling off assets? What are you talking about?"

He waved his hand, trying to put a smile on his face. "Just business, son. Don't worry about it."

"What aren't you telling me, Pops, and don't lie to me. You know I can't tolerate liars."

He took a deep breath, holding it for several seconds before expelling. "The stock drop hurt us. Business is down significantly from a year ago. And…"

"And?" I hissed, my patience all but gone.

"The company has received a couple of recent threats."

"The company?"

"Well, the words were directed at me, but I know the intent is to defame and destroy me."

I cocked my head, knowing I was going to have to pry the information out of him. Maybe the caller hadn't been some freak after all, but why warn me? "What were the contents of these threats?"

He appeared even more nervous than before. "I haven't always been a good man, son."

"Tell me something I don't know. What did you do?"

His face grew red, a snarl erupting from his throat as he glared at me, but within seconds, his fury faded away, much like his resolve. "I've done some things, what some would call illegal activities, although I didn't consider them as such at the time. Whoever sent the emails seems to have details, maybe even evidence. Damning evidence."

"The person could be bluffing."

He shook his head vehemently. "He knew things, details that I've kept secret."

"He. You sound so certain."

My father slammed his hand on his desk, physically shaking. "I'm not certain of anything except I can't allow the information to be disclosed. It would ruin me. It would completely tear apart this company. You and your brother and sister would have nothing left. This… individual even accused me of murder. Can you believe that?"

"Actually, yes, I can."

He stared at me, incredulous, his eyes shimmering with anger. He pointed a finger at me, his entire body shaking. "Don't you dare say that shit to me! I'm your father. I did what I had to do."

His vehemence alone was enough to confirm my beliefs.

He'd purposely had at least two of his enemies killed. The tension was high, both of us remaining silent for at least a full minute.

"What does this person want?" I asked bitterly.

"He is trying to blackmail me."

"For cash?"

"I don't know at this point. The asshole is toying with me, leading me on saying I'll learn soon enough. You're the only one who knows this. You can't talk to anyone about it. I mean anyone."

While I wasn't certain why he hadn't included Chase in on the conversation, if I had to guess, I'd say my father had determined I couldn't be behind the blackmail attempt. However, what my father didn't know was that I was also aware of certain discrepancies that he'd been the instigator of, although nothing that would derail the company entirely. "Is there a time limit?"

"No, at least not yet. I think the asshole wants to keep me on edge and it's working. I just wish I knew what the asshole wanted. I can't sleep. I can't eat."

Yeah, Pops. Imagine what the two men you destroyed feel.

"What you've neglected to tell me as that you've also received death threats. I will have to assume it's from the same person, but maybe you have several individuals attempting to take you down. Isn't that the case?"

He didn't react at first, his expression almost blank. Then he slowly fell into his chair, his breathing ragged. "How the hell would you know that?"

"Because I was warned by some unknown caller prior to your attorney providing the good news about the trust fund." I walked closer, slamming my hands on the desk. "What the fuck is going on?"

"I swear to you, I don't know, at least not entirely. I don't think it's about the defense contract. This goes way beyond any recent business activities."

I laughed, shaking my head. "You might be a good poker player when it comes to business, Pops, but you're a shitty liar. My question is why the hell would this entity call me? There has to be a reason."

"I said. I. Don't. Know."

It was easy to see he wasn't ready to tell me anything useful. I took my time, thinking about what little he'd told me. "You need to send me those emails, Pops."

"I'd prefer not to."

"If you want my help, then you will send them to me. I'm here under false pretenses and that pisses me off."

An actual smile crossed his face and he took a few seconds to look me in the eyes. "I knew I could count on you, son. No matter our differences, blood is always thicker than water."

I knew better than to think I'd get any additional platitudes from my father. I'd already received more compliments, however jaded they were, than I'd gotten my entire life. As I walked to the door, I could barely contain my laughter.

Or my anger.

Whoever was attempting to blackmail or annihilate my father would be forced to deal with me. And my form of retaliation had nothing to do with stroking a pen or opening a bank account.

While he'd refused to tell me what this was about, I thought it went far deeper than the recent accusations regarding his contract with the military.

"Oh, and son. While Bristol appears to be a nice girl, she's not the one for you. Besides, I have a feeling that she's nothing but an actress you hired in order to get your hands on your trust fund. If that's the case, toss her. You don't need a noose around your neck. I'll gladly sign away the fund, especially since I don't want the blackmailer to get a hold of it."

There was no reason for his words to bother me in the least, but they did on two levels. Whatever he'd done was extremely egregious. The other reason was more disturbing personally. I thought about his second offer and the answer was easy. "I love Bristol, Pops. While you may not believe it, there is such a thing as wanting to spend your life with someone who's better than you."

As I walked out of the door, I realized that a part of me believed what I'd spouted off.

God help me.

CHAPTER 8

ristol

Lies.

I felt embroiled in them, the weight pushing me under the water. The fight to stay afloat was difficult, leaving me aching inside, my throat closing.

"I'm famished. Let's grab a late lunch and a very tall glass of wine." Ashley tugged my arm, dragging me across the street and into a bistro.

We'd shopped for over four hours, the whirlwind trip taking us to a half dozen stores. I had to give the lively girl credit. She knew her way around San Diego. At least I'd managed to select several rooms full of furniture, although I had to admit that at this point every fabric and detail was nothing but a blur in my mind. She's also insisted I try on and purchase several pieces of clothing.

And lingerie.

I'd felt like such a hypocrite, but I'd gone along with the charade, trying to keep up the pretense as well as the banter. Now, exhausted, I had to admit I wasn't that good of an actress after all. At least she hadn't seemed to notice.

"This is perfect," she said as she pulled me toward a table near the front window. "Now, we can search for hunky men." Giggling, she flopped her shopping bags onto the floor then gasped. "I'm sorry. I guess you can't ogle sexy men any longer. My brother would have a cow."

Grinning, I eased the shopping bags next to hers and leaned over the table. "There is no harm in looking or fantasizing for that matter."

Her laugh was genuine, her eyes sparkling in the bright sun streaming in through the window. I genuinely liked the girl. Her spunk reminded me of myself just a few years before. She immediately waved for a waiter and we ordered the wine that I had to admit I was looking forward to.

"Now, you need to tell me all the juicy details about how you two met. I mean the juicy parts. Not the watered down crap you were kind enough to tell at the godawful dinner last night." When she rolled her eyes, it was all I could do to keep my laughter down to a minimum.

"Um, let's just say that your brother refuses to take no for an answer."

"That's the way of the Powers men. They truly believe they're all that and a bag of chips. I'm surprised you can tolerate him, although he does have a soft little underbelly that he refuses to allow anyone to see." Her eyes opened wide. "And if you dare tell my brother I said that, I'm going to kill you."

I pretended to zip my lips, already able to relax. "Not a single word."

"Good. I like you a hell of a lot."

"Well, I like you too."

When the wine arrived, she took her time taking several sips then slid the glass away, folding her arms across the table. "Are you certain you want to get involved with this family?"

"Why do you say that?"

"Come on, Bristol. You're one smart cookie. That's easy to tell. My family is insufferable. Charity is a mess and Riley has always been treated like a second class citizen. I won't tell you what I really think about Chase, other than he's an insufferable asshole, more so now that he decided to end the only decent relationship he's ever had."

"The fiancée?"

She nodded. "Bridgett was so sweet and loving, the kindest person in the world. She put up with his sorry ass for months. Then he just texted her one day and poof, it was over."

"Cold bastard."

"That's why he's so angry you're here. Believe it or not, our father really does want a grandchild. I know. It sounds nuts. It's something about continuing the Powers family legacy. Old school stuff. Now, Houston is happy, getting married and he's returned to the fold. Trust me. He'll start pushing for grandchildren as soon as you've returned from your honeymoon. You are going on a honeymoon, right?"

I realized I'd been holding my breath. The ruse had far too many consequences. "I... I'm not certain. This really was so unexpected." I must have seemed flustered by the look on her face.

She bit her lip, making a face. "I know. I talk too much. That's always been my problem, but I do worry about you. I'm not certain love can conquer all evils."

I thought about her statement, watching as she tried to portray such confidence. She could have been Houston's twin, the same shade of sandy blonde hair, only hers was in curls spilling all the way down her back. Her large eyes seemed laced with innocence, but I could tell she was masking a good portion of her emotions. I would if I had a family like the Powers. "You know what? I do believe love and respect can conquer all in a relationship as long as there is communication and trust. Without all of those together, a couple doesn't have the ability to form a bond of any kind, let alone a friendship. It's so important to enjoy the little things in life, like holding hands or kissing in the moonlight." I mused over what I was saying.

She took a deep breath.

"Even waking up on a Sunday morning when it's raining outside and deciding that there's no place to go. Watching old movies and listening to music while enjoying a glass of wine together or making dinner when there doesn't seem to be anything in the house that's edible. That's what matters. Not money. Not power. Not large houses with beautiful views of the ocean. Just being together is all that matters." Sighing, I reached for my wine, visions of Houston's face crowding my thoughts. As if that kind of a man would ever enjoy the little things in life.

I had to be out of my mind.

"That's wonderful, Bristol. I can see how much love is between the two of you. You've just given me something to dream about."

Dream. I wanted to tell her that the reality was cold and bleak, but how could I burst her bubble?

Besides, I'd obviously sold her a bill of goods that would likely gather me points.

"I don't know how you did it, but I think you've grounded him."

"I'm not sure about that."

"However…" she purred. "What about his dominating side?"

I bit my lip, purposely rolling my eyes in an exaggerated manner. "Well, there is that."

We laughed together again, the conversation moving away from Houston.

Sadly, I couldn't seem to get the man out of my mind.

Brutal.

Dangerous.

Nasty.

Sexy…

Houston.

The late lunch was amazing, allowing me to forget for a little while that I was nothing but a boosted Girl Friday, planning an arranged marriage with a man I knew little about. While Ashley had provided a few details about their past, I didn't feel it was prudent to riddle her with questions.

As we walked out into the late afternoon sun, I realized a tiny part of me had missed him. I was also apprehensive about spending an entire evening with him alone.

"By the way, since I knew you guys didn't have anything in the new house, I took the liberty of sending you a few things. They should be there by the time we return." She squeezed my hand, once again pulling me in the direction of wherever she wanted to go.

"Do I want to ask where you're taking me next? Shoe shopping?"

"Nothing like that. Just a last stop before I take you home."

As she stopped in front of a store a full block long, I grimaced. A bridal shop. I'd tried to convince myself that I was prepared to go through with the ruse of marriage, but my entire body was trembling. The lie would mean we were married in name only, but the actual act would make it legal. While I didn't know all the rules with regard to California, I certainly understood divorce took time.

"What's wrong? You don't have to purchase anything today, but you do need to narrow down some choices. My brother has absolutely zero patience. Come on. This is the finest location in town."

"You set me up."

Laughing, she winked before pulling on the brass handle. "Maybe a little. Just take a look. If you see something you like, try it on. Price is no object, remember."

The thought of sliding into a white gown, one meant for lovers who couldn't handle spending the rest of their lives without each other was debilitating.

"Can I help you, ladies?"

The store clerk was pleasant, making me cringe even more.

"My beautiful friend is marrying my brother, Houston Powers, of the Powers family? She'd love to look at a few dresses." There was no doubt Ashley was throwing the influence card, which surprised me, the clerk's response shocking me even more.

"Oh, my goodness. We have a guest of honor in our midst. Please allow me to show you some of our most gorgeous dresses. You're a size eight. Correct?"

I nodded, unable to find my voice.

"I have a vision of you as a bride. Come with me."

While I trailed behind dutifully, I was shaking to my core. How in God's name was I going to be able to get through this? I didn't love him. Surely someone would notice at the wedding if not before. There was no way I was that good of an actress.

The clerk was fastidious, pulling out five dresses within seconds. Every one of them was gorgeous, ornate with rhinestones and several feet of train. I felt sick to my stomach, the two glasses of wine threatening to force me to run into the bathroom. When the older woman held one of them in front of me, pushing me gently toward the three-way mirror, I couldn't hide my feelings of disgust.

She frowned, darting a glance in Ashley's direction. "You're not a traditional bride. Are you?"

"Not even close. I can't see myself in something so… frilly." I chose my words carefully, realizing they'd likely get back to Houston.

"Then I think I have something that's simply perfect for you."

Perfect.

There was nothing perfect in this life, although I was shocked at the dress the clerk had presented. Sleek and beautiful, the simple design was exactly like the dress I would choose.

If I was getting married to the man of my dreams.

I did as a good girl would do. I tried it on.

As I stood in front of the mirror, all the thoughts about a perfect relationship I'd shared with Ashley swept into my mind. That wasn't going to happen.

"That's the one, Bristol." Ashley squeezed my arms, her words of encouragement creating a wave of sadness.

"I think you're right," I managed.

"Excellent." The store clerk clapped her hands. "I'll set it aside for you, unless you'd like to finish the fitting today."

"No, a later time. I just got into town."

"Very well."

As I headed for the dressing room, I realized I'd just sealed the deal, allowing the lie to continue.

For some reason, I envisioned my signature written in blood.

A cold chill trickled down my spine the second I got out of the passenger seat. The sun was slowly fading, yet still bright enough I continued to wear my sunglasses. Ashley continued to jabber as she started to remove packages from her car.

I couldn't get the odd feeling out of my system. After removing my shades, I scanned the area surrounding the house. The tree-lined driveway was filled with tropical foliage, various flowering shrubs that had been well maintained. The house was far removed from any others, the privacy something I was certain Houston paid a pretty penny for.

Still, I couldn't shake the feeling that we were being watched. I'd noticed a car in the side mirror, swearing that it had been following us after we left the bridal shop. I wasn't prone to succumbing to this kind of fear, but my instinct was never wrong.

There was someone hiding in the trees.

"I think we should get inside," I half whispered.

Ashley followed my gaze, tugging the hair out of her face. "Do you see something?"

"I… Maybe just a deer." I had no idea whether San Diego even had roaming deer in the city or anywhere else for that matter, but she took my statement at face value, chatting away as she grabbed packages out of the back of the car.

Whatever she'd ordered had been delivered, the oversized boxes piled on the expansive porch.

"What did you do?" I asked, trying to shove aside the prickles still trickling down my back.

"Just a little housewarming gift. Besides, I thought the both of you might need a romantic night after the shitshow last night." She rolled her eyes and laughed as I unlocked the door. It took several trips before we got everything inside.

"It's time I got out of your hair. I'm certain Houston will be home soon," she half purred then pointed toward two of the boxes. "Make certain and open those first. They'll need some special care."

"You don't want to stay? I did purchase some wine. I'm not certain we have any glasses but chugging out of the bottle I've done before."

She grinned, shaking her head. "Nope. It's your first night in a beautiful new home with the man of your dreams. I'm not going to spoil it, even though I'd love to be a fly on the wall."

Home.

How many times had she used the word over the course of the day? As far as man of my dreams, Houston was more like the boogeyman in my worst nightmare. "Thank you for everything."

Ashley squeezed my arm then backed away. "Just don't allow either my father or Chase to get under your skin. That's what drove Houston away."

"How do you do it?"

"I have certain methods. You'll find yours. Try and remember love conquers all. At least that's what I've heard." Giggling, she almost raced to the door as if Houston wouldn't want her to be in his house upon his return.

After she closed the door, I rubbed my arms, moving toward the glorious set of French doors and throwing them open. The warm breeze did little to calm my nerves or the chill that continued to shift down the length of my body. I indulged for a few minutes, watching the ocean waves before remembering I needed to open the boxes.

What I found warmed my heart. Ashley was entirely different than everyone else in her family, a caring individual. I had no idea how she'd managed to remain so levelheaded.

She'd provided an entire picnic of meats, cheeses, fruits and bread, seafood salad, and olives of three different types. There was a case of wine, bottles of liquor, and fresh squeezed orange juice. There was even a box of dishes and utensils along with the most gorgeous set of fine crystal I'd ever seen. She'd even purchased a coffeemaker and six different gourmet coffees along with cookies and the most expensive chocolates in the world. In the other boxes were items for the house from the softest pillows I'd ever squeezed to other decorative pillows, sheets, and an exquisite comforter in the richest shade of ruby red. And the number of candles she'd purchased had the capacity of burning down the house.

What made me laugh was the small stereo system she'd purchased so we'd be able to have music. The compact design had everything.

Ashley had spent a fortune on a hope and dream that didn't really exist. I hated myself even more for partaking in the ruse.

After placing the grocery items in the kitchen and unpacking a portion of the wineglasses, I pulled out one of the bottles I'd purchased, a favorite that I'd rarely been allowed to buy. The fifty-dollar price tag was a big no-no. Now it seemed like little more than allowance money. How ridiculous.

I poured a hefty amount and found a soothing jazz station before returning to the deck, determined to relax.

As if that was going to happen.

What had already nagged at my respectable self was that I could see myself actually living in such a gorgeous house, making every room special. I was even able to envision a few of the rooms; splashes of vivid colors on accent walls, gorgeous pieces of art purchased at galleries, and beachy yet elegant furniture. And that's exactly what I'd purchased with Houston's money.

The visions were so dazzling and real that I had to remind myself I was only a guest for a short period of time.

Strings of colors dotted the sky as the afternoon gave way, the breeze remaining as well as the chill. The glass of wine had done little to calm my nerves, the innate feeling that tonight would be even more difficult. I'd suddenly never felt so alone in the world, drifting into a sea of unknown. I leaned over the railing, taking a deep breath of the salty sea.

There was nothing but pristine beach as far as the eye could see. There were no other houses or commercial buildings breaking up the spectacular view. The setting was as close to paradise as I'd ever seen. Sighing, I'd had just about as much serenity as I could tolerate. For whatever time alone I had left, I'd put away the rest of the things, pretending the next few days wouldn't be difficult.

As I started to turn away, a slight scent wafted in my direction, the odor not made by nature. A cigar. I'd know the rich aroma anywhere. I'd always been drawn to a man smoking a cigar for some insane reason. However, it was out of place in the secluded area. Unable to see anything, I carefully walked down the flight of stairs, moving around the pool in order to see more of the shoreline. Houston didn't seem like the type of man to smoke cigars. Besides, I hadn't heard a car or been given any indication of his arrival.

I scanned both sides of the beach, including shifting my gaze to the few trees dotting one side of the property. The uncanny sensations had returned, the hair standing up on the back of my neck. There was nothing that I could see, but as before, I knew I was being watched. There was no doubt in my mind. Swallowing hard, I took a deep whiff, but there was no way of determining from which direction the trail of smoke was coming.

However, it was obvious that Houston had left out some crucial details about the contract. After another two minutes of searching, I slowly turned around. Another series of sensations coursed through me, only this time they were entirely electric in nature. I didn't need to glance at the upper deck to know he was there. Houston. My soon to be husband.

But when I did, my heart thumped more rapidly.

The powerful man stood with his hands in his pockets, his jacket open, his tie removed. Even though twilight was preparing to descend on the horizon, he still wore dark sunglasses, but there was no doubt he was staring at me. An aura of danger surrounded him as well as one of utter sensuality.

He didn't move or acknowledge me in any way, but I could swear I was able to read his thoughts.

The man wanted to devour me.

As soon as I started to walk up the stairs, he disappeared into the house. Shadows and sadness surrounded the man. Even with all his dominating tendencies and power, there was a darkness furrowing inside of him that was threatening to eat him alive.

I took my time before going inside. He was nowhere to be seen, but I heard a sound coming from another part of the house. I found him standing with a glass in one hand, the other planted on the counter. He was staring at the bottle of scotch, unblinking, his entire body tense.

"You will not leave this house without my permission." While his words were said quietly with almost no inflection, I sensed his anger increasing.

"That wasn't part of the deal we made."

"Well, it is now." Snapping his head in my direction, his eyes pierced mine in such a commanding way that I was forced to suck in my breath.

"Has something happened?"

His jaw was clenched, his chest heaving. Then he chuckled and took a swig of his drink as he lifted his glass, swirling the liquid. "A remarkable selection."

"A housewarming gift from your sister, along with all the boxes you see in the living room." He was hiding something from me.

He snorted, still remaining in the same position. "That's my sister for you. A true angel in a sea full of monsters."

I could tell the conversation wasn't going anywhere. "At some point we have to talk."

"You didn't acknowledge the new rule."

Exasperated, I inched closer, deciding to refill my wine. "Then you need to tell me what's going on."

When he slammed his hand on the counter, I jumped, immediately inching away. He shook his head before raking his fingers through his hair. "Do. You. Understand?"

"Yes. I do. But why? At least tell me that."

Houston took a deep breath, holding it in his lungs as he walked around me, heading toward the open door and standing in the entrance. I don't know why I bothered to trail behind him, almost desperate to hear the answer, other than my nerves remaining on edge from the cigar smoke.

He took his time before answering. "There are certain entities determined to destroy my father's corporation."

"A corporation you don't care about." That much he'd already told me.

"Maybe so, but the thought of it being ripped apart piece by piece doesn't sit well."

"Are you so terrified I'll divulge the terms of our contract that you're going to treat me as nothing but a prisoner?"

"You're not a prisoner, Bristol. You know without requiring a reminder what's at stake. You have nothing in your life without the deal we made."

I took a deep breath in order to curtail my anger. "It's funny. Just when I think you might have a decent bone in your body, you remind me all over again that you're nothing but a control freak." I couldn't stand the sight of him any longer. Huffing, I turned away, determined to get as much space between us as possible.

He grabbed my arm, jerking me against him, immediately lowering his head. The feel of his hot breath slicing across the nape of my neck was titillating, but all I wanted to do was get away from him.

"You don't understand my world, Bristol. There is always someone prepared to take what belongs to our family and they will use any method necessary in order to do so, any weakness that comes to light."

"Am I your weakness, Houston?" I was tingling all over, my nipples scraping against the lace of my bra. The thought of being aroused while he treated me like nothing but an object was disgusting.

As well as humiliating.

When he pressed his lips against my skin, I shuddered visibly, a single slight moan slipping past my lips. Electricity surged through me, his touch searing every nerve ending. And I hated myself for it.

"You are an unexpected delight, a creature of exquisite beauty and sensuality, but that changes nothing. You will do as I say." He dragged his tongue down the length of my neck with a husky growl. I wasn't certain if he was trying to scare me or usurp his authority.

But I jerked away, sloshing strings of wine over the edge of the glass.

"When you're ready to talk to me about what the hell I'm supposed to do other than simply be your freaking arm candy, let me know. Otherwise, leave me the hell alone."

Before I'd taken two steps, I heard another series of growls, but the tone was entirely different. They were ones of frustration and uncertainty.

"Perhaps you are my weakness, Bristol, what some would consider my kryptonite. Whatever the case, there are things happening that need attention, dangers that I hadn't fully anticipated. While you're little more than a delightful employee, I don't want anything to happen to you."

"Is that why you have someone watching me?"

The dead silence was the only thing that forced me to turn toward him. I'd obviously struck a nerve.

"What are you talking about?" His tone was demanding.

I instantly regretted having said anything. "I don't know for certain, but I could swear someone was outside when Ashley and I returned home. When I was outside just now, I was positive that I caught a scent of a cigar."

His nostrils flared and he immediately walked outside, staring down at the beach as if he'd be able to see anything in the deepening shadows. He seemed to sense my approach, twisting his head. "I don't have anyone watching you. There is a level of trust that is implied with the contract."

"Then who could it be?"

"That I don't know, but I intend on finding out. I have some phone calls to make. After that, we'll go to dinner."

"Why don't we have something here? Ashley made certain we had everything we needed for the night."

He said nothing at first then walked back inside, staring at the remaining boxes with disdain. "As you wish. Stay on the property. Do not go to the beach without my permission. Are we clear?"

"Yes." He shot me an undistinguishable look before retreating to another part of the house.

Leaving me entirely alone.

What was really going on?

I shifted my attention to the rolling waters for a few additional seconds before deciding to ignore his arrogance. At least I could enjoy pretending we both gave a damn.

There was no reason for me to enjoy placing all the purchased items, including preparing a makeshift bed complete with positioning several candles, but I did. Over the course of almost two hours, I managed to wash and put away the dishes and break down the boxes as well. I hadn't caught sight of him, although his booming voice had filtered down the hallway while I'd been in the bedroom.

When I was satisfied that at least we'd have a fairly comfortable bed for the night, I hung up a few pieces of clothing before changing. Whether or not he liked my selection of a tee shirt and shorts, I didn't give a damn.

I almost laughed when I took the picnic basket to the pool, spreading out a blanket and several of the flameless candles nearby. They flickered as if dancing in the light breeze, adding the perfect touch to the shimmering lights of the pool. The beautiful day had turned into a gorgeous night, stars sparkling in the sky. I stood for a few minutes doing nothing but gazing at them. I used to wish upon stars as a wide-eyed kid who thought she could conquer the world. Now they held an entirely different meaning.

A faraway place where anything could happen.

I smirked at the thought, realizing I'd be forced to interrupt whatever business dealings Houston was engaging in. Maybe there was some irrational side of me that hungered to find a way to rip aside his defenses, for once seeing what made him tick. Would that make me like him any better? There was no telling, but at least it would provide some level of peace.

Maybe.

"You do realize our relationship isn't about romance." Houston issued a statement as if it was a mandate.

"Do you remember you said this didn't have to be unpleasant or difficult?" I shivered as I turned to face him, surprised that he'd actually changed clothes, now wearing blue jeans and a polo. He looked less like a ruthless millionaire than before, his casual attire suiting him, highlighting his chiseled body.

Houston peered down at the blanket. "You're right. We can enjoy ourselves."

My God, the man was giving permission.

He stood over me, waiting until I'd eased onto the blanket, curling my legs under me before he did the same. As he yanked open the basket, I found it necessary to hold my breath. His bout of anger indicated whatever he'd learned at his meetings had driven him to the edge of his usual rational behavior.

The quiet settling between us was just as difficult as every other aspect of the time we'd spent together. I was shocked when he carefully opened the wine then began to place the various items in an artistic array on the blanket. He finally lifted his gaze, handing me a glass. When our fingers touched, there was such an erotic feel to the way he brushed his index finger across mine that I was momentarily stunned.

Then he issued a statement that pulled me into his darkness, allowing me a glimpse of what the deal was really about.

"There will be an attempt made on my father's life. If the assassin is successful, that will leave me in charge of the company. That will also place my life as well as anyone in my world in danger, including you. If you are being watched, it's because someone wants you out of my life. That's never going to happen. No one takes what belongs to me. Ever."

CHAPTER 9

*H*ouston

Disbelief.

I could see Bristol's utter disbelief at the statement I'd made. Her eyes flashed in the same way they'd done on the night we'd met, a mixture of anger and immediate dislike. I'd never been one to mince words and I certainly wasn't going to start now. While certain women were prone to histrionics, she wasn't one of them. That left the reality that she was being watched.

As to the full understanding of why, I had yet to ascertain. It was obvious my father had lured me here under false pretenses. He'd know that his threat of removing my inheritance altogether was the only thing that would pull me back into the fold.

Bristol stared at me wide-eyed, her mouth twisting. "What are you talking about?"

"I'm saying that my father has made his share of enemies over the years and it would appear that one or more of them want him dead, not just ruined." I knew my words held a cold edge, as if I didn't care, but during the course of the last few hours, I'd been forced to realize that I actually did give a damn. Maybe time spent away from the powerful man had given me an entirely different perspective. I was angry, even more so because after the dozen phone calls I'd made, I'd heard lots of angry voices, but I didn't believe that any of his direct competitors could be capable of performing such a heinous act.

Including hiring someone to do the job.

"You say that as if it's no big deal."

"It's a very big deal."

She took a sip of her wine and to my surprise, her hand wasn't shaking. She was as calm and collected as she'd acted the majority of the time. I had even more respect for her, although I was furious with myself that I'd brought her into the damning problem. If I'd known just how serious the situation truly was, I would never have put her life on hold or in jeopardy.

Maybe.

I looked away, shaking my head. I couldn't get over the fact I'd turned more like my father than I would have ever believed. That pissed me off almost as much.

"Then what are you going to do about it? And don't you dare tell me that you want your father killed over money."

I abhorred the tone of her voice, the accusation she tossed my way. "My father confided only a small portion of what he's dealing with, and from what I can tell, not to my brother or my sister."

"Why?"

"Beats the shit out of me."

"You have two brothers. Why do you hate your stepbrother so much?"

I'd never been asked the question. "I don't hate him, Bristol. I think it's all about what we were taught as children."

"Right. Blood is thicker than water. That's why you'll never get married to anyone you care about. You're too terrified they'll manage to take away your money. That's one of the reasons you specifically requested an attorney, isn't it? So I could check for all the loopholes in your trust fund paperwork and whatever contracts you might enter into. You're so damn greedy that you don't want any other human being to have the possibility of getting what you believe rightfully belongs to you."

She almost had a shimmer of glee in her eyes. Huffing, I tamped back my natural retort, vicious words that wouldn't have meant a damn thing. At minimum, she deserved the truth regarding the deal we'd made. "I did request an attorney and yes, I wanted to make certain there weren't any loopholes, but it had more to do with the barbs thrown and the games my father enjoys playing, not the money."

"You expect me to believe that."

"I expect you to do the job I paid you to do."

A smile crossed her face while she eased the wine onto the blanket and jerked up. "Enjoy dinner. After all, you're nothing but a pig."

I closed my eyes, sucking in my breath. "Don't go."

"Is that a fucking order?"

"That's a request, Bristol. I'm sorry I sound like an asshole."

"That's because you are an asshole."

A laugh bubbled to the surface. "You're right. That's all I've ever been and something I've taken pride in becoming. Would you please sit down, and I will rein in the nasty side of me? Okay?"

She hesitated for over a minute then walked back slowly, sitting down and keeping her hateful glare. "I'm not your enemy. I will try and help you, but you have to tell me the truth, at least whatever truth you're aware of. If it makes you feel any better, remember that I signed a nondisclosure, and that includes any aspect of whatever I learn or that we talk about. If I would break that agreement, I could be sued as well as disbarred. Does that help you understand just how serious I take legal contracts?"

She could be all business, another aspect I admired. I held up my glass, cocking my head when she didn't immediately retrieve hers. "Yes, Bristol, it does."

Rolling her eyes, she allowed our glasses to touch then immediately pulled away. "Then talk. If your father's life has really been threatened, then the police should be brought in. I know exactly what you're going to say. The family can handle the problem, the all-powerful Powers family. What if you can't? What if you get a call in the middle of the night informing you that your father was murdered? Are you going to give a damn?"

My thoughts drifted to the phone call over a month before. By all rights, I should tell her what had transpired.

But I didn't.

"Yes, I will care," I managed. I watched as she sipped her wine, her body finally relaxing to a degree. She would always be tense around me, but in truth, I didn't blame her.

"Then act like it. Talk. Tell me about this trust fund at least."

"The trust fund was created just after I was born and mostly from my mother's money. Her parents were well off and left her with a significant inheritance. Same with Chase and Ashley. I don't know the circumstances around if or what amount Riley was provided. After that, my father used his business acumen to parlay the funds, the amounts now worth as much as twenty times what has originally been indicated."

"That's why your father feels he has control over the options."

"Yes. When I left five years ago after a bitter argument, my father threatened me, but never said anything about the trust fund. Then I received notification from his attorney that the terms had changed."

She laughed. "Including that you had to get married."

"Yes. I balked at first, but from what the attorney I hired to look into it told me there was nothing I could do about it given my birth mother was dead."

"So, you figured why not invest two million to gain more money?"

"Thirty-five million, or so I was told. I've yet to be given access to the fund itself, even to check the balance."

"Wow. I always knew that everyone had a price. Thirty-five million is yours."

The same old anger rushed into my system. "It's not just about the money, Bristol. It's also about the principle, believe it or not. My father can't rule everyone around him."

"Like you attempt to do."

Now I couldn't help but laugh. She'd seen right through me. "Maybe you're right. I arrived prepared for a battle and because my curiosity had been piqued. Instead, my father begged for my help. He's never asked a single soul on this planet for help."

"Which means he takes the threat seriously."

Sighing, I nodded. "Likely. He wants me to take over a significant portion of the corporation, with plans that I'll eventually be made CEO of the entire organization."

"Interesting. Doesn't Chase believe he's the heir apparent?"

"Absolutely," I mused. The lady was more observant than I gave her credit for. "Chase has acted like I'm his enemy for years. When I moved away, I can't imagine how glad he was to see me go. He's followed in my father's footsteps his entire life."

"Did your father mention any terms of this new agreement?"

"I have a contract I've glanced over, but I want you to take a good look at it. In addition, he's offered to void the new codicil with regard to the trust. It's a win-win according to my father."

Bristol inched closer. "How did you find out your father had been threatened?"

"He told me as much, although I had to drag it out of him. I would have laughed it off because my father is the master of game playing, but there was absolute terror in his eyes. He's being blackmailed, although the terms have yet to be disclosed. I've never seen him as broken as he was standing in the middle of his office. He says he has no idea who it could be."

"You always know your enemies, Houston. That's rule number one of playing corporate games, especially in a high dollar world that your father plays in. Billions of dollars can be won and lost without breaking a sweat."

"But only if you're ruthless, even unscrupulous."

"Exactly, which shouldn't be difficult for you. Has your father been involved in illegal activities?"

Damn if her terse words didn't excite the hell out of me.

"I've always suspected he has including insider trading, but he's hidden his tracks well. Granted, he's being accused of stealing intellectual property involving a military contract worth a significant amount of money, but I have no idea whether that is true or not."

She rubbed her finger across her lips, blinking several times. "It would appear he doesn't hide his discrepancies well enough. In other words, someone is holding information or even evidence over his head and whatever it is, the chance being taken is worth the risk. If I had to guess, given the amount of money on the table, whoever is threatening your father will likely use rougher methods in order to get what they want."

"Including murder." I didn't offer the words as a question. I made a statement. "I don't deserve your help, Bristol. I realize that. I've been less than forthcoming, not to mention my surly attitude. However, if you'd be willing to continue, I will offer you another million dollars."

The look on her face was one of condemnation, not disbelief. "Let me give you a piece of advice, Houston. While you've never known suffering in your life, the majority of people have. Money is important in order to keep a roof over people's heads and food on the table, but it's not everything. In fact, it's only a small part of life and can't buy happiness. That's something you've never learned and I feel sorry for you."

"As I've told you before, don't feel sorry for me. I've enjoyed my life. Have you?" I instantly regretted the ugly words. She didn't deserve my anger because of the shit I'd be forced to deal with.

"You're such a bastard. I don't believe you." She tossed the glass, her aim perfect. Wine splashed across my face and down my shirt. Snarling, she shifted to her feet, walking quickly toward the house.

I reacted, jerking up and snagging her arm, dragging her against the heat of my body. Fisting her hair, I yanked with enough force she hissed, pummeling her fists against me.

"Get off me," she demanded.

"That's not going to happen." My breathing heavy, I slid one hand down her back, cupping her bottom and grinding my hips against her.

She continued fighting me, wiggling in my hold as she struggled for her freedom. "I hate you."

"I don't care if you hate me. I need you to obey me."

Her laugh was infuriating, driving the beast that I'd become to the surface. She seemed tiny in my arms, like a delicate flower that should be cared for. I wasn't that kind of person. All I knew how to do was take what I wanted.

And today was no exception.

I crushed my mouth over hers, savoring the strangled moans she made as I pushed my throbbing cock against her stomach. She felt so damn good in my arms, as if she'd always belonged against me. As I fought to push her lips apart, she wrapped one hand around my neck, digging her fingernails into my skin.

There was no pain, only a surge of electricity that became blinding. I had to have her. I refused to allow her to get away from me. When I managed to thrust my tongue past her voluptuous lips, the combination of red wine and cinnamon fueled every one of my senses. Just the touch of her showered both of us with white-hot flames, licking down every inch of our bodies. Nothing had ever felt so damn good.

Pushing and pulling, she couldn't budge at first, yet the little hellion refused to give up. She raked her nails down my back, her moans turning into ragged whimpers. Her refusal to submit to me tossed gasoline onto the roaring fire.

I was blinded by my needs, dominating her tongue as I explored the dark recesses of her mouth. She could have no way of knowing what she was doing to me. I shifted my hips back and forth, the friction even more powerful than the kiss. And I took my time, waiting until she finally allowed her body to mold against mine, acquiescing to the point of acting as if she enjoyed the moment of passion.

When I broke the kiss, I nipped her lower lip, allowing a string of growls to permeate the night air.

"Oh…" The single syllable slipped out of her mouth. She closed her eyes, panting as I dragged my tongue from one side of her jaw to the other, biting down on her earlobe then licking very slowly around the shell of her ear.

"You're all mine," I breathed, barely able to contain my raw needs. I was going to take her in every tight hole, forcing her to suck my cock before plunging it deep into her pretty pink pussy. Then I'd claim her ass, spanking her in order to insure her obedience. After that, I'd tie her to my bed, keeping her naked and waiting for my use. My thoughts were vile and sadistic, filthy and delicious and I knew I couldn't resist her any longer.

I should have known the little brat had something up her sleeve. She would never truly give in to me. The second I pulled away, she managed to throw a hard punch to my chest, immediately twisting in order to get out of my clutches.

However, she didn't understand my power on any level. The second I snagged her forearm, she reeled around, smacking my face. The force of her actions pummeled us backward, tossing us into the pool.

The shock of the water as well as her actions dragged at my rage. I still had my grip on her arm, but she was quick with her actions, kicking out and breaking my hold. As soon as I popped up to the surface, I let out a deep roar. The little brat had already started to swim away.

Hell, no.

She wasn't going to get away from me.

Not now.

Not ever.

Reaching out, I snagged her leg, easily able to drag her backwards.

"Bastard," she hissed.

"You're right." I slapped my hand around the back of her neck, wrapping one leg around her. "You're going to stop fighting me."

Her eyes darted back and forth, her breath skipping. My God, she was absolutely stunning in the lighting of the pool. Everything about her was exactly what I'd craved my entire life. She'd managed to break through some insane barrier, crashing against the armor that I'd invested time and effort into securing around myself.

And I wanted every inch of her.

"You're such a horrible person," she whispered, some of the fight slipping away.

"But this horrible bastard you can't resist."

Her mouth twisted as she clung to me, her nose wrinkling as she tried to think of some retort. "I will always resist you."

"You're lying to me, Bristol. I could smell your desire the moment I walked in the door. Tell me you crave my cock sliding deep inside of you."

"No."

"Tell me." My command was deep, the sound more like a beast than a man.

"I…"

Her single hesitation was all I needed, my hunger increasing to the point I wasn't going to be able to hold back. "One last time. Tell me."

"Yes. God, yes!"

I captured her mouth, wasting no time whisking my tongue inside as I turned her in a full circle. Her hands clung to me as if I was a lifeline, her body tensing and pushing away, but only for a few seconds. When she wrapped both arms around my neck, pulling me in closer, I felt vindicated from being the monstrous bastard she'd accused me of being.

Our connection, the soaring electricity was unequaled, my desire rocketing off the charts. I could no longer think clearly, my needs were so intense. As the kiss became a wild moment of fantasy and indulgency, our bodies twisting together and water splashing over us, I realized I could lose myself in this woman.

Forever.

The kiss becoming close to violent, I finally pushed her away, jerking at her top until I was able to drag it over her head.

She laughed, her eyes glistening in the darkness, and all I could think about was ravaging every inch of her sensuous body. She had no idea what I was capable of, but she'd soon learn. Within the next few seconds, we tore at our clothing until we were finally free of the hindrance. I shoved her against the side of the pool, smacking my hands on the edge as I ground my hips against her.

Laughing nervously, she tangled her fingers in my hair, darting her eyes back and forth. "Fuck me."

Her command was like music to my ears, although she'd never be in charge. I could feel a crooked smile crossing my face as I dragged one of her legs around me, pushing my cock against her swollen folds.

The expression on her face was one of torment as well as blissful longing, allowing her to enjoy being taken by a beast. When I slipped my cockhead inside, she threw her head back, allowing the light breeze to float her ragged moan toward the heavens. The sound was sweeter than any music, further igniting the savage deep within.

I drove into her with fury, her muscles immediately straining to accept my girth. I was thrown into my own moment of sheer ecstasy, my body shaking violently as I remained inside of her. But I wanted more.

Required more.

She was my kryptonite, a powerful entity who could garner far too much control. I couldn't allow her to do that. I pulled out, holding just the tip inside, teasing her. I wanted her to beg for my cock.

As usual, her defiance forbade her surrender. She jutted her hips forward, forcing my cock inside. Moaning, her eyelids fluttered as she pursed her lips. The little brat was doing everything in her power to cut through what remained of my defenses.

I slammed her against the wall, driving my cock in several times. Her winded gasps were my reward. With every brutal plunge, she lowered her head more, her moans becoming rampant. I adored the way her skin shimmered in the festive lighting. She was so alive and warm, electrifying every cell in my body.

As I thrust into her like a crazed man, our bodies melding together, she tossed her head from side to side, her eyes remaining closed.

"I'm going to do filthy things to you," I managed.

"Mmm…"

"Shackle you to my bed."

"Yes."

"Use your body every time I need it." I was breathless, barely able to speak, my hunger knowing no bounds.

"Do it," she purred, further exciting the beast.

I was thrown by how much I hungered, unable to get enough. The way her pussy yielded to me was incredible, spurring me on as a burst of heat wrapped around both our bodies. While there was nothing that I wanted more than to explode inside her tight channel, I wanted to experience every aspect of her luscious body.

I wouldn't stop until she came, slathering my cock with her juice. Nothing was going to stop me from yanking her into raw bliss.

Her pants increased, her eyes glassing over. I knew she was close.

"Do you want to come for me, little brat?" I whispered.

"Uh-huh." Her head bobbed as the pleasure shifted through every inch of her body.

"Are you going to be a good girl?"

"Yes. Yes!"

I pounded into her harder and faster, every synapse on fire, my muscles hard as rocks. "Then come for me. Let go."

"I…"

"Surrender, now. Now!"

My words seemed to ignite another fire within her. In seconds, her body began to shake uncontrollably; her face pinched as she opened her mouth on a ragged cry. Her pussy muscles clamped and released several times, a scream erupting from her throat.

And still, I refused to stop, thrusting into her intense heat with all the fury of a barbarian. She yielded to my brutal actions, a single climax erupting into a swelling wave crashing over her. She was even more beautiful than before, her eyelids fluttering and her body quivering against mine.

As she sagged against me, her breathing still scattered, I nuzzled her neck, sliding my tongue up and down.

Now it was my turn.

When I pulled away, she whimpered, trying to focus as she reached for me. Without hesitation, I jumped onto the edge of the pool, snagging a handful of her beautiful hair and dragging her between my open legs. "Suck me, sweetheart. Take every inch of my cock inside that hot mouth of yours."

The look she gave me could melt a man straight into the ground, but she obeyed, rolling her fingers on the insides of my legs as she blew across my aching cockhead. I watched as she slid the tip of her finger back and forth across my slit, licking her lips as if in anticipation.

I was barely able to contain my patience as she toyed with me, raking her nail along the side of my shaft before cupping my balls. When she rolled them between her fingers, I let off a ragged hiss, stars floating in front of my eyes. We were combustible together, our needs exploding to the point that there was no return. I would never be able to get enough of her.

"Don't tease me too long, my pet, or you're going to face my belt."

She winked as she looked up at me, her challenge one I wouldn't soon forget. When she squeezed my balls to the point of discomfort, I let off a single growl. The moment she added additional pressure, a roar erupted. There was no doubt she was enjoying her moment of control and freedom, but it would be short lived.

I held back a series of guttural sounds, trying to keep my gaze pinned on her as she slowly lifted my cock, first darting her tongue across my slit then sliding it down the underside of my shaft. I opened my legs even wider, leaning back as she blew across my swollen balls. The ache was quickly moving to anguish, my testicles full of seed.

"Fuck," I hissed the second she took one ball into her mouth, swishing her tongue back and forth before using her strong jaw muscles to clamp down. Even the noises she made, while exaggerated, were sexy as fuck, keeping me on the edge. She knew exactly what she was doing, turning me on then pulling back, driving me to the point of madness. The little girl would face a round of punishment. The thought made me smile as she shifted her open mouth to my other testicle.

"Mmm…"

I couldn't help but smile, my body so tense I couldn't stop shaking. She was testing my resolve, pushing as no other woman had ever done. And fuck, I wanted more.

When she finally zigzagged her tongue as she dragged it closer to my tip, I was ready to take over, forcing her heated mouth to take every inch.

"Suck. Me." My words were little more than a raspy whisper.

She turned her eyes upward and I could swear they were nothing more than liquid pools of fire. Opening her mouth wide, she took only my cockhead inside, taking her damn sweet time to engulf the tip.

Growling, I reached down, fisting her hair as a reminder that I was in charge. The moment she took me down another inch, I had to fight to keep from driving my cock all the way inside. Her mouth was molten fire, explosive heat resonating from every pore in her delicious body.

Bristol issued a series of purrs as she took my cock in deeper. When she was only an inch from the base, I pushed her head down until her lower lip rested on my balls.

"Fuck. So hot." Panting, I held her in place for a full ten seconds before releasing my hold, trying to catch my breath as she lifted her head, her tongue constantly swirling. I planted my hands on the deck, jutting my hips in jarring motions, face fucking her savagely.

She didn't fight me, merely placing her hands on my thighs, allowing my brutal actions to continue. Her slight gagging sounds as she was forced to accept all of me added fuel to the fire. I became lost in the moment, keeping my fingers tangled in her hair, trying to catch my breath as I drove into her mouth.

I could fuck her for hours. Days. Maybe that's exactly what I would do, foregoing anything but taking her over and over again. Another grin slid across my face as the adrenaline rush sparked an entirely new set of electric jolts. I'd never been this turned on in my freaking life. As I powered into her hot little mouth, all I could think about was driving my cock into her ass, the ultimate moment of control.

While the experience was damn good, I shoved her away, immediately sliding into the water. As I wrapped my arms around her, pulling her toward the set of curved concrete steps, she bit her lower lip. At that moment she seemed even more vulnerable, but I knew the woman wasn't as innocent as she portrayed. She was a wildcat in disguise, never finding the kind of man who could suit her needs.

Or her raging hunger.

I was that man and after tonight, she would never want another.

"What are you doing?" she dared to ask, darting a look from one side to the other.

I lowered my head until I could whisper in her ear, "First I'm spanking you for being the bad little girl you are. Then I'm fucking you in the ass."

The look on her face was priceless, her breath skipping and her eyes opening wide. "Bastard." While she'd used the word countless times, the meaning was entirely different.

"Yes. Never forget that."

She didn't fight me until I eased her onto the stairs. Then she proceeded to try to escape, grabbing the metal handrail and attempting to scamper up the few stairs.

With ease I grabbed and pulled, planting her onto her hands and knees and wrapping my hand around her neck. "Not so fast, little girl." When I brought my hand down against her rounded bottom, she whisked her hand through the water, splashing a wave across my heated body. "Tsk. Tsk. That's going to cost you." I brought my hand down several times, moving from one side of her buttocks to the other, her refusal to stop fighting only fueling me on.

"Oh. That hurts."

"As it should." I gave her several more in rapid succession, adoring the blossom of red on her perfect skin. The sound as

I smacked my palm against her wet skin was just as enticing as her quivering body. I was one sadistic man.

She wiggled and clawed at the stairs, splashing water in all directions. "Oh. Oh!" Her wails filled the night air, causing me to smile even more.

"You will learn to be very good. Won't you?" I peppered her ass with hard strikes until my hand ached, but not nearly as much as my cock. My balls hung low, my shaft twitching from the continued agony.

"Yes. Yes! Stop. I will be good."

"Somehow, I don't believe you."

I continued the spanking for another two minutes until I couldn't take the wait or the anticipation any longer. The second I kicked her legs wide open, she looked over her shoulder, panting and dragging her tongue across her lips.

As I gripped her hip with one hand, she threw her head back, closing her eyes and parting those lovely lips of hers. Every move she made was so damn enticing. I could barely contain my actions as I slipped the tip of my cock just inside her tight asshole. Then I took a deep breath, fighting the natural urge to take her like the true savage I was.

She whimpered, taking several exaggerated breaths as I pushed another inch inside.

"Relax and breathe for me." I no longer recognized my voice, the guttural tone deep and laced with a hint of evil. I did everything I could to control my actions as I slowly slid inside, pushing past the tight ring of muscle. Then it became clear I couldn't hold back any longer. When I thrust the remaining two inches inside, our combined roars were in perfect orchestration.

"Oh. Oh. Oh…" She undulated her hips, arching her back as she tossed her head back and forth.

I couldn't breathe, didn't give a damn about anything else. I simply wanted to strip away her last resolve, making her mine.

All mine.

There would never be another.

Growling, I pulled out, slamming into her again.

And again.

Until my actions turned just as brutal as my nature. The heat and tightness pulled me into a surreal world, my mind no longer able to process my actions. Nor did I care. I took exactly what I wanted, digging my fingers into her neck as I held her in place. I could no longer breathe and as I lost the last of my control, I threw my head back and roared, filling her with my seed.

Another moment of reckoning rushed into my system.

If I wasn't careful, I would never be able to fulfill the terms of our contract because I was falling hard for the feisty woman.

That couldn't happen. If I did, my beautiful kryptonite would become nothing more than a pawn in the world of power and greed.

CHAPTER 10

ristol

A beautiful sunrise.

There was nothing more I enjoyed than the first light of day as it crept up over the horizon. Today was one of those days, the string of colors floating across the sky more delightful than I'd seen in a long time. I stood on the balcony of the master bedroom, drinking in the cool air and fragrance of the ocean, forced to admit that San Diego was gorgeous. I'd forgotten just how much I missed the beach.

It was also so quiet, the only sound the water lapping at the shore as well as a few seagulls in the distance. I took a deep breath as I leaned over, my skin prickled from the slight chill. Then I sensed his presence behind me. The night hadn't gone as I'd planned, although with Houston, nothing was as it seemed.

We'd enjoyed a night together. After the early heated discussion, there'd been no other talk of business or contracts. We simply savored the food that Ashley had provided around the firepit, huddling in blankets she'd also arranged for. While he certainly didn't open up about his life in many regards, I'd realized that unlike what I'd thought, he had a deep commitment to his family. Did that make him less of a brute? Maybe not, but I gathered a small sense of why he'd handled his life the way he had, including the decisions he'd made.

That meant nothing. I knew that. Our business arrangement would end soon enough, and he'd be left with a company he'd never wanted anything to do with and perhaps be forced to face whatever recriminations his father had left behind. That was none of my business and I refused to care.

Although I was extremely curious about the limited information he'd told me. Threats? What in God's name had his father done to warrant that kind of behavior? And what if that placed Houston's life in danger? His father had brought him here for more than just torturing him with his trust fund or handing over the company.

William Powers was prepared to die for his merciless actions.

A cold shiver skated down my spine.

While green in terms of full contract negotiations, I was eager to delve into the one his father had given him. Were there any hidden clues as to what was going on? What troubled me the most was that there could be enough evidence not only to destroy Houston's father, the company bankrupted, but to trickle down to everyone involved.

The game being played was dangerous as hell.

I shuddered at the thought, visions of the night before once again rushing to the forefront of my mind. Houston was far too irresistible.

I'd allowed myself to surrender in a way that I'd never planned on. While I'd enjoyed every second of our wild, savage sex, that's all it had been. My need to tighten and keep my resolve was even stronger than before. I refused to lose my heart to a man with no understanding of love.

"You're up early," he said quietly, his tone entirely different than his usual demanding one.

"I couldn't sleep."

"I assume you ordered a bed, maybe a mattress and box springs?" His laugh was genuine and as he flanked my side, leaning over the railing, I was taken aback by his muscular body all over again. He'd remained naked while I'd insisted on donning one of my nightgowns. The thought of sharing a makeshift bed on the floor remaining without clothes had been entirely too intimate.

Normal.

And we were anything but.

I realized my nipples had already hardened from the sight of him alone and that pissed me off. When a rush of heat and blossoming desire shifted up my legs, another wave of shame came over me. Somewhere deep inside I knew my body's reaction was perfectly acceptable, but I'd promised myself I'd remain in control of both my emotions as well as any physical attraction.

"Of course I did. That was first thing." I laughed with him, although mine was stilted.

He took a deep breath, holding it in before stretching out his arms. "It's going to be a beautiful day." With his tousled hair and two-day stubble, his appearance was far too tempting. And his eyes. Geesh. I could get lost in them for days.

Every move he made was sexy as hell, creating a flutter deep inside my pussy. "I didn't think you noticed such things. What happened to your attitude from last night?"

"You really don't know a thing about me, Bristol."

After turning toward me, a mischievous glint in his eyes, I hated what I'd just said. "I'm sorry. That was shitty."

"Yes, it was, but you're right. I lived here until I was twenty-five and never gave a damn about the beach or the ocean, other than longing to surf when I was a kid. I guess it's past time I enjoyed my surroundings." With that, he gave me a longing gaze, allowing his eyes to fall down to my bare feet. "I could get used to this."

"Well, don't. I'm certain you'd prefer to have your own room."

He sighed then shifted toward the door. "Did I see a coffeemaker?"

"Yes."

"I'll make us a cup."

There was no question as to whether I wanted one or would accept. That was his usual way of handling everything. I wanted to keep hating him but with every passing hour, it was becoming more difficult. He simply had a commanding way about him that was natural, even inviting.

By the time I made it into the kitchen, he'd thrown on a pair of light sweatpants, hiding his gorgeous cock. I chastised my thoughts as the scent of coffee filled my nostrils. He stood over the counter; papers stretched across several inches. The contracts.

"I didn't know what you liked in your coffee," he said absently without looking at me.

"That was one of those pieces of information you were supposed to learn about me. Remember? Cream, no sugar." I reached into the refrigerator, feeling his weighted stare.

"Oh, yeah? And what exactly do you know about me?"

I took my time pouring in some cream, finding a spoon in the box of utensils and stirring before answering. "I know you prefer cheeseburgers on the grill to the perfect rare steak. You prefer sports cars, but only if they're considered antiques. You don't read books and rarely have time for movies, but if you're in the mood, it's all about a thriller, the bloodier the better. You enjoy your coffee black and very strong. You adore classical music, although you rarely allow anyone to know that. You always wanted to be a rock star and even tried out for a band just after high school, guitar your instrument of choice. How am I doing?"

His face had remained pinched when I rattled on from the information I'd memorized. Then he grinned like a kid, highlighting the two dimples I rarely saw. "You actually took that stuff seriously."

"Yeah, I did so I do know you to some degree. That was part of my job. Wasn't it?" When he didn't answer, I realized he was undressing me with his eyes. The same heat and desire as the night before nearly gutted me. This wasn't about sex, even though the chemistry we shared was off the chain. I purposely looked away, studying the papers in front of me. Given the heavy volume, I'd say that whoever had prepared them hadn't missed a beat. "I'll need to take some time looking at these. I don't want to give you an off the cuff response."

Damn if he didn't walk closer, sliding strands of hair from my face over my shoulder. "You don't have to be afraid of looking at me, Bristol. I'm not always an evil man."

"No, you're not, which is what bothers me." I realized I was shaking like a leaf. This was getting ridiculous. "Is that all right? To take some time, I mean? There are subtle ways to add conditions that could easily be overlooked. I need to be thorough in order to give you the best advice."

Sighing, he backed away. "Of course and I appreciate your due diligence. I'm going to take a short tour of the other facilities today that are highlighted in the contract. Then maybe we can go out to lunch and talk."

"The furniture is arriving sometime today. They wouldn't tell me when."

"Ah, yes. The great furniture so we can continue playing house." I heard the discord in his voice, even a hint of anger.

"That's what you told me to do."

"Yes, I know. That's fine. Maybe I'll bring something home for dinner." He laughed, shifting away from me and walking into the living room.

I couldn't stand leaving the conversation this way. We certainly didn't need to be at each other's throats. As I trailed after him, I was fascinated that he scanned every wall. Was he actually debating what it could look like full of furniture?

"You know, I bet our tastes are remarkably similar," he said.

"Why would you think that?"

"Just a hunch." He flashed his million-dollar smile in my direction before throwing open the doors, breathing in the air all over again.

What the hell was up with him today? Was he actually considering enjoying life? I found that hard to believe.

"Well, I hope you'll like what I purchased. You're going to have to live with my choices or trash them after I'm gone."

He laughed, the deep baritone floating into every cell in my body. The way the man ignited my senses was disruptive. As he casually leaned against the doorjamb, sipping on his coffee, I couldn't take my eyes off him.

"What if it was real after all?"

His question was so out of the blue and completely foreign that I was shocked. "It? You mean the game we're playing?"

He shot me another heated look, narrowing his eyes. "Is that so hard to imagine?"

"Hell… Never." I shut my mouth and thought about what he was asking. "No, it's not. I just don't think we're compatible. What's important to you isn't to me." Why the hell was I bothering to explain that to him? I wasn't going to fall in love with him any more than he was with me. That was certain.

My answer seemed to please him, the fabulous grin returning. "Someone very wise told me a long time ago never to say never. I'd remember that if I were you. Besides, I adore a challenge. Wasn't that in whatever notes Mr. Darke prepared for you?"

I could think of no curt answer. "Well, I wouldn't worry about it. Let's just figure out what your father really has planned. Maybe I can find something useful. I'll also need to know everything you've learned about the company and the threats. Anything you can glean will be helpful."

"I can do that."

Was he actually going to share details with me? Now I was confused.

"Okay, good. I'll make notes and if necessary, I can add a codicil to the contract with agreed upon revisions."

Sighing, he seemed to respect I no longer wanted to carry on with the conversation. "That's fine. I'll take a shower and leave. You can have the house all to yourself."

I nodded and backed away until he tensed, hissing under his breath. Every muscle in his body tensed. "What's wrong?"

"Take this." Houston shoved the coffee mug into my hand, immediately racing down the stairs and onto the beach.

I rushed onto the deck, fumbling to put the mugs on the surface then shielding my eyes from the sun. What in the hell was the man doing? As I scanned the beach, I finally realized he'd seen someone else. A cold shiver trickled through me. I'd been right. Someone had been watching me.

As he flew toward the mysterious person, I strained to see what was going on. Within seconds, Houston had snagged the stranger by the collar, ripping something from the person's hand. I was finally able to decipher the unwanted guest had to be a male by his size and stature. I didn't need to hear them to realize they were arguing.

When Houston threw a punch, knocking the man to the sand, I reacted, rushing down the stairs and flying toward them. By that point, Houston was already tromping in my direction, still carrying whatever he'd taken from the man.

When he was only twenty feet away, he threw out his arm, pointing toward the house.

I remained where I was, shaking my head, darting my gaze from the man I was supposed to marry to the person struggling to get to his feet.

"I thought I told you to get into the house," Houston snarled, pointing a second time. I could easily see how furious he was.

While I backed away, I didn't turn and run like he expected. The hesitation allowed me to see that in his hand was a camera, the long lens indicating whoever the photographer was, he'd had no intention of being caught.

Houston grabbed my arm, yanking me toward the house. "You need to learn to obey me."

"What the hell is going on?"

He said nothing as we both trudged up the stairs, but before yanking me inside, he turned toward the ocean again. "The asshole better leave or I'll continue what I started."

When we were inside, he glared at me before ripping out the data card. I was shocked when he crushed it in his bare hands then tossed the camera to the side, the smashing sound jarring. He remained enraged, pacing the floor like a panther ready to pounce.

"Who was that?" I asked, trying to remain calm.

"How the hell do I know? Likely some goddamn reporter. When I tell you to do something, you will do it."

My God, the man was not just angry, he was so furious that his face was red. I also detected a hint of fear. Jesus Christ.

What was really going on? Had his father placed him in peril?

"What are you afraid of?"

"I'm not afraid of anything, but I do expect respect in my house," he snapped as he paced the floor. I gazed down at the camera then back toward Houston.

"Look, I—"

"Don't," he interrupted then closed his eyes. "I'm sorry. Okay? But the last thing we need is some freaking reporter snapping pictures of us. I can't have us as frontpage freaking news right now."

"Isn't that what you want, for everyone to think we're madly in love?"

"Don't be naïve, Bristol. It just doesn't suit you. This isn't about an actress marrying a rock star. This is a billion-dollar company that has sharks who likely smell blood in the water. You've seen the tabloids that still exist. It doesn't matter if the majority are gone from supermarket shelves. That asshole could do anything with them, including selling them to the highest bidder. Or, he could be working for the same entity who's trying to get dirt on the family. I lived with that shit for the majority of my life. You haven't. That's why you follow my orders."

His fervor was shocking, but it allowed me further insight into the kind of life he'd been forced to live.

"Hell," he continued. "He could be working for the asshole determined to hunt and kill my father. Why not take out the entire family?"

"I don't know what you want me to say."

"Say you're listening to me. Tell me that you will do what I tell you to do." After a few seconds, he exhaled, his voice no longer holding the level of anger as it had before. "I'm not trying to scare you. Just stay inside until I return. Okay? I need to figure out what that asshole really wants. The bastard photographer refused to tell me who he was or the person he was working for, although he was quick to threaten me. And you were right. We can't pretend our relationship is anything but what it is. Business."

Wow. And there it was. Business. The man was all about the money. I'd been such a fool to think even for a second it could be about anything else.

"You could have just looked at the pictures. Then you would have had a good idea what he was doing here."

He turned his head, sucking in his breath. Even his stance was disturbing. His words hurt more than they should. The yin and yang of his statements was far too draining. I couldn't handle playing more than one game at a time. I simply wasn't wired that way.

"Okay. I'll do what you ask." I couldn't tolerate any additional beratement. Fuck him. My stomach was already churning, my heart unable to stop thudding. There had to be more to his reaction than just being hounded by some reporter. Now wasn't the time to push him.

I headed toward the bedroom, moving quickly into the bathroom, closing and locking the door. I needed time to think and process.

After splashing water in my face, I stood in front of the mirror, glaring at my own reflection. For a few minutes, he'd allowed me to see the man inside. Not the one he wanted everyone else to see, but the man who enjoyed the simpler things in life, including laughter. Then anxiety that he'd carried with him for years had taken over.

I wasn't certain I'd ever see the soft and fuzzy man that Ashley insisted did exist.

The light rapping on the door actually produced a moan. I squelched it, shaking my head. "Just go. Okay?"

"Bristol. I really am sorry. Can we talk?"

"I don't think we have anything to talk about right now. You made it clear what I can and can't do. I intend on following your rules to the letter."

When at least a full thirty seconds had passed, I actually thought he'd left. Then I heard a crashing sound and backed away from the door, expecting him to come smashing through at any minute.

A few minutes passed, the sound of grumbling continuing.

Then there was silence. The lack of noise was even worse.

I had no idea how long I remained behind the locked door. My reluctance to venture out had nothing to do with being afraid of the man. I knew in my gut he wasn't going to hurt me, but I couldn't handle his abrasiveness.

Or his damn sex appeal.

Finally, I'd had enough of hiding and opened the door, taking cautious steps outside. In his fit of anger, he'd smashed one of his suitcases against the closet door. The contents remained spilled onto the floor, a hole in the flimsy door. What in the hell was going on with him?

He'd already left. There were signs he'd taken a shower in another bathroom, his sweatpants hanging over a towel bar.

For some crazy reason, I pulled them into my hands, holding them against my face. His sweat sent tingles dancing throughout my body. He was so masculine and so damn infuriating.

When I walked back into the kitchen, I was surprised that he'd brought in and washed the coffee cups. He'd also left me a note.

Forgive me.

The two simple words sent a sharp jab into my heart. Damn the man.

His ruggedness.

His sexiness.

His dominating tendencies.

Damn him.

If I wasn't careful, I'd fall hard for Houston Powers.

* * *

New furniture.

There was something incredible about getting new furniture. Up to this point, I'd managed a few select purchases from Ikea, but I'd never had anything like the pieces that had begun to arrive. They were spectacular.

The second I'd started to pore over the contract, the doorbell had rung, delivery drivers standing by.

At least by noon, almost everything had arrived. I was shocked at how efficient the drivers were, and I'd even able to sweet talk a few of them to rearrange my original placement. Only one more delivery was expected. Then I could spend the rest if the afternoon going over the paperwork while sitting on a brand new deck chair.

Why that thought made me giddy was ridiculous, but at least I'd smiled the majority of the morning. As I folded several of the pieces of plastic that had covered some of the pieces, my thoughts shifted back to Houston's bout of fury. Maybe his anger had been caused by nothing more than the photographer, but I had my doubts.

The sound of the doorbell dragged me out of my procedural thinking process. At least the last load had arrived. When I swung open the door, it was the second time I was shocked in one day.

My instinct kicked into overdrive. This was no social call.

"Chase. What are you doing here?"

He looked over my shoulder, an ugly smirk on his face.

"If you're looking for Houston, he had some kind of meeting." My gut told me not to share Houston's itinerary with his brother.

"I'm not looking for Houston. I came to talk with you. Can I come in?"

The sudden polite tone in his voice initiated a red flag. "Of course. I apologize for the mess, but everything is arriving at once."

Don't do it. Don't do it.

I ignored my inner voice, if for no other reason than a chance to gain more information.

He immediately walked out of the foyer and into the living room, turning in a full circle. The fact he remained quiet was just as disturbing as his terse appearance.

"Would you like something to drink?"

"This isn't a social call."

Here we go.

I cocked my head, realizing he was taking a mental picture of the entire room. I thought about the paperwork in plain view in the kitchen and grimaced. Chase had no idea what their father had offered to Houston. I would bet on it. "Okay, Chase. I actually have a lot of work to do so if you don't mind, get to the point regarding your visit."

"Do you like playing games?" he asked.

"I'm sorry? What are you talking about?"

With a huge knowing smile on his face, he turned to face me. "I know all about you, Bristol."

The fact he'd taken the time to take a close look at my identity wasn't surprising. Houston had said the first person to do so would be his brother. Maybe he was prepared to finish his earlier threat. *Go ahead, big boy. I can take it.* "Then you know that I don't play games. Ever."

He laughed, the sound pissing me off. The man was a know-it-all and I wanted to wipe the smirk off his face. "In some regards, you don't. However, I think you're one damn good actress. Or maybe not. Maybe that's why you were fired from your prestigious job and on the first day I might add. Bravo."

I glared at him, trying to keep from ripping the asshole a new one. "Do you have a point, Chase?"

"My point is that I'm well aware of your little affair you had with a married senator. I'm certain my brother wouldn't want that to get out to the press."

I was shocked that he'd learned, which meant he had some kind of connection to my old boss. What lengths did the man go through to find out information about me and more important, why? The rift between brothers must be much more significant than Houston had led me to believe.

And the statement he made was far too close to what had occurred that morning. The press. Had he been the one to send the reporter? That was a possibility and something I wouldn't let on we were aware of. Unless the mysterious person had called him. "Houston is well aware of what happened in my position. That's why he suggested we make a permanent move to his hometown."

He laughed, as if the asshole could see right through my statement.

I stood my ground, folding my arms and making my glare even harsher. With his ability to gather private information, I was fearful he'd found out about Dark Overture.

"No, I think that's why you grasped onto my brother. You knew that one day someone would find out and you could be ruined. What better way than to grab onto a real catch, a man who might have more money than you could ever dream of."

While I was furious, forced to temper my anger, I was hopeful that the game he mentioned was one of greed, not the indecent invitation I'd received. "And what about tossing your fiancée to the wolves?"

The second I made the statement, his entire demeanor changed. I could see white-hot fury building to the point I expected him to lash out violently. A moment of fear swept through me.

He lifted his arm as if he was going to hit me then pointed a finger, his mouth twisting until his features made him appear like a monster. "Don't. You. *Ever.* Mention. Her. Again."

"Hmmm… What a shame. No grandchildren." The words slipped past my mouth before I could stop them. I was playing with fire while a gasoline can stood between us.

Back down. Back down. Back down.

I wasn't certain I could calm the situation.

His flash of rage remained. Then his face relaxed, his body no longer shaking.

"I assure you that I will find the right woman, but she won't be a plastic Barbie doll searching for a new life."

I had to give him credit for regrouping.

"You know, I don't need to explain anything about my relationship with your brother, Chase. He and I are in the relationship. But how about this? If you're so damn worried, then talk to him yourself. My guess is that your brother will laugh at you for acting like an idiot." The flash in his eyes made me chuckle. "That's right. You're the brother that's all talk and no action. You hide behind your wealth instead of trying to make yourself a better man. Then again, that's likely impossible to do."

I realized the instant I'd issued the words I'd made another huge mistake, but I hadn't been able to help myself. With two strides, he stood only inches from me, still moving forward in an effort to shove me against the wall. I refused, smashing my hand against him.

He slowly looked down at my actions, exhaling in an exaggerated manner. "I suggest you learn to be very careful, Bristol. While my brother might be fooled by your actions, I know better than to think a woman of your... virtue could fall in love with a man like Houston."

Now I'd reached my limit.

"How dare you." I was even more pissed, prepared to cold cock the bastard. "He's intelligent and funny, passionate and devoted. He's exactly the kind of man I've hoped for." The compliments had come so easily, which was confusing as hell.

"I'll repeat my advice. Get out while you still can."

"Is that a threat, Chase? Is that something you'd like me to tell your brother as well? I'm certain he'll enjoy providing a reply of his own."

He acted as if he was going to stroke the side of my face then pulled away. "Tell him anything you would like. That doesn't change the message. Let's see how long your relationship lasts when he's penniless, forced to spend time behind bars."

"What?" While I'd been warned about the entire family to some degree, this was something I couldn't fathom. "What are you suggesting?"

"I'm not suggesting anything. I'm stating facts." Chase shifted around me, stopping long enough to give me a long look, one billowing with desire. "However, if you're good in bed, I might decide to keep my brother's leftovers."

I was appalled but there was no way I was going to allow the asshole to get under my skin. I stood where I was, giving him a sweet smile. "Nice offer, Chase, but nothing about you appeals to me. Nothing. Now that I've been close to you, I can no longer stand your stench. Get out."

He took a deep breath before heading toward the door. It took everything I had not to race after the asshole. As another laugh pushed up from his throat, I managed to hold back a series of shivers.

But only until he closed the door.

I moved toward the couch then could swear the sun glinted off something metal. As I headed toward the back doors, I hesitated before walking outside, remembering Houston's request. While I didn't see anything, my gut told me there was someone lying in wait. I backed away, even angrier than before.

What in the hell had I gotten myself into?

CHAPTER 11

Houston

Retaliation.

I was the kind of man who thrived on the concept, although in my previous line of work, that had only entailed shutting down other traders before they had the opportunity to jump on a promising tip. Although I was ruthless in my gathering of new clients, ensuring they had intel on other more unscrupulous traders in the business.

I'd taken pride in the fact I'd squelched more than a few careers along the way.

This was entirely different.

I remained furious that some asshole would invade my space, taking photographs in a reckless pursuit of fame and fortune. Whether Chase was behind the egregious move or not, I was determined to find out. An ugly thought shifted into my mind.

Could my brother have the nerve to try to have our father assassinated? My initial answer was disturbing but one I could believe.

However, I would follow through with my predisposed plans. I'd spent the better part of the morning touring facilities that I'd never had any interest in before. Two of them had been purchased in a tactical maneuver by my father only a couple of years before. He'd enjoyed every moment of dismantling the upper echelon of management, destroying careers as well as lives along the way.

While it would appear the companies were thriving, the moment I'd stepped foot into the organization, the tension was so thick, I'd been able to smell it in the air. Everyone was afraid of anyone with the last name of Powers.

Management had been less than forthcoming, providing me with a set of financials that I would bet didn't give the entire picture.

Given they were under Chase's supervision, I knew they had reason to fear for their jobs, perhaps even their lives.

The fact two CEOs had disappeared shortly after bitter takeovers remained in the back of my mind. The news had been sensational several months ago, but as with all aspects of scandal, with no news feeding the piranhas, the focus had been dropped. After reading every article I could find, one thing was certain, at least in my mind.

Their vanishing act had been unexpected to everyone who knew them. While there'd been vast speculation that they'd taken the millions of dollars they'd received and moved to a tropical island or another glorious destination, I didn't buy the bullshit for a single second.

And why?

Because the two men had done everything in their power to thwart my father's takeover, including accusing him of blackmail and extortion. I had to wonder if either my father or Chase had paid off the most vocal reporters in an effort to squelch the stories.

Then I hadn't heard about a single additional report or any wind of another volley of accusations. Until the oddities of a month before, I hadn't given the corporation much thought.

There was no sign of Chase, but I had no doubt my unexpected visit would be reported to him. I remained in the rental car, studying the smaller building housing some of the essential components used for the defense system chips included in the military contracts. What surprised me was that Riley had been placed in charge of this single operation. Was my father testing the man's resolve or loyalty? It seemed odd that my father would place that much faith in a son he'd never given a shit about.

Everything I'd seen and heard seemed off for my father's typical handling of business.

I exited the vehicle, studying the sleek glass building for a few seconds before heading for the entrance. The security was even tighter than the other buildings I'd visited, forcing me to remain outside until a representative not only approved my entrance but escorted me inside. As I waited, my thoughts turned to Bristol, including the night we'd shared.

There was no way I could say I was a good man on any level. In fact, her use of the term 'bastard' was entirely appropriate. Her continued rebellious attitude didn't surprise me. What did was her determination to break through some shell she was convinced kept me a prisoner in my own world.

She was a spitfire of seduction, her ability to drive me to almost losing all control keeping my cock twitching from the visions that refused to leave my mind. Wanting her was easy.

Keeping her was something else entirely.

Bristol was right in that we were two different people. That made me crave her even more.

"Houston."

The sound of Riley's voice actually made me smile. As I turned to face him, removing my sunglasses, I could see a certain level of anxiety in his eyes. "I'm sorry to come unannounced."

He chuckled as he walked closer, shoving his hands into his pockets. "I knew you'd drop by, no doubt directed by your father."

"My decision given I've been away for so long."

The look of amusement remained on his face. "I don't buy it. You have no interest in this shit. Why are you really here?"

After taking a deep breath, I decided it was time to find out what he knew. If he crossed me, he would suffer the consequences. "To find out what the hell is really going on."

"And you trust me to tell you?"

I inched closer, thinking about my answer. "You know how I feel about Chase. From what you said the other night, you feel the same way."

Riley took his time answering, studying my eyes as if searching for my soul. "Chase doesn't give a shit about the employees of any of the companies. He'll do whatever it takes to increase profits."

"That much I already figured out, Riley. Don't bullshit me. I know every trick, every opportunity. Our father has been threatened, which is something I think you're already aware of. Call it a gut feeling. Now, do you want to provide me with your perspective or am I wasting my time?"

Inhaling, he glanced from one side of the parking lot to another. "Walk with me." He didn't wait for me to respond, moving away from the parking lot and toward what appeared to be a small path leading into a sanctuary of trees. He seemed tense, remaining quiet until we were a solid hundred yards away from the facility.

"Look, I wasn't made aware you were returning until the day before you arrived."

"Okay. And?" I was already growing impatient.

"And while I'd not privy to certain company information, I've certainly heard the rumors from employees as well as colleagues. I have a group of friends that I keep in touch with, the kind of people involved in similar businesses, all of them in the know. They've provided a wealth of information that William refused to share."

He was even using my father's first name. I could tell just how furious he was for being shortchanged over the years.

Did that make me feel sorry for him? Hell, no. Maybe I just had trust issues. "What are these… colleagues telling you?"

"That William has been hiding accurate numbers from the corporation for one."

"How the hell would they know that?"

"Honestly, they refused to divulge that information."

I laughed. "Don't you find that curious? Throw out a few accusations without backup?"

Riley inched closer. "You might have been gone for a few years, Houston, but you know how degenerate this world of specialized computer technology can be. There is limited loyalty, a high turnover and secrets are bought and sold no matter the heightened level of security."

"You're trying to tell me that one of my father's employees has sold him out?"

"That's exactly what I'm telling you."

"Then that means whoever it was held a high-ranking position." He nodded after I issued the words. "Okay. What else? Do the rumors the particular technology you're working on was stolen from a rival company hold any merit?"

His laugh was genuine, although the sound bitter. "I've spent the last year and a half working nights and weekends, doing everything I could to push the employees through various testing and delays, disappointments and issues with getting supplies from overseas. They worked their butts off in order to vie for even the chance to bid on that military contract. There is no freaking way a single scrap of it was stolen from anyone."

"Including the design?"

He hesitated, closing his eyes and sighing. "It's my damn design."

"What?" If that was the case, Chase had to be beside himself with fury.

"Yup. Not a single person in the house had any idea how much I loved working with computers and every other piece of electronics I could get my hands on. They were black and white, no emotions needed. I even graduated with my electronics engineering degree a year early, not that anyone gave a damn. By then, I'd already developed several designs, including working examples that could completely change the course of defense technology. It was the single time William took me seriously."

"Which is why he put you in charge of this portion of the company."

"Maybe so," he said more in passing.

I had to admire the man. He'd surpassed all of us in his ability to forge a life of his own. Maybe I hadn't given him enough credit over the years. "What do you think is the biggest threat to the corporation?"

"You mean other than basic greed?" Riley shook his head. "From what I've been told, there is an entity determined to bring down the company. I don't know the reason why, and depending on who you ask, they'll give you a different answer. William isn't a popular man by anyone's standards."

An entity. His statement was nothing more than a confirmation of what I'd already suspected. "Any idea who?"

"No. However, from the increasingly tense atmosphere within the company as well as William's sudden change in behavior, I'd say he is or was personal with whoever it is."

"Do you have any proof of wrongdoing?"

"Other than meetings regarding the new military contract I wasn't allowed to participate in? Not much."

"I need whatever you have, including names of any disgruntled employees. Any enemies, even if you believe not to be an issue."

"Why, Houston? What are you trying to accomplish, destroying your father's legacy?"

The answer didn't come easily nor was I certain of my intent. "I honestly don't have an answer for you other than I would hate to see all our father worked for going down in flames because of bullshit rivalries." I suspected Riley had no idea our father's life had been threatened.

"You think Chase is behind this. Don't you?"

"I have no doubt he's a part of whatever is going on and I don't plan on allowing him to follow through with that pleasure."

He studied me intently, finally shaking his head. "You've changed."

"We've all changed. Perhaps by getting older, we learn what's most important."

"Defeating your brother."

"It might be necessary, Riley. However, I've learned recently that there's more to life than money and power."

"Whatever Bristol has brought to your life, it would appear it's a change for the better. I only hope you don't allow either Chase or William to destroy it."

"Don't worry. That isn't going to happen. I want everything you have, notes on what you suspect."

Nodding, Riley has a faraway look in his eyes. "What a shame we couldn't be a family."

I thought about his comment and for the first time began to see how difficult life had been on him. "What do you want?"

"Out of the company or life in general?"

"Maybe both because our professional life is usually entwined with our personal joys."

"I'll let you know when I figure that out."

The awkward tension between us had increased over the years. "Understood. Let me know when you've gathered information. We'll meet privately."

"What are you going to do with that information?"

"I'll let you know when I've figured that out." I laughed, repeating his words, although even the sound was bitter. As I started to walk away, my curiosity continued to spike. "Do you enjoy what you do within the company?"

"Actually, I do. I think I'm damn good at it as well. It's a shame your father hasn't noticed."

"You know, William is your father too. And I think you've answered my question. You're a right fit for the company, much more so than I could ever be."

Riley had always hidden his emotions, likely terrified as to the repercussions from his sentiments. Seeing the angst in his eyes wasn't just surprising.

It bothered the fuck out of me.

Maybe he was right in that Bristol had already managed some kind of change within my blackened soul, although the more time I spent close to my family, the more I realized it wasn't in my best interest to indulge in a single weakness.

He looked away, taking a deep breath. "No, he's not, Houston. My father would never toss me aside as if my life didn't matter. Don't worry. I used to cry myself to sleep at night when I was a little boy, longing to secure William's good graces." When he shifted his head, his eyes were hard and cold. He also wore the same expression that had been reflected in every mirror I'd glanced into.

Hunger.

But not for money or power.

For retaliation.

My instinct also told me that Riley had been keeping tabs on my father and perhaps Chase as well for a longer period of time than he wanted me to believe. With no trust between us, he had zero reason to be straightforward. After all, as far as he was concerned, I was the playboy returning for the money. Or maybe he'd already caught wind of my father's change of heart, one that didn't include Riley to any degree. Yeah, if I were him, I'd be pissed as shit.

"Now I'm a man. Maybe what they say is true about going through hardships in your life. It makes you stronger. I assure you that William can't hurt me any longer. As far as continuing my involvement in the company? I doubt it'll have the same charm in the future," Riley huffed. My God. The sweet young boy with a verve for life had become an exact replica of his two brothers.

The legacy of the Powers family continued.

And I had the distinct feeling we'd all burn in hell.

* * *

After the meeting with Riley, I'd actually driven to La Jolla Shores, the pristine beach far removed from the hustling and bustling of the city. There was something almost cathartic about standing on the small pier, watching a few surfers as they tried to catch a wave. Memories blasted to the surface, including my early desires to become a champion surfer. Even my basic chatter as a young boy had been met with discouragement, angry words from my father.

I'd learned to keep my thoughts to myself.

A 'what-if' moment shifted into my mind. Maybe I'd be a hell of a lot happier if I'd followed my childhood dream. As I leaned over the wooden railing, I had to laugh. Just what the world needed, another aging surfer.

Turning away, an odd sense of knowing kicked in.

I was being watched, followed to every destination.

Now I was pissed.

And there was something else.

Danger.

I was worried, anxious that by bringing Bristol into this nightmare, I could also destroy her life. No. that wasn't acceptable.

The drive took longer than expected, a level of anxiety kicking into high gear, which was entirely different than my normal reaction to any difficult situation. By the time I swung the car into the driveway, my blood pressure had risen enough a headache had formed.

I stared down at my recent purchase, the Beretta remaining on the passenger seat. Money could buy anything even if there were rules in an attempt to prevent unwarranted purchases. My one act of defiance after I'd turned eighteen had been the purchase of a gun. I'd spent enough time at the shooting range to understand and respect the craft. I loaded the weapon, sliding the remaining ammunition under the seat then easing the gun into my pocket. I'd seen no evidence that someone had followed me, but the nagging feeling had remained the entire afternoon.

By the time I'd arrived back at the house, the sun was already starting to set. I stood outside for a few seconds, staring at the bank of trees flanking the other side of the driveway. Given the location of the house, if someone had actually been watching Bristol from this vantage point, they would have been forced to park a good distance away, either hiking up the side of hill covered in rocks on finding an access point from the beachside. I doubted the reporter I'd accosted could handle such a maneuver. Was there someone else keeping tabs on my arrival into town?

I walked closer, scanning the area. There were no clear indications that anyone had hidden in the trees, but that meant little for a professional.

Not that the photographer had the look of anything but an aging reporter giving it one last effort to make a name for himself.

Although looks could certainly be deceiving.

After entering the house, I was struck by the fact there was no noise, no sound whatsoever. There were also no lights on that I could see. Bristling, I kept my hand on the weapon, moving through the house quietly, finally finding the contract as well as Bristol's laptop strewn across the new coffee table. I placed the financials beside them, which I'd scour over later.

Every nerve on edge, I shifted the weapon into both hands, finally catching sight of her long hair flowing in the breeze as she stood on the deck. She turned toward me before I had a chance to shove the gun out of sight, her eyes falling to the cold hard steel in my hand. There was no exclamation of shock as she returned her gaze to my eyes.

I walked onto the deck, leaning over the railing and studying the turbulent ocean as high tide rolled in. The quiet between us was unnerving. Time to trust her. I only hoped I was doing the right thing.

"I wasn't completely honest with you," I finally offered.

"About?"

"The reason I returned to San Diego. Sure, I refuse to allow my brother to get his hands on the money my mother had set aside, but that was only part of the reason for my decision."

She remained quiet, the only sound the lapping water.

"I had a call in the middle of the night about a month ago, a deep voice telling me my father was going to die. Trust me, it wasn't some proclamation that he was in poor health. I could tell there was menace in the man's tone. When he issued a single dark chuckle, all the hairs had stood up on the back of my neck."

"You're kidding?"

I shook my head. "I wish I were. When the events unfolded, including the call from my father's attorney about the trust, I realized I had no choice. If I had to guess, I'd say I've been lured here."

"Lured. That's an interesting word."

Chuckling, I turned my head. "I can tell you have a reason for saying that."

"We are required to stay married for at least a year."

I was caught off guard by her words. I could finally tell either something had occurred or whatever had driven her to that realization was troubling the hell out of her. "That's not what we agreed on."

"That's what your father requires in his contract regarding the offer he made to oversee portions of his company. Yes, the trust fund papers haven't been altered to reflect the change, which means we could continue our ruse and you'd still be a wealthy man, but not in the same terms as the contract for his corporation implies."

"What the hell?" I snarled.

"He was clever how he introduced the single sentence, burying it in the footnotes. If we don't stay married at least for that long, the contract will become null and void, rights and revisions transferring to Chase."

"Jesus Christ." What the hell was my father up to? I swung my head toward the door, glaring at the papers on the table.

"Grandchildren."

I knew I was gawking at her. "I don't understand."

"According to your sister, your father is almost desperate to have grandchildren. Given Chase ended his upcoming marriage, the burden fell on your shoulders. I know it is a stretch, but if he's under some kind of duress, he's likely not thinking rationally."

I was not only incensed but outraged by such a ridiculous requirement. "I don't buy it completely. What else did you find?"

"If you follow through with his terms, that would mean you'd eventually get everything. His position, a significant portion of his assets, and complete control of the company's future. Granted, it's a tiered contract, meaning you have certain goals to complete; however, when you do, the entire corporation will be yours, including a majority hold of the stock as well as control of the options."

"My siblings?"

"There are no arrangements for them, at least from what I can tell. However, as disturbing as a certain portion of the contract might be, it's not what I found that bothers the hell out of me. It's what I learned." She lifted the glass of wine in her hand. While she did her best to hide the fact her entire body was trembling, the slosh of liquid in the glass gave it away.

"What are you talking about?"

She took a sip of wine before answering. "Did Mr. Darke tell you why I was terminated from the law firm?"

"No. What does that have to do with anything?"

"I'm not entirely certain other than your brother found out the reason why, which should have been kept confidential."

"I'm not following you."

Exhaling, her eyes shimmered with fury. "Chase paid me a little visit a few hours ago. First of all, he warned me about you. When that didn't work, he threw in my face that he knew why I'd been terminated on my first day on the job."

Fisting my hands, rage unlike any I'd felt in a hell of a long time rushed into my system. "What. The. Fuck? I'm going to kill him." When she reached out, grabbing my arm, I issued a series of growls. "He needs to understand that his kind of behavior isn't going to be tolerated."

"There's nothing you can do right now, Houston. I held my own, but your brother is a time bomb ready to explode."

"He has several reasons, including the fact my father is shutting him out of a portion of the company. That is, if he knows and given his behavior when I met with my father, I'd say he found out. That being said, I'm not going to tolerate the man hurting you." Huffing, I jerked away, taking several deep breaths. "I'm sorry. I'm not trying to take this out on you. I had no idea just how volatile this damn trip was going to be. You certainly don't deserve the crap being tossed in your direction."

"I already told you. I can handle myself. I'm not helpless."

"But you are my responsibility," I snapped, pressing my fingers against my chest for emphasis. "Mine."

"I don't belong to you."

After a few seconds, I half laughed. "You're right. You don't. Besides, it must be obvious now that I'm just as damaged as the rest of my family." Goddamn this shit. I'd allowed my family to get under my skin just like before, only this time, the stakes were much higher. For all the bullshit I'd told myself, there was almost no difference in my actions than my father's or Chase's for that matter.

"Look, if you want my educated guess, I don't think your brother's concern that you're back in town is the only reason his fuse is getting shorter, his broken engagement to Bridgett aside, but I certainly don't like what he was insinuating. If he finds out how I got here, not only will your trust fund be yanked, but the offer will be tossed as well. I don't think you want that to happen. If you're hotheaded like usual, I have no doubt it will."

Hotheaded. She'd seen nothing yet. Chase and I were going to have the kind of discussion that would leave him hurting for one hell of a long time. Fuck the family. What the hell did I care about his broken engagement?

However, she was right. I took a deep breath, inching closer. "Tell me everything. What about this job and what would it matter?"

"Maybe to further discredit me in an attempt to force your father to reconsider."

"What happened?"

"You see, somehow my employer in a different city found out that I'd been foolish enough to get involved with a handsome older man. We had a torrid affair, only I didn't realize how appropriate the term really was. He'd neglected to tell me he was married. If that wasn't bad enough, I also learned that he was a Maryland State senator. Now, I broke it off as soon as I learned. While he called me a couple of times, he finally got the message I didn't want to see him. I've thought nothing about it until my boss at the law firm threw it in my face."

"What the goddamn hell would that matter to your freaking boss?"

She wagged her finger. "Oh, but there was this nasty little morality clause in my employment papers that I'd thought nothing of. How stupid of me."

I slammed my fist on the railing, snarling under my breath. "How did Chase find out?"

"That's what I want to know."

What had occurred over the last month didn't make a damn bit of sense other than the fact my father was terrified of losing everything. Damn the secrets he continued to hide.

"That's what I was so angry about at the club the other night. Chase acted like he had something on me. I suspected it was about Dark Overture. I didn't think he'd stoop so low as to toss my unsavory affair in my face. What is his point? What can he gain from the knowledge?"

I turned my gaze toward the ocean once again, doing everything I could to curtail my increasing anger. While Chase was a complete asshole as far as I was concerned, I knew him well enough to realize he was under the kind of pressure that could break a man. But why?

It didn't matter. He would still face my wrath.

Before I had a chance to answer, the single ding of my phone indicated an incoming email. Grabbing my phone, I navigated to the correct application, curious as to what my father had sent me.

My father hadn't bothered to add a tagline or any notations regarding the forwarded mail he'd sent, a single line that made my hackles raise.

The message was clear.

And chilling.

You are going to die, your entire family destroyed. Be. Afraid.

CHAPTER 12

ristol

Destruction.

While I was no computer expert by any means, I would guess the address listed on the email forwarded from Houston's father was either no longer in use or not trackable. The look on Houston's face was cold and dark, as if the rage had furrowed deep inside of him, resurrecting a beast who'd been asleep in his lair.

A cold chill trickled down my spine, my heart racing.

"What the hell is going on?" I asked as I watched him scan the perimeter of the beach. He'd purchased a gun, for God's sake. I was antsy, finding it difficult to focus.

"I'm not certain, but we are going to find out. I had a long chat with Riley today. It's funny that my father neglected to tell me that Riley was in charge of the same company that's been accused of stealing trade secrets."

"Do you think that's possible? Is Riley pissed enough at the lifelong treatment he's received that he would actually threaten your father?"

He shook his head several times. "No, I don't. The design of the computer chip was his brainchild. I doubt he'd do anything stupid to risk what he's spent months trying to accomplish."

"Which leaves Chase."

"No, we're missing a piece of this ridiculous puzzle. However, I've made a difficult decision and you're not going to fight me on this."

When he closed the distance, placing his hands on my arms and gently brushing the tips of his fingers up and down, I couldn't help but shiver. There was so much electricity surging between us, but he'd shifted into an entirely different level of emotions.

"What?"

He cocked his head, rubbing his knuckle across my jaw. "I'm not going to risk your life to honor my father's wishes. I'll have the second money drop wired to your account. I want you to leave on the first flight available."

"You're really worried. You suddenly show up with a gun and now you want me to leave. Are you hiding something from me?" I eased my wine onto one of the new outdoor tables I'd purchased, going over everything I'd read in the contracts in my mind. There was nothing blatant, other than the one-year marriage clause. There had to be more.

"I'm not hiding anything, Bristol. I'm as confused as you are. However, until I know what's going on, I can't rule out that the threat made against my father's life is real. As far as destroying the family, there are any number of methods in doing so, including taking additional lives. It's too risky having you in the middle of this shit."

"I'm not leaving."

"You will do as I say."

I pushed my palms against his chest, digging my fingers into his shirt. "You don't have a choice." Why didn't I take the offer and run? What was wrong with me? Was I so attracted to him or was it about taking the risk? I didn't have an answer.

"Then I'll throw you out."

"No. You won't. I can tell you don't want me to leave."

"Why in God's name would you stay? You've already been treated as if you're a second-class citizen. Your life might be in danger. And for certain, my family is going to make your life miserable. Go home. Salvage your career. Enjoy your life. You get a one-time reprieve."

I slid my hands up to his shoulders, allowing my fingers to tangle in his long strands of hair. "Does that mean you want me to go?"

He remained unblinking for several seconds then huffed in the same aggravating way he'd done since we'd met. "You're going to do what I tell you to do."

"Always the man in charge. Aren't you?" I spouted. "Fine. If you really want me to leave, then tell me that's what you want. Find some actual courage." Every part of me was on edge. He was just as volatile as the situation we were in. I couldn't take the back and forth. His eyes pierced deep inside, driving a stake through my heart. Why? Why did I give a damn about him when it was obvious that he didn't give a damn about anyone else?

"Why the hell would you stay? It's ridiculous."

"Is it any more ridiculous than the fact you spent over two million dollars to fake a marriage?"

His face contorted, his mouth twisting out of anger and frustration. Then he fisted my hair, dragging me onto my toes as he lowered his head. "Goddamn it, woman. You are hardheaded as fuck."

"That's why I was handpicked for you." I glared into his eyes, refusing to back down. "Tell me to leave with a reason. Do it."

Seconds ticked by.

Awkward.

Horrible.

Seconds.

"No. You're mine. All mine."

Growling, he crushed his mouth over mine, wrapping his other arm around me. The scent of him was more intoxicating than ever, filling my nostrils, the exotic fragrance rushing into every cell. I was instantly lightheaded as I clawed at his neck, digging my nails into his skin.

The kiss was filled with desperate passion, the kind of unforgiving hunger that would never burn out. Stars floated behind my closed eyes, pulling me into a beautifully colored vacuum. As he thrust his tongue inside my mouth, I yielded to him, clinging to him as if he was a lifeline.

Or the man I was falling in love with.

There was no rhyme or reason to the insanity of the way I was feeling, and I felt blindsided by the intense emotions rolling through me. Everything about him was so powerful, the dominating man refusing to accept anything but what he wanted.

And I knew he hungered for me.

As unconventional as our relationship had started, there was no denying our connection. He was the only liquid that could quench my thirst.

Our bodies melded together, his throbbing cock pressing against my stomach. I couldn't seem to get enough of him, swishing my tongue back and forth against his even though he controlled every move I made, including the brutal kiss.

He kept his savage hold on my hair, refusing to let me go, grinding his hips back and forth. The sensations skyrocketed, my heart racing. I wanted nothing more than to yield to his desires, to feel his thick shaft driving inside of me. The taste of him created a wave of tingles, my nipples aching as they scraped against my tee shirt.

When he finally broke the kiss, he issued a series of husky growls, the guttural sounds echoing in my ears. "Damn it, woman. I want you."

"Then don't push me away. I don't deserve that."

He closed his eyes, taking several deep breaths. "I don't know what's going to happen."

"Then we need to figure it out together."

Sighing, he pulled away, still keeping his fingers entwined in my hair as his eyes darted back and forth. "It's risky as hell."

"But worth it."

"Yes, and I can't seem to get enough of you, but hear me. You will follow my orders. Do you understand me?"

"Yes, sir."

His nostrils flaring, he narrowed his eyes. "I will devour you and there's nothing you can do about it."

"Good." I pushed away from him with more force, able to break free then walking into the house, beckoning him with a single finger. "Then come with me. We have work to do."

He shook his head, the look on his face carnal. "Such a damn bad girl. I'm going to have to do something about that."

"Uh-huh. We shall see."

"Yes, you will."

* * *

Mine.

The word just sat there in the front lobes of my mind; the very word I'd longed to have a man say to me.

But not this way.

Concentrate. You were hired to do a damn job.

"I don't see anything odd with the financials. In fact, they are crystal clear, although the company is struggling financially. They need new contracts, or they won't be able to make payroll in the upcoming months." He rubbed his eyes, hissing under his breath.

"So your father's stock has slipped significantly, almost twenty percent in the last two months. I would say he's desperate for a spark. Maybe that spark is you."

Sighing, he looked away. "I'm no expert, but it's possible he waited too long. That's why he's selling off assets."

"That's a shame. Word of mouth can damage a reputation more than almost anything. This blackmailer knew how to begin destroying your father. Unfortunately, I also can't see a way around the fact we need to get married." I shifted my gaze from my laptop to his face, uncertain of his expression.

"I know you don't want to be committed to me in a formal marriage for up to a year. I certainly wouldn't want to be." He chuckled, although I could tell he was serious.

"There has to be a way around the clause, but we need to keep up the charade for now." The inner voice inside of me was calling me assorted names including stupid. There was no doubt I should take Houston up on his offer and get the hell out now, but I wasn't going to do that. Our attraction might be intense, but we were both in a precarious position. Still, I felt loyalty to him in a strange way.

Precarious. My God, the word wasn't strong enough for whatever game was being played and I was firmly convinced someone had planned a method of derailing the entire family. Maybe I was along for the ride by accident, although I hadn't been able to rule out the possibility that Daniel Darke wasn't as discreet as his promises had indicated.

He chuckled as he swirled his drink, staring at me with his dark eyes, his dominant side bursting through the seams. Then he lifted his glass. "To a happy life together, my beautiful, bratty fiancée."

I ignored his hint of arrogance, returning my attention to what limited information we'd been provided. "I need the full financial records for the entire corporation as well as copies of current contracts. Did Riley have anything to say of any importance?"

"He has knowledge of the people he considers my father's most vicious enemies."

The way he said the words was almost as if he no longer cared. I was too tired to argue with him, the fury of being forced to deal with Chase as well as worry about a family that wasn't even mine exhausting. "I hope that means he's going to provide some sort of documentation."

"Yes. Trust me, he will," Houston stated in his usual authoritative voice. His eyes never left me, the hunger remaining in them as he licked the rim of his glass. "If he doesn't, I'm going to drag it out of him." His anger remained, furrowing inside of him, simply waiting for the right moment to explode.

I forced myself to look away, pushing the computer further across the coffee table then grabbing my glass of wine.

He leaned forward, shifting his glass from one hand to the other, his heated gaze remaining. "I'm sorry. As I told you before, you don't deserve to deal with any of this bullshit."

"Maybe not but here we both are. We need to make a plan. You brought me here for my expertise, so you need to let me do what I was paid for." Every time he looked at me, I quivered, but the formidable man held such anger inside. Even though the reasons were obvious, he was the damaged man he'd learned to accept. "I'm going to ask Ashley to help me make some arrangements. I guess you don't care about the wedding."

"You're certain you want to do this?"

I wasn't certain of anything except I couldn't get my mind off the surly, gorgeous man. For all his pontificating, he'd managed to slide into my psyche, leaving me hot and breathless any time he was in close proximity.

Sadly, I was terrified that he'd already captured my heart.

"You're not going to stop me." I glared down at the damn weapon he'd bought, furious that he'd felt the need.

"Then so be it. Have the ceremony and the reception wherever you want."

"Let me guess. Money is no object." I hated the terseness in my tone, but there was nothing worse than feeling utter lack of control.

He laughed, the sound far too seductive. "Yes, spend whatever you want to make it the lavish event of the year. But you're right. There's nothing we can do right now. We'll have to wait until in the morning. Then we are going to find answers. I suggest we go to dinner."

I thought about his request then closed the lid on the computer. "How about we order in pizza? We could actually act for a little while that we're the loving couple we pretend to be. Maybe watch an old movie?" Right. As if the man would actually say yes.

When he rose to a standing position, reaching for my almost empty wine, I shuddered all over again. "Why not?"

As he walked away, I glanced outside at the dark sky. Night had fallen, the moon merely a sliver, and from where I was sitting, I could only see a few stars. I used to take comfort in the darkness, allowing my imagination to wander to distance places. Only I hadn't included San Diego as a location where every girl's fantasy could come true. I pressed my fingers across my mouth, trying my best to keep from bursting into laughter.

There was certainly nothing funny about what we were going through, or about Houston's life in general, but at this point, there was nothing left to do.

When he returned, all I had to do was glance at his rugged, gorgeous face and suddenly, there was no way of holding back the laughter.

Houston narrowed his eyes as he placed the drinks on the table, standing over me, his larger than life presence only adding to the ridiculous fit.

"What's so funny?" he asked.

Unable to answer him, I simply pressed my other hand on top of the first, the sound still managing to slip through my fingers.

His expression turned to annoyance. Just the way he placed his hands on his hips brought another round of giggles. At this point, my stomach hurt. I lay down on the sofa, pushing my face into one of the accent pillows. I could hear nothing but the raucous sounds bursting up from my throat. I closed my eyes, the laughter producing tears. It was obvious my nerves had gotten the better of me.

When I felt hands pressing against me, I yelped, still unable to stop cackling.

"You are one bad girl," he said, the sound of his voice slipping over me like the softest Sherpa blanket. I was pulled into a lull, enjoying the way he rubbed his hands down my legs.

Then the bastard decided to tickle me.

"What?" Screeching, I tried to jerk up only to be pushed down, the weight of his massive hand pressing against my chest. I blinked several times, tears continuing to trickle down my cheeks. A moment of disbelief settled in from the sight of his dazzling amused eyes and the way his mouth pursed in frustration.

"You heard me." A grin popping on his face, he tickled me with the kind of ferocity that once again, I couldn't stop laughing.

"No. No! Stop. You have to stop." I twisted and pitched, trying everything to get him to stop including slamming my knees into his chest.

"Nice try, bad girl." Houston refused to stop, driving me to the point of madness.

I had zero control over my muscles. None. When I managed to jerk my knees all the way to my chest, kicking out with the ferocity of a boxer, I could hear the shock in his voice.

"Fuck!"

Blinking furiously, I took gasping breaths as I stared at him. The force I'd used had pitched him away several feet. And I laughed again.

He took several deep breaths, his nostrils flaring as his beast rose to the surface. Then he pounced, managing to flip me over onto my stomach, easily wrangling with my shorts until they were pulled down to my knees. "You're never going to learn."

"What are you doing?"

I didn't have to wait for the answer for long. When he brought his hand down, the cracking sound seemed so exaggerated.

"Ouch!" I yelped, although all I could feel was the remnants of stomach cramps from the tickling event. Maybe I was still in shock that this was the same man who'd been so rude and forceful the night I'd met him. Whatever the case, I had difficulty trying to convince my muscles to help me escape.

"That's exactly what you're supposed to say. Punishments are supposed to hurt," he proclaimed than proceeded to smack me at least a dozen times, moving from one side of my bottom to the other.

I wiggled, smashing my fists against the couch, but I knew it was no use. "I hate you."

I heard him chuckling. "That's what you've said before." He refused to stop, bringing his hand down in rapid motions. I was lost to the actions, let alone the pain.

The sting was starting to build, becoming full blown pain, the increasing heat rushing into every cell in my body. I finally closed my eyes, taking several deep breaths then realizing just how aroused I'd become. There was no doubt he could gather a whiff of my desire and the feel of my pussy juice trickling between my legs was embarrassing. There was going to be a stain on the new couch.

His breathing was ragged; I concentrated on the sound, blocking out my moans as I clawed at the pillow. There wasn't a single inch of my body that wasn't tingling.

I sensed his needs were increasing, his ability to maintain control fading. We were far too explosive together, our needs insatiable. When the weight on the couch shifted, I couldn't move. Everything about the moment was sinful, a filthy reminder just how desperate the man could make me.

Then I heard the distinct sound of his belt being unfastened. I didn't have the energy to look as I tried to catch my breath.

Seconds later, he ripped my shorts and panties all the way off, wasting no time before jerking me up, forcing me to straddle his legs. His expression primal and his smile laced with a hint of evil, he rubbed his hands under my shirt, sliding it along with his fingers over my shoulders, yanking and pitching the unwanted material.

"Mmm… I could feast on you for days. This is what I want every day I come home from work."

"Me entirely naked?" I purred as I brushed the tip of my index finger down the side of his neck.

"Yes. Naked and ready to suck my cock. After that, I'll slide inside that wet little pussy of yours." His tone gravelly, he rubbed his hands up from my waist, taking his time and shifting his palms back and forth across my fully erect nipples.

The sensations were powerful, a wave of excitement and anticipation coursing through me. I closed my eyes, tipping my head and enjoying the pulse of electricity as his cock throbbed against my legs.

"You know I'm not a good man," he whispered, as if he was sharing a secret.

"I know."

"But you crave me anyway."

I dragged my tongue across my lips, uncertain he wanted the answer.

But I gave him one anyway.

"Yes. More than anything."

"Mmm... That's good since you're never getting away from me." When he pinched my nipples, an eruption of pain twisted together with the delicious wave of pleasure, the combination leaving me breathless.

"I..." I dug my fingers into his shoulders, arching my back as he twisted and plucked both until they were over-sensitized. He was even more controlling, taking what he wanted, his dominating actions only adding gasoline to the fire burning deep within.

I managed to lift my head, taking rapid breaths as I shifted back and forth across his legs, slickening his skin.

After lowering his head, he shifted his hands until he cupped both breasts, allowing his heated breath to cascade from one side to the other. All the while he kept his gaze locked on me, his eyes like liquid pools, able to pull me into a magical place.

He swirled his tongue around my bruised nipple before pulling the tender tissue into his mouth, taking his time to lick and suck.

"My God..." I whispered, no longer able to focus. Everything was a huge blur, the rough and tumble sounds of the ocean just as ragged as the timbre of his animalistic growls. He'd never been this hungry, his muscles tense, hard as a rock.

Within seconds, he shifted to my other nipple, the roughness of his tongue sending a concentrated bolt of electricity to the tips of my toes.

I crawled my fingers down his chest, scooting just enough I was able to wrap my hand around the top of his cock, fingering his sensitive slit.

"Be careful teasing me."

"Or what?" I murmured. The way his shaft throbbed in my hand created even more need. I twisted my fingers, creating enough friction, his body stiffened even more.

Another growl was his only answer as he licked and sucked, biting down hard enough I threw my head back and screamed.

He couldn't seem to maintain control any longer. A smile crossing his face, he gripped my hips, lifting and holding me in the air. "Do you need to ask?" As he brought me down, impaling my pussy with the entire length of his cock, I realized I'd never felt so alive, free of the straitjacket I'd kept myself in.

"Yes. Yes. Yes." I couldn't stop my ragged moans, my pulse skipping. The feel of having him inside of me, pushing my muscles until they accepted the thick invasion was incredible. Lightheaded, I couldn't stop shaking.

"What do you want, Bristol?"

I laughed as I tried to focus. "Fuck me. Just don't stop."

"So tight. So damn wet." Houston lifted me again until the tip was just inside, keeping me above him for several seconds then yanking me down.

I was breathless, clinging to him as the rush of heat and fire continued to build. Everything around me was spinning, pushing me to the point of absolute bliss.

He refused to stop, repeating his actions, fucking me long and hard. My pussy clamped and released, pulling him in even deeper. I was so close to coming, my heart hammering against my chest creating a series of vibrations as well as echoes in my ears.

"I can't... I'm going to..." Unable to form any words, I lolled my head, my entire body shuddering as a climax pounded into my system. "Yes. Yes. Yes. Yes!"

His roars matched my strangled moans, his actions even more brutal. The sound of skin slapping against skin was so sweet, lingering in my ears.

"Come again for me. Slicken my cock," he commanded, continuing to pump me up and down like a wild man.

There was no way to hold back, no ability to disobey. As the giant wave splashed over me, I noticed the first bolt of lightning far out to sea. The dazzling colors crisscrossed the sky like a beautiful work of art.

"Oh. Oh!"

He held me in place as my body continued to shake. Only when I lowered my head until our lips were mere centimeters apart did he make another demand.

"Ride me, baby."

As I bucked against him, I darted my tongue across the seam of his mouth, enjoying the taste of bourbon, the hint of my wine. The flavors were a powerful aphrodisiac, pushing my desire to the limits as I squeezed my legs against his.

I kissed his lips, brushing them back and forth, slipping my tongue just inside his hot, wet mouth. For a few precious minutes, we were as one. For some crazy reason, another single tear slipped past my lashes. My heart ached for him; for the dreams he'd never been allowed to have and for the passion he was just beginning to understand.

Easing back, I took several shallow breaths, purposely clamping then releasing my muscles.

He rubbed his hands up and down my back, a barbaric smile remaining on his face. I could tell he was close to coming, his body shaking more than before.

"So bad," he managed, his breath skipping, and his eyelids now half closed. "You will soon learn just how much so."

"Uh-huh."

As his face became pinched, he fisted my hair, holding me in place. His eyes dilated, he released a deep bellow, the sound reverberating around us. When his body tensed, I threw my head back, riding him like a wild stallion.

There was nothing like the sound of his roar as he erupted deep inside, filling me with his seed.

Then he issued the single word once again, sending another wave of shivers dancing down my body.

"Mine."

* * *

Pizza.

Wine.

A chilling movie.

And a passionate, sexy man.

What could be better on a stormy night?

Very few things in life surprised me any longer. After the invitation I'd received from Dark Overture, I'd thought I could never be so surprised again. However, as we relaxed on the couch, the box of half-eaten pizza on the coffee table, the scent of pepperoni and spicy tomato sauce still wafting in the air, I was more than just surprised.

I was shocked.

He'd grabbed a blanket, making certain we could huddle under the softness as we started to watch movie number two. While I hadn't paid any attention to the name, I certainly knew it was another thriller, one packed with action and bloodshed. I'd found a small weakness in Houston after all.

He stared wide-eyed at the television, his bare feet crossed and propped up on the table, slouched against the couch as if he was actually comfortable.

My legs folded, I rested against him, my hand firmly planted around my wineglass. I was happy, as strange as the thought was in my mind. While my bottom still ached from the spanking, I'd even enjoyed the hint of rekindled pain as the material of the couch scraped back and forth across my skin.

As a particularly gruesome portion flashed across the screen, I lifted my head, smiling from the way his eyes were glistening. He had a smile on his face, his expression like that of a little kid enjoying the big screen for the first time.

Yawning, I was surprised just how tired I was.

When I eased from the covers, managing to place my glass on the table, he reached for me, tugging me backward almost immediately. As I settled against him, I realized there was nothing like the warmth of his body combined with the fluffy blanket to lull me into a slight daze. I could almost envision the moment turning into something deeper.

And longer lasting.

Stop it. Just stop.

My inner voice would never allow me real peace.

I finally closed my eyes as the sound of gunfire popped from the speakers. Even though I tried to stay awake, I finally couldn't stare at the television or the bloody scenes any longer. Mmm… So good. So warm. So…

"You need to run," Houston instructed. He swung in a wide arc, his weapon firmly planted in both hands.

Pop! Pop! Pop!

The sound of gunfire came from behind. The asshole was catching up.

"Go. Go. Go!" He pushed my back, forcing me to spring into action.

I took off running, racing into the shadowed light as night began to fall. The forest was dense, the cracking of limbs beneath my feet unable to hide the hard pounding of my heart. The air was humid, sucking away my breath. Strings of perspiration slipped down both sides of my face from the exertion, but we had to keep going.

We had to get away.

"Keep going. Keep going!" he hissed.

When I no longer felt him behind me, I stopped short, gasping for air. The second I turned around, I caught the muzzle flash as he popped off three shots in a row.

"Damn it," he snarled, then bolted in my direction, grabbing my arm and yanking me into the densest portion of the forest.

"We're not going to get away," I managed, limbs smacking against my face as my feet became tangled in the dense underbrush.

"Like hell we won't."

The sound of his voice was guttural, riddled with anger.

We continued on, but I sensed the perpetrator was getting closer. God help us.

Seconds passed, maybe minutes, the only sound creaks and chirps within the forest.

Then I heard a single crack, the air suddenly turning still.

I was pulled into a vacuum as the stench of blood filled the air.

No longer able to sense his presence, I jerked to a stop, slowly turning around.

"No!"

What the... Jerking up, light rushed across my face, forcing me to wince. Too bright. Too much. I took several deep breaths, realizing my heart was racing, vivid images of what must have been a nightmare spinning through my mind. I blinked several times until I was finally able to focus.

But the ugly dream refused to go away.

As if it had been a warning.

He's going to die.

A moment of absolute panic settled in, the vision of his blood-soaked shirt remaining in the forefront of my mind.

After a few seconds, I realized I must have fallen asleep. A cold shiver snaked down the entire length of my body, the ugliness of the nightmare refusing to back down. My God. The dream had been some crazy kind of epiphany.

Whoever was threatening the family wanted revenge, but not just on Houston's father.

This was about destroying the family in any way possible.

I had to stop thinking about it. It was just a damn dream.

Very slowly I turned my head, almost able to smile at the sight of Houston in his slumber. The slight sound of his quiet snores was masked by the continued blare of the television. I stared at him for a few seconds, admiring the way strands of hair had slipped into his face. He looked serene, more so than any time before.

Wow. I couldn't believe we'd been out for hours.

Easing from the covers, I reached for the remote, ready to face the day.

Until I glanced at the screen, another chill coursing down my spine, anger bursting to the surface.

"Oh. My. God."

CHAPTER 13

Houston

Rage.

I'd felt it more times in the last few days than I had for five full years. I sat staring at the television, wide awake as the fury pushed my adrenaline into overdrive.

Is the Empire of the Powers Family Finally Crumbling or is there a New Prince Ready to Take the Helm?

"The pictures," I said absently as the red block lettering of the headline remained on the bottom of the screen, a female reporter standing in front of my father's office building. The photographs had obviously been taken by the same asshole who'd been outside the house.

The vivid images detailed both Bristol and me from checking into the hotel to leaving the club after the family dinner. Then there were the pictures taken just outside the house as well as my visit to the freaking beach. And my purchase of a weapon. Even worse were the accusations that the reporter on television came very close to making without providing a real opportunity for a lawsuit.

"My God. What is she trying to get at?" Bristol stood close to the television while I remained seated.

"From what our sources have told us, a criminal investigation has been underway for some time involving insider trading as well as the theft of intellectual property. While an investigation was confirmed by a member of the local branch of the FBI, no details were provided because of the ongoing case. However, it would appear that the family's attempt at providing new leadership had been too little, too late, stocks of Powers Enterprise plummeting."

I rubbed both sides of my face, surprised the phone hadn't already started to ring.

She turned to look at me, walking closer. "If that's the truth, you can't sign that contract, at least not until we know what you're dealing with. I need to find out who the reporter talked to. At very minimum, I might be able to secure some details. I have some contacts that I might be able to access, FBI agents who might be helpful."

As I rose to my feet, I took a deep breath. "I may take you up on that. In the meantime, the family's attorney is also the corporate attorney. He should have warned my father. But he will handle this situation now."

"Maybe he did," she said quietly. "Maybe that's why your father wanted you to sign the papers quickly."

I thought about what she was suggesting and realized it made sense. "The station was obviously tipped off by whoever is attempting to blackmail my father. While the reporter doesn't seem to know your identity, that's only a matter of time."

"Don't worry. I won't talk to anyone. However, I still think we should go through with the wedding and as soon as possible. Your father suspected a leak was coming. Whether or not his scheme to get you here is about his knowledge of possible criminal action or some truth behind the blackmail, you can't take either lightly."

Hissing, I moved toward the window just as my phone started to ring. "For what it's worth, I would never have put you in this position had I known."

"I know that, Houston, but I'm here. We made a deal. I plan on sticking to my end of it. I suggest you do the same. Whatever happens, the family will need a strong leader as well as someone who can handle the corporation. That appears to be you."

"Maybe. Maybe not." I answered the phone on the fourth ring. "Hello, Pops. I expected you to call."

A freaking Saturday. The last thing I'd wanted to do was to spend any time on this bullshit. The night before had given me a taste of a real life, one I hungered to experience. Now this.

"Do you realize I had to come in through the back door of the building? Even then, at least one of the reporters figured out what I was doing. It's a basic mob scene out there." I glared out the window, the damn vipers nothing more than ants from this height, but I knew the bloodsucking leeches would do everything in their power to continue the sensationalized story.

At least my father had managed to find some damn common sense, demanding the attorney who'd worked for him for years be present.

"Mr. Hapshire has been instructed to write a cease and desist letter to the station," my father said. Even the tone of his voice had changed, as if he'd resigned himself to going to prison. For what?

"And I'm certain your glorious attorney had advised you that up to this point, nothing that was reported in the morning news is slanderous. Or am I wrong?" I asked as I turned to face him. "Is this investigation into the company a basic lie?"

The look shared between the two men was all I needed, not only to confirm the truth but to rile me even more.

"Goddamn it. Why the fuck did you lure me here, Pops? Huh? Did you just need some kind of warm body to take over until the shit could be worked out?" When he didn't say anything, I moved closer, slamming my hands on the surface of his desk. "You need to tell me the truth. I lost my patience the second I was forced to wake up to that bullshit!"

"Calm down, Houston. This has been very disconcerting for your father."

I snapped my head in the attorney's direction, half laughing. "You calm down, Gregory. Here's the facts as I know them.

My trust fund was altered on purpose in an attempt to lure me here under false pretenses. Because you already knew about my success entirely away from the corporation, you added another bonus item to ensure I'd return by asking someone to make a call in the middle of the night warning me about your impending death. Now, if I had to guess, I'd say that *you* made the call, Gregory. Same deep inflection in your tone." I paused for a moment, noting my father didn't seem to have any reaction at all.

"You don't know what you're talking about, son," Gregory said.

"Yes, I do, and I think I'm actually hitting my stride. Because of the fact you realized that I could never work with Chase, you threw another carrot to get me to stay with your more than generous offer of attaching myself to a company that's bleeding money. However, you were very clever in adding the passage that I stay married for at least a year. Why? Did you really distrust me that much? Did you think I'd hire someone to play my wife just to get my hands on the money?"

Bile formed in my mouth from issuing the lie. That's all the Powers family was, it would seem. Liars.

"Actually, I'm sad to say but yes, son. When Chase found out about Bristol's termination and why, I allowed his suspicions to become mine. I'm sorry for that."

I took a deep breath, trying to hold in my anger. "Is there an ongoing investigation for wrongdoing?"

Another hesitation was about all I would take.

"Tell. Me."

"Yes, there is and has been for almost three months. The Feds can't find anything because there isn't any criminal activity going on." Gregory seemed so smug, so certain of what he was telling me.

"Then why the subterfuge?"

My father drummed his fingers on the desk. "I had to make certain I had someone here I could count on."

"What about Chase? He's been your lapdog for years."

"Chase is… Every concern I mentioned to you is entirely true. He's not capable of running this company in my absence. Besides, since you haven't been involved for years, the continuation of the company is possible under your helm. All of you can have a future together."

I looked from one man to the other. "You think they're not only going to arrest you, but that the charge is going to stick. Right?"

"There's always that possibility," my father half whispered. "I think the Feds are building a case that includes some damaging information from an insider."

"Are you trying to suggest that Chase is attempting to blackmail you, including sending enough evidence to the police to have them interested in filing charges?"

"No, I don't think Chase would stoop that low, but it's obvious that the person who threatened me has some kind of real information."

I thought about what Riley had told me, as well as the information he was supposed to provide. Right now, I couldn't trust anyone.

Including my father.

I wasn't ready to divulge anything. "At least I know what I'm up against. I am getting married, Pops, but I couldn't care less about the money in that trust. If you want to steal it from me, then do that. You'll have that on your conscience for the rest of your life. However," I said, stopping short and thinking about what I was about to say. "I do care about the company. Why? I have no fucking idea other than I'm aware that Riley is the sole reason you have an opportunity for a contract that could take the corporation into a lucrative future. You need that contract, just like you need to secure several others just to keep this damn corporation afloat. And there's Ashley. She doesn't deserve to have a black cloud hanging over her head for any reason. So, I'm going to play along, including attempting to help clear your name, but when this fiasco is over, our personal relationship is too. This time for good. Do you understand the terms of my deal?"

I could tell my soliloquy hit my father hard. I also realized I honestly didn't care. He'd played dirty for years. I wanted no part of that in my life.

"That's fine. You do what you need to do in your life. If you're really happy and you love Bristol, then I'm ecstatic you found someone to share your life with."

"But you have no intentions on altering either the codicil with the trust fund or the contract. Do you?"

"I advised your father that wouldn't be in his best interest."

I stared at Gregory, bursting into laughter. All of this for grandchildren? What a crock of shit. "You know what? Whatever. I've yet to make my decision regarding taking over a portion of the company, Pops. As I told you yesterday, I'll let you know when I do."

"Son. Can we talk about this?"

"I don't think there's anything left to talk about. But I do have one question for you, and I want the truth."

"What?" my father asked, his tone full of exasperation.

"Did you kill the two men you destroyed?"

This time, he didn't bother glancing in Gregory's direction. He stood, no expression on his face. "No, I did not."

"Then where the hell are they?"

He huffed, eyeing me carefully. "I don't know and I don't care. What I do know is that I'm not a murderer."

Uh-huh. I was beginning to think otherwise.

I headed for the door, unable to stomach any more bullshit. Just before I walked out, I laughed before issuing a few final words. "For what it's worth, I think you're underestimating Chase. He just needed the same thing I did for all those years. Your blessing."

* * *

Bristol

"I'm sorry you have to go through this."

The massive mirror allowed me to see Ashley's concerned reflection. She stood directly behind me, her arms folded, constantly checking over her shoulder. So far, there hadn't been any reporters tailing us. I think given the mood I was in, I'd not only break their cameras but their faces as well.

"It's okay."

"No, it's not."

I shifted as the seamstress returned to the room. The dress was just as gorgeous as I'd remembered, but I felt even more like a fraud. If I had any common sense, I would have accepted the out, leaving the city and never looking back.

There was only one reason why I didn't.

Love.

There was no sense of denying it any longer nor could I explain why I could feel so strongly, but the final reality had occurred sometime over the man licking pizza sauce off my lips the night before. My heart continued to do pitter-patters as I glared at myself in the mirror.

Ashley walked away, shaking her head, neither one of us wanting to air the dirty laundry in front of the woman helping me.

"I think we have everything. There wasn't much that had to be altered." The seamstress smiled as she finished unbuttoning the dress. "Just be careful taking it off. I'll have your dress ready for you in a couple days."

"Thank you. I appreciate you pushing this up on the schedule."

"Anything for the Powers family. They are like superstars around here."

Even Ashley turned around, her face contorted as if prepared for a fight. "What does that mean?"

The woman seemed confused. "Just that with all the money your father has provided for various businesses, including this one, as well as several charities, I think he's an incredible human being." She glanced in my direction. "I mean, I know he doesn't like to advertise how much help he's given to people, but since my sister is the owner, I know that she wouldn't have been able to keep her doors open without his help."

"You mean a loan at a high rate of interest," Ashley snarked.

"No, a gift. He gave my sister over forty thousand dollars."

"What?" Ashley laughed. "You're kidding me."

"I'm sorry. Did I say something wrong?" Her face paling, she blinked several times.

"No," Ashley breathed. "Not at all. Thank you for telling us."

The lovely lady smiled although there was confusion in her eyes. After she left the room, Ashley and I looked at each other.

"That's different," I said.

"That's amazing." Ashley half laughed. "Maybe there is some good in my father after all."

Why would a man who gave freely to others extort from anyone? None of this was making any sense. "I'm going to change."

"Then I suggest we get the hell out of here."

I finally smiled for the first time that morning. "Agreed."

I couldn't get my thoughts off Houston as I placed the dress on the hanger. Was I being foolish? Likely. But I'd made a deal and I knew the man I was marrying actually needed my help.

As I walked out into the shop, I could see Ashley frowning. "What's wrong?"

"I have a very bad feeling."

"You and me both."

"I know it's only noon, but I could use a Bloody Mary. You game?" She grinned as she turned in my direction.

"Why not? I agree with you. Things are going to get dark and ugly."

"But," she said as she walked closer, "we have to think about a wedding cake. I know the perfect baker."

"I would guess you know the perfect everything."

Ashley rolled her eyes. "Except for men."

She had no idea how much I felt the same way.

The second we made it to the corner of the street, it was as if locusts appeared from the shadows, swarming over us, tossing questions from several directions.

"How does it feel marrying into the Powers family?"

"Are you aware of the unscrupulous dealings within Powers Enterprises?"

"Is your fiancé a part of the investigation?"

"Jesus Christ," Ashley huffed. "This is getting out of hand."

I was shocked at the level of force used, the reporters pushing so close I had difficulty breathing. "We need to get the hell out of here."

"Yeah, we do. I think I know how to get us out of this." She tugged me toward the bridal shop, stopping short before returning inside.

I followed her gaze as she pulled away from me, taking a few steps, shoving her hand in front of one of the cameras. Through the crowd of people, I was able to catch a glimpse of a woman who didn't appear to be with the group of reporters. While she was still taking pictures, she was dressed far too casually.

"Bridgett. What the hell?" Ashley huffed. Then she shook her head, backing away and yanking me into the store.

"What was that?"

"Just something to piss me off. Come on." Ashley guided me to the back door, opening it slowly and darting her head into the sunlight. "We're clear. Just follow me."

Crowding close to the backs of the various stores, we crept along then she darted toward another street, bounding into a coffee shop.

We both backed further into the establishment and away from the massive window fronting the street. Even from where we stood, I could see the reporters hounding the owner of the bridal shop as she attempted to get them to leave.

"That was insane," Ashley snarled.

"Who was that woman?"

She hesitated before answering. "I'm not certain, but it looked a hell of a lot like Bridgett."

I thought about the name. "As in Chase's ex-fiancée?"

"The very one."

"Why did they break up?"

Laughing, she glanced in my direction. "Do you honestly think Chase and I have regular conversations? He lives in his big house with his fancy toys and doesn't give me the time of day. If I had to guess, I'd say she challenged the fact he wasn't spending enough time with her."

"Then she'd be angry."

"My guess is she's probably grateful she didn't fall into marrying into our fucked-up family." Gasping, she gripped my arm. "I'm sorry. That was totally inappropriate."

"Don't worry about it," I said as I watched the reporters beginning to disperse. Every nagging feeling I'd had earlier was heightened. "I love your brother; however, I'm no wallflower. I won't stand for bullshit."

"God, I knew I'd like you. We're going to order a coffee and wait this out. Then you're going to take me home. I don't think we should finish our shopping trip with the assholes trying to follow us."

"Take you home? What does that mean?"

"I think you need some wheels not only to finish your wedding planning but to find a little solace of your own. If I had to guess, I'd say we're all in for one hell of a ride."

Another bad feeling formed in the pit of my stomach, my throat tightening. Ashley was right. This was only the beginning, the nightmare about to get much worse.

Houston

I found Riley's house easily enough, although I was surprised at the modest structure he'd chosen. It would seem my stepbrother was completely down to earth, far removed from the glorious lifestyle my father as well as Chase enjoyed living.

When he opened the door, I could tell he was just as pensive as before, his mouth pinched as he darted his eyes back and forth across my face.

"I'm going to assume you weren't followed," he said as he opened the door wider.

"Not to my knowledge, although it's become painfully obvious that since the moment that I set foot in the damned city that I've been followed."

"You knew it was bound to happen. Anything having to do with the Powers Empire is big news around here."

He closed the door behind me, heading for another part of the house. As he guided me into the kitchen, I was struck by just how normal everything appeared. I'd lived in a sparkling new condo in Atlanta for only six months, yet I hadn't cooked a single meal. The furniture I'd purchased was stylish, even posh by some standards, but I'd spent little time in any other room than the bedroom.

Then I'd left it without looking back, uncertain of whether I'd end up selling the place or not. At this point, the thought of returning to the austere environment wasn't any more enjoyable than staying in San Diego.

"Nice place," I said absently.

He snorted. "Right. I'm certain you're used to living in a mansion. The place suits me. I brought what you asked for. Keep in mind that I wasn't allowed into your father and Chase's secret society, but I'm pretty certain I know the identity of the two individuals your father crushed. What I can't find is anything regarding their disappearance." He pointed toward the two fairly thick files on his kitchen table.

I moved closer, shifting through them quickly, shocked as hell as some of the information he'd provided. Not only were there details regarding the takeovers of the two companies, there was also highly detailed personal information on the two former owners. "These aren't typical records you'd secure on the internet. Did Pops have all this backup on Wallace Harlow and Broderick Young?"

Riley remained stoic for a few seconds then grinned. "I told you I have friends, including a good buddy who knows his way around every secure computer system in the business."

I couldn't help but laugh. "You're one resourceful man. I'll give you credit."

He sat down at the table, yanking one of the files closer. "You have to be in this damn family. I'll take Mr. Young. You take Harlow. Maybe we can find something your father doesn't want us to know."

At this point, I could only hope so.

We remained quiet as we searched the documentation, but Chase and his visit to see Bristol continued to piss me off. "Do you know anything about Chase?"

Sighing, he lifted his head. "What kind of things? It's obvious he and I aren't buddies and we don't run in the same circle."

"But given you work for the company, you've had to deal with him in business as well as some family gatherings. Right?"

"Unfortunately, yes. He's not that forthcoming, but as you've witnessed, he also can't keep his anger in check." Riley narrowed his eyes. "Did something happen?"

"He paid a visit to Bristol at our new home. From what I heard, he threatened her."

"He's an asshole, but I don't need to tell you that."

"Chase is a dangerous man. Don't ever think otherwise, Riley." For a few seconds, we shared a look. "I'm sorry about never getting to know you better."

While the statement seemed to surprise him, he shook his head. "Don't worry about it, Houston. We live in different worlds."

"Maybe I don't want to live in a glass house any longer."

Smirking, he shrugged. "Then don't. Follow your heart. That's the best thing you can do for yourself as well as your lovely fiancée."

His words were more profound than he had any idea of. I continued to look through Wallace Harlow's complete work history, including how he'd brought the small company into the forefront almost ten years before. Then a series of risky decisions had placed his company in harm's way, allowing my father to purchase the company for one fifth of what I would guess it was worth. No wonder the man had been pissed.

"What happened with Chase's fiancée? Did that change him in some way?"

Riley exhaled, leaning back in his chair. "I didn't honestly know Bridgett Quinlan very well. She seemed nice. From what I could tell, your father thought highly of her. She did good work for the company, at least that's what I was told, but she'd only been working there for a few months."

"Wait a minute. She worked for the company?"

"Yeah, which is what made the entire situation sticky. I don't know the details, but she worked directly for your father for a short period of time. When Chase dumped her, I heard he also fired her."

A cold chill shifted down my spine. "Bridgett Quinlan." I repeated the name as I frantically flipped through several pages, half laughing when I found the one that I was looking for. "Fuck."

"What is it?" He eased off his seat, moving over the table.

"Harlow's daughter is named Bridgett."

"The name isn't that odd."

"Yeah, but look at the name in parentheses next to her last name."

He peered over my shoulder. "Quinlan. Wait a minute. That's far too coincidental."

"Exactly." I slammed the file shut, rising to my feet.

"What are you going to do?"

"She went by her mother's maiden name for a reason. There has to be a connection since some of the information that was leaked came directly from the company's records."

"Ah, shit."

"Don't say a word yet, Riley. I need to trust you on this. Things aren't as they seem. I'm going to have a long chat with Chase. I think Bridgett Quinlan was out for revenge and if I had to guess, I think Chase had some knowledge of her intentions."

"If he did, then he's complicit."

"Let's hope the hell not, for his sake."

While Chase was my brother and supposedly blood was thicker than water, right now I was more concerned with it in the literal sense.

Including spilling his if necessary.

CHAPTER 14

ouston

Fury had wrapped itself around me like a blanket of steel, keeping my adrenaline high and my muscles constricted. I powered the rental car through the streets of San Diego, taking the highway at a high rate of speed. I no longer gave a shit Chase was my brother. If he'd knowingly allowed his ex to purposely set out to destroy my family, he would never see the light of day again.

No matter the consequences.

The bastard lived in the same house he'd purchased just before I'd left, the grandiose mansion meant for a freaking king.

Only he wasn't even close to claiming the throne.

Now within only five miles of my brother's house, I peered into the rearview mirror, daring the asshole photographer to follow me. Why the hell not? Maybe he'd get his fifteen minutes of fame when I beat the crap out of Chase.

The sound of my phone did nothing but push my anger into another level. After yanking it into my hand, I laughed. "I'm in no mood, Pops. Save your bullshit for later." I had to wonder if my father had been smart enough to make the connection of Bridgett to her father. While it was painfully obvious that she'd used her middle name, deciding not to disclose her true identity, my father and his minion attorney should have spent more time checking on Harlow's background.

"Your brother has been arrested."

The statement wasn't anything like what I would have expected. "What did you say?"

"I just got the call. Gregory is on his way, but I need you, son. Now. You have to go to the police station. This is all bullshit."

"Yeah, because someone is out to destroy the entire family." My anger was to the point I was shaking. "Where the hell is he?" There was no way to avoid adding another layer to the already scandalous situation.

As he stated the address, I was barely listening. If Bridgett was behind everything from the anonymous call to the threats made on my father, the ridiculous news report and now this? It meant she was after everyone in the entire family.

And my family included the love of my life.

"I'll see what I can do." I ended the call, taking several deep breaths then dialing Bristol. "Where are you?" I could tell she was in the car. Against my better judgment, I'd allowed her to contact Ashley. My God. I continued to put her in harm's way.

"Driving back to the house. Why?"

"Have Ashley stay with you when you get there and lock the freaking doors."

"What's going on?"

"I'll tell you when I get there." I veered off the interstate, taking an exit. I was determined to make certain both Ashley and Bristol were safe and secure.

"Ashley's not with me. She had me drop her off so I could take my time shopping. What is wrong?"

Fuck. "Just go to the house. Okay?"

"Okay, but you're scaring me."

Gunning the engine, I shifted back onto the interstate, heading in the direction of the beach. "Just get inside and lock the doors."

"Houston. Please… What the hell?"

"What's happening?" I could tell her sudden exasperation had nothing to do with our conversation.

"I don't know. The car is acting strange."

Oh, my God. "Where are you?" My heart racing, I listened as she tried to describe her location, managing to give me enough I realized where she was. "Listen to me right now. Pull over. Just get somewhere safe and wait for me. You got it?" Damn it. Her GPS had taken her over one of the mountains.

"Goddamn it, Houston. What is going on?"

"Do it!"

"Okay. I'm trying to find a place. There's a pull off."

Exhaling, I pressed down on the accelerator, shifting around several cars. "Tell me when you've managed to pull off."

"Just a quarter mile. Okay, I'm... No. No."

"What?" I demanded.

"The brakes. I don't have any brakes."

In just a few seconds, my entire world fell into an abyss. My body shaking, I took several deep breaths. "Bristol. Bristol!"

As everything fell into slow motion, the sound of her screams followed by the crush of metal pounding into my ears, I threw my head back and roared.

* * *

Sirens.

They blasted all around me, the echo far too intense. I was stunned, my mind and body functioning while my heart had all but stopped. A vacuum remained over my eyes, the haze narrowing my vision, but I pressed on. I would get to her.

I would save her.

Then I would kill everyone responsible for putting her life in danger.

Several vehicles had stopped, a crowd hovering near a smashed guardrail. But they were doing nothing. Not a goddamn thing. When I jerked to a stop, I could see the front wheels of the car were perched dangerously over the edge of the limited terrain bordering the side of the winding road.

With the back of the vehicle higher than the front, it was only a matter of time before the car would plummet to the surface floor.

I jumped out, shoving the ridiculous spectators away, cursing at the ones taking pictures. "Get away. Get the fuck out of here." While the sirens had gotten louder, indicating help was close, the single shift of her car as it lurched forward a few inches, a few rocks tumbling down the mountainside meant there was no time to waste.

As I approached the driver's door, rage continuing to pulse, the sight of her leaning forward, blood splattered on the windshield was almost too much to bear. And why hadn't the goddamn airbags gone off? The door was locked, the car still engaged in drive, the only thing keeping her from going over the edge the twisted steel from the guardrail caught under the tires.

And the creaking sounds continued.

"Bristol. Can you hear me?" I tapped on the window, then quickly realized she'd lost consciousness. I had no other choice but to break the glass. I stumbled back to the rental, struggling to get inside the truck. I nearly ripped the interior upholstery in an effort to find the freaking jack. With no time to waste, I powered back to the driver's side, saying a silent prayer as the car began to totter even more.

Help me, God. Freaking help me.

After two brutal slams of the metal bar, the window shattered.

"The car is going to go!" someone screamed.

"Mister, you got to get away. You can't save her."

Like fucking hell I couldn't. Reaching inside, I pulled her away from the steering wheel, fighting the goddamn seatbelt. Blood streamed down her face from the gash in her forehead. "Come on. Come on! Stay with me, Bristol."

She offered a single moan, her eyelids fluttering.

The car shifted forward another few inches.

I held my breath, finally yanking the belt away, pulling her into my arms. "Okay, honey. Hold on. Just hold."

The sound of tires screeching behind me, sirens blasting couldn't mask the continuous creaking sound as the vehicle shifted and pitched forward.

With one hard yank, I pulled her free, tumbling backwards onto the pavement as the car lurched forward, pitching down the mountainside. Within seconds, the loud explosion vibrated beneath my feet. I wrapped my arms around her, taking several deep breaths, closing my eyes for a few seconds as I felt her warm body against mine.

"Mmm..." Bristol whimpered, shifting in my arms.

As two fire engines and several police cars approached, the entire group of spectators clapping as if this had all been nothing more than a scene from a movie, I peered down at the beautiful woman. "I almost lost you. I love you. God, I love you."

She managed to press her hand against my chest, taking shallow breaths as she tried to smile. "I'm not... going... anywhere."

* * *

Bristol looked so damn pale, as if the shimmering light within her had been yanked away. She'd been lucky, only bumps and bruises, a slight concussion, yet the doctors wanted to keep her overnight for observation.

The damn police hadn't been helpful, although they'd seemed shocked that I'd been able to save her. At least they'd taken my statement. Unfortunately, the press had gotten wind of the accident within minutes, likely based on uploaded photographs from one of the bystanders.

I sat by her bed, holding her cold fingers in my hand, thinking about everything that had happened. With little left of the car, I knew it would be difficult to prove that anyone had tampered with the brakes, but I would bet my life on it.

Lowering my head, I couldn't get rid of the fury, my body remaining tense. It was only a matter of time until Bridgett tried again.

"Don't look so forlorn."

Hearing her voice, I chuckled as I lifted my head. "You're supposed to be resting."

"I am. I'm stuck in this bed, aren't I?" Her voice was weak, keeping me just as pissed off as before.

"Where you're going to stay put or else."

Bristol smiled. The light in her beautiful eyes had returned. "You can't boss me around."

"Wanna make a bet?"

"Not going to happen."

"Oh, I don't think we need to bet on that one, baby. I rule the house. Remember?"

She laughed, wincing after doing so. "I think the brake lines were tampered with. They were fine at first then I heard a strange sound. After that, almost nothing. I tried to stop, even attempting to pull the emergency brake."

"That's what I believe happened, but I'm not certain it can be proven. There's almost nothing left of the car, although Ashley is on her way. Maybe she has some idea of what the hell happened."

"What about your father? Is he okay?"

"At this point, although I'm not certain I care. However, Chase was arrested."

"He's really behind this?" Every breath she took was labored.

I gave her a long look before answering. "I don't believe so, but I do think he knows more than he's told anyone."

Bristol strained as she tried to sit up.

"Nope. I'll tie you to the bed if necessary."

She issued another one of her rebellious looks, which gave me another sigh of relief. "Your father isn't all you think he is."

"You don't need to tell me that."

"Listen to me. Did you know he regularly gives to charities? That he's provided cash, not a loan for several local businesses?"

I snorted, shaking my head. "Not a chance. My father is far too greedy."

Entwining her fingers with mine, she squeezed, her lovely mouth twisting. "Listen to me. I'm serious. I think he sold his assets in order to be able to do that without taking company money. Sometimes people aren't who we think they are."

Nothing could have surprised me anymore but if I knew my father, he had some nefarious reason, like being able to avoid paying taxes. "Yeah, well, that doesn't make him father of the year."

"No, but it could mean you give yourself a chance to get to know him. I'll bug you about it until you do." Her eyes were full of mischief.

"Such a freaking bad girl." I pulled her hand to my mouth, pressing my lips against her knuckles. I was never going to allow her out of my sight again.

"Your bad girl."

The sound of the door made me bristle.

"Oh, God. I am so sorry," Ashley murmured. "I'm so glad you're okay. This is my fault."

"It's not your fault, Ashley. Things happen," Bristol said, a weak smile crossing her face.

"Hell, yes, it is. I knew something was wrong after I had that work done. I should have followed my instincts."

I moved to a standing position, walking closer. "What are you talking about?"

"I had the car serviced. You know, new brakes and all the bells and whistles." Ashley looked back and forth from Bristol and into my eyes. I hadn't told her what had occurred over the phone, only that Bristol had been in an accident. "Why are you looking at me that way, Houston?"

"The brakes could have been tampered with," I growled.

Ashley slapped her hand over her mouth, tears immediately filling her eyes. "Oh, my God. It's my fault."

"Listen to me. You can't break down, not now. I need the name of the shop you used. Can you get that for me?"

"Of course. Do you have an idea who did this?"

"Maybe, but I need to have a conversation with the FBI."

"They're waiting outside." Ashley narrowed her eyes. "Did Bristol tell you about Bridgett?"

As soon as my sister mentioned the name, I hissed under my breath. "What are you talking about?"

"I think we saw her outside of the bridal shop. We were basically attacked by reporters."

I turned my head, locking eyes with Bristol. The pieces of the puzzle were falling together. "I'm going to have a conversation with the Feds. Can you stay with her?"

"Of course. What's going on? Dad called. Chase was arrested? This is getting crazy."

"Just stay with her until I return. Whatever happens, there are to be no visitors."

"Wait. Aren't you going to tell us what's going on?" Ashley asked, her tone more demanding than before.

"I'm going to end this. Take care of her, Ashley. She's very special to me." As I gave Bristol a longing look, my heart racing, I realized that I was entirely too calm.

There was something to the old adage of the calm before the storm. If the FBI didn't provide any assistance, I would take matters into my own hands. The threat on my family was finished.

* * *

Polite.

The Feds had been very polite, listening to my ideas and concerns. They'd even written notes, but I could tell by the looks on their faces that they'd already made up their minds that whatever evidence that they'd refused to share with me was enough to implicate both my father as well as Chase. If I had to guess, they really believed that my father had murdered the two men.

And so did I.

At least I'd learned the great attorney had been able to use his influence with a judge on a Saturday, allowing Chase to get out of prison late in the afternoon. Somehow, the man always got lucky.

Twilight had settled over the city, bright stars in the sky.

As I pulled into Chase's driveway, a growl formed in my throat. My father had arrived. Killing two birds with one stone was a perfect ending to this dreadful fucking day.

I'd spent a couple of hours tracking down the photographer, and although he'd initially been reluctant to talk to me, I'd been able to convince him that it was in his best interest. I'd even been kind enough to return his camera, although I had doubts that he'd be able to use it in the future. Chuckling, I would never forget the look on his face when I'd managed to corner him just outside his car.

At least I'd learned who'd hired him in the first place.

I leaned against one of the giant columns flanking the set of double mahogany front doors before ringing the bell. I half expected a maid or some other employee to open the door.

My brother had always been grandiose in everything he did.

No answer.

Interesting.

The door was unlocked. I walked inside, refusing any additional courtesies. Within seconds, I heard loud voices. My father and brother to be exact. With a smile on my face, I wandered closer, taking my time before moving into the doorway of my brother's office. The heated argument was fascinating, especially given the fact Chase had just been released from jail.

"You're not taking what belongs to me, Dad. I don't give a shit about the reasons you have. My attorney is already preparing a fight that you're not going to win," Chase hissed.

"It's my company, Chase. You have no say in who I decide to allow to run the organization. If you'd kept up your end of the deal, then none of this shit would be happening," my father challenged.

"My end?"

"You should have gone through with the goddamned marriage like I requested. That was the single thing I asked you to do."

Chase fisted his hands, moving toward my father, rage continuing to build on his face. "I didn't love her, Dad. Hell, she didn't love me. She was out for the money and you know it."

"Get out of my face, son. It was the easiest way to keep our reputation."

"Yeah, a lot of good that did. All Bridgett wanted was revenge and you knew that all along. You freaking set me up then brought in Houston, forcing him to marry someone he likely met in a damn bar."

I started clapping as I walked into the room, keeping the smile glued to my face, although my anger was at an all-time high. "Do you want to know what's funny? I actually did meet Bristol in a bar, but that was only in preparation of signing a contract with her for two million dollars to pretend we were in love. I fully intended on keeping my end of the bargain, then tossing her aside after three months of marriage. I figured what the hell. I could endure that period of time even if I hated the woman."

As my brother slowly turned in my direction, I expected glee on his face. Instead, there was a level of remorse that I wasn't used to.

"My God," my father whispered.

"It was necessary. She was perfect in every regard, including being able to advise me on the loopholes and bullshit you tried to pull on me, Pops, which of course you did." I rubbed my jaw as I swaggered closer. "A funny thing happened, something that you're probably going to enjoy teasing me about for some time to come. Not that I give a shit. I fell in love with her. But do you want to know why? Not because she's beautiful, which she is. Not even because the chemistry we share is off the charts. I fell in love because she has integrity, something this family lost a hell of a long time ago."

My father took several deep breaths, his face turning red.

What a shame.

I did so hate seeing my father disturbed.

"Anyway, I tried to get her to return home, especially since Chase already made good on his treats to discredit her. If I had to guess, I'd say you spilled more dirty laundry to Bridgett than you want to mention. Am I right? You certainly don't want our father to know just how conniving the two you were, both of you plotting to destroy him. Now, you had entirely different reasons. You want the company, Chase. All of it. Bridgett wanted to avenge her father's death and I have no doubt you had something to do with that, Pops. I guess Bridgett's frustration with you continues since I'm certain she's the person responsible for having you arrested."

"What the hell are you talking about?" Chase demanded.

"Let me continue. The fun is just getting started. Chase, I think you're the one who actually spread the information that the company stole the technology, thereby destroying any chances for the defense contract."

Chase laughed. "Why the hell would I do that?"

"Because if stocks dropped, which they did, you knew exactly how frantic our father would become. You simply didn't realize that he actually still believes in the company he built from the ground up. That's why he wanted me to take control. That's when things really got messy."

"You're fucking crazy," Chase huffed.

"Is he?" my father demanded.

Chase snarled. "Get out of my house. Both of you. This is bullshit."

"Not so fast. I do know for certain that you hired a photographer to spy on me. Fortunately, he came to his senses, but that was only after I threatened to beat the crap out of him. At that point, Bridgett was left to do the dirty work, following Bristol while she was planning our fucking wedding." Goddamn, I was pissed. Taking a few seconds, I calmed my level of anger. "Hell, I even purchased a freaking weapon. Isn't that funny? Oh, and my guess is that Pops didn't tell you that the brakes on Ashley's car were tampered with. I think Bridgett decided on her own that since she was tossed out of the money-making deal and the joy of wreaking the retaliation she'd counted on having, she decided to get revenge of her own. Sound familiar?"

Chase swallowed several times, his earlier look of arrogance no longer visible. I watched as my father shifted his gaze, horror on his face.

"Yes, our sister could have died. Instead, I almost lost my fiancée, a woman who is much better than all of us. Fortunately, I was able to save her, but that doesn't mean emotional scars won't remain. I doubt she's going to remain by my side after this fucking bullshit she's had to deal with, but I'm actually going to try because I love her. By all rights, I should allow the federal agents to haul your asses to jail. However, I don't think you intended anything to get this far, which is why you actually terminated your relationship."

Now the quiet in the room was almost deafening.

"As I said, Bristol is a better person than all of us. I'm sorry that I brought her in under false pretenses, but I'm damn glad I at least had the opportunity to meet her. She's taught me a thing or two, including that everyone has two sides. Even you, Chase."

"What do you want, son?" my father asked.

I took a deep breath, thinking about what Bristol had told me in the hospital. "Is it true that you've provided financial aid for several businesses, even given to charities, Pops?"

He seemed embarrassed at the question. "I felt it was the least I could do."

"And did you kill those men?"

"No! I told you that. I would never kill anyone. Broderick died of a goddamn heart attack two months after the deal was signed. Have I felt guilty as fuck ever since? Hell, yes. But he was a bad businessman who not only tried to recant our deal, he also spread lies about our company. So I did everything I could to crush him. As far as Bridgett's father, the old bastard took the money and left the country, leaving his wife and daughter behind. He's on some fucking tropical island sucking down drinks with a girl younger than Bridgett."

"What?" Chase demanded. "You never told me that."

"Because I didn't want Bridgett to know. She deserved better, which is why I hired her in the first place. I knew from day one who she was. I'm no fool," my father huffed. "I didn't expect she was capable of revenge. I thought that when you took interest in her that she could find happiness. I guess I was wrong."

"You wanted to buy her loyalty with the Powers money," Chase stated quietly.

"Yes. Maybe I just wanted to protect her. When all the rumors started to fly, I thought they'd go away at first."

"When they didn't, you made certain you made an alternate plan to ensure Powers Enterprises would stay afloat," I offered.

My father nodded. "I know what I did was wrong, but I felt I had no other choice. And do you really want to know why? Because Chase is in love with Bridgett."

Chase sighed, turning and walking toward the set of double doors. "I thought she was the one. Isn't that stupid?"

I shook my head. The power of greed was what had almost destroyed the company. "I'm going to make both of you an offer. This is a onetime deal. If you don't accept, then I will walk out the door and you'll never see me again. I couldn't give a shit about this company or the money. If you accept, you will make certain that every member of this family is treated as if they matter, including Riley and Charity."

As I allowed the concept to sweep through their minds, I realized that I was more at peace than I'd felt in a long time.

"After I give you the details, you'll have two minutes to give me your answer. Then I'll walk out that door."

Only moments later, I took a deep breath as I headed out of my brother's house. The air was crisp, even cool, the night beautiful.

At this point, I had only one thing on my mind.

Fighting for the woman I loved.

"Are you sure you can handle this?" I asked without bothering to look in Chase's direction. During the ride over, he'd remained completely quiet, doing little more than staring out the windshield.

Chase removed his sunglasses, shoving them into the pocket of his jacket as I killed the engine. "I think there was a part of me that knew Bridgett had a hidden agenda, although for the life of me I couldn't figure out why I felt that way. However, I should have followed my instincts. I hope at some point you'll accept my apology."

I thought about his words, and while I remained angry, it was time to allow the family to heal. "No apologies necessary." I noticed the single police car pulling to the curb outside Bridgett's house. At my request, no flashing lights had been used. While Bridgett had taken advantage of the entire family, she'd almost destroyed my brother. Still, she'd had her reasons.

"Let's get this over with." He climbed out of the car, taking a deep breath before walking toward her door. He waited until I'd flanked his side before knocking on the door.

The moment Bridgett opened the door, her face fell. "I was expecting you."

Chase took his time before answering. "A part of me needs to ask you why, but I already know the answer."

"I'm sorry, Chase." Bridgett's words were barely mumbled.

"I do have one question for you," he continued. "Did you ever give a shit about me?"

Her lower lip quivering, Bridgett glanced into my eyes before returning her attention to my brother. "More than I can tell you."

Inhaling, he shifted to his right, allowing her to see the two officers as they walked closer. I was surprised how calm she was, although there was a single tear slipping past her lashes.

"I appreciate you telling me. Good luck, Bridgett. I do hope you manage to salvage your life." Chase turned without saying anything else, immediately heading for the car.

I gave her a hard look before doing the same, easing onto the driver's seat. "Are you okay?"

"You know what?" Chase asked. "I will be. At least I've finally learned that blood is much thicker than water."

There was no doubt my brother would heal, although it would take some time. Maybe we'd find a way to act as brothers again.

As I pulled out of the driveway, my thoughts shifted to Bristol. She'd become my family. Now it was time to give her my heart.

CHAPTER 15

ristol

I stood on the deck, gazing out at the ocean, the morning light casting a shimmer across the water. Sadly, I still felt as if a black cloud was on the horizon.

Lies.

I would never forget my mother's condemnation of lies. She reminded me that while no relationship is perfect, the ones beginning with a subterfuge of any kind were destined to fail.

Perhaps she was right.

Maybe I should heed her advice.

But the truth was I'd not only fallen in love with the rugged man with eyes the color of the lightest sapphire, I'd come to like as well as respect him. Although he'd come clean to his family, that didn't mean we could continue our charade. He had his world and I had mine.

I no longer knew what to do, which wasn't like me.

In the two weeks since the accident, he'd changed even more, helping his father weed through the ugliness that had enshrouded the corporation. He'd worked tirelessly late into the night, sharing ideas for improvements as well as overseeing the possibility of new contracts. He'd asked for my advice, using my expertise to guide them into making certain global changes with their contracts.

Our passion had increased, his needs bordering on sadistic, but I could tell he'd locked a part of him away, as if fearful of getting any closer. Maybe I'd done the same thing, relying on our insane chemistry to form a more significant bond.

Right now, it was all about saving the Powers Enterprise.

While the stocks hadn't completely rebounded, they were on the way, allowing for a brighter future. Yet even though I could sense satisfaction in him from helping to save his father's legacy, he wasn't himself, as if the decisions he was forcing himself to make had wrapped around his soul.

As far as our wedding, he'd been the one to call it off, saying he'd wanted to give me more time.

In truth, he'd been right.

Maybe marriage wasn't in our best interest.

Given his father had removed all codicils regarding marriage, there was no remaining requirement. The great William Powers had even given his blessing to our engagement, as long as we were in love. Were we? I liked to think both of us felt the same way, but I was no longer certain. I remained by his side, enjoying spending time with Ashley as well as making the home, our home, something special.

But I wasn't certain about what the future would bring.

At least Bridgett had learned the truth about her father. While I could only imagine that the news had crushed her, maybe she'd find a way of healing. While somewhat surprising, Chase had remained by her side even though she was still facing criminal charges. I'd been surprised the damning evidence the Feds had was all about actions she'd taken, all discovered during their investigation. While her initial activities had been severe enough, the fact she'd convinced a mechanic to tamper with the brakes could force her to spend time in prison.

I took a deep breath as I walked through the house, smoothing down my dress. Later this morning was the beginning of a celebration, a rebirth of a portion of the company. There were no additional black clouds hanging over the Powers name.

At least for now.

I found Houston on the deck, leaning over the railing, his eyes glued to the rolling waters. He'd spent more time outdoors than I would have ever imagined, but the quiet time seemed to give him a sense of peace.

A growl slipped past his lips as he turned to face me, shaking his head as his heated gaze fell to my high heels then back to my face. "You look good enough to eat." Reaching out, he snagged my arm, dragging me against his chest.

Every time he spoke, shivers trickled down my spine. "Be careful, handsome man. We can't be late."

"I get to decide." He lowered his head, nipping my earlobe then inhaling. "You're wearing that perfume again."

"Your favorite? Yes, of course. All in an effort to tempt you."

"Well, it's working."

I pushed away, giving him a mischievous look. "You seem tense. Are you happy about this?"

"I've had to make some tough decisions. At least my father has listened to my advice, which actually surprises me."

"What's going on with Bridgett?"

Houston half smiled. "Chase hired the best attorney in the industry. Given her grief about her father, whatever time she's forced to serve will be minimal."

"I'm glad for both Chase as well as Bridgett."

"Yeah, it's funny to see my brother in love but I'm happy for him. Now, I have a question for you."

"Okay. Should I be sitting down?" I laughed, although I could see he was serious.

"If I returned to Atlanta, working my old job, do you think you'd want to return?"

I thought about his question. I'd thought seriously about returning, but I wasn't certain what I would have to look forward to. "I love it here, Houston. I'm not going to lie. The ocean. The gorgeous weather. Even the house. But I don't want to be here without you. I don't know about Atlanta. In truth, I'm still angry about what happened. I still don't know how Chase found out."

"Didn't you tell me that everyone has a price? It would appear your former boss did as well. However, they aren't the only firm in town."

"That depends on who you talk to. I'm just not sure what's best for me at this point."

Sighing, I could see a hint of sadness in his eyes. "I understand."

"Why? Are you thinking about going back?"

He took a deep breath, glancing away for a few seconds. "I have. There's no more investigation. From what I was told, the Feds officially closed it. Chase is really stepping up to the plate and doing a damn good job. At some point, maybe we'll be able to mend the rift between us. Only time will tell. He's talented and my dad seems to appreciate what he's bringing to the table. Hell, my dad had even established more permanent funding methods for the small businesses he loves so much."

"And Riley?"

"Oh, he's going to get all the acclaim he deserves in about an hour. I think he'll become the powerhouse of the company. Anyway, it was just a question. We should go."

"Why do I feel like you have something up your sleeve?" I hated the moment of tension between us. We weren't getting any closer, only further apart.

Grinning, his eyes twinkled. "Because you know me too well."

"That's what I'm afraid of."

As he brushed a strand of hair from my face, his thoughtful look returned. "You've made me very happy these last few weeks. You've also forced me to realize that there's more to life than money. That being said, I've decided to give a portion of my trust fund to my dad's favorite charity."

I slid my arms around him, tilting my head. "You really are a marshmallow inside."

"Who told you that?"

"Ashley."

"I'm going to kick her ass." He lowered his head, pressing his lips against mine. "I think we can be a few minutes late." As he captured my mouth, pulling me onto my toes, a shudder shifted down my legs.

His kisses were more passionate than anything and as he slipped his tongue past my lips, I moaned into his mouth, my body on fire. Just the feel of his fingers was enough to ignite the flames until they were white hot, searing every inch of my skin.

He ground his hips against me, causing an immediate reaction, my nipples fully aroused and my pussy aching. As he rolled his fingers down my side, I shuddered, lights flashing before my eyes. He dominated my tongue, exploring the dark recesses of my mouth as if it was for the last time.

His actions became brutal.

Unforgiving.

Demanding.

And I loved every second of it.

As he crumpled the hem of my dress, tugging it up my thighs, the light breeze wafted across my skin creating goosebumps. The second he slipped his fingers under the thin elastic of my panties, I pushed against him one last time in some crazy effort to break our connection.

He was having none of it.

Breaking the kiss, he dragged his tongue across my lips then whispered a command. "Remove your panties."

"We're going to be late."

"We have time. Do it."

His commanding tone sent another wave of shivers through me. Taking several deep breaths, I slipped my hands under my dress, sliding the thin lace down my legs, struggling to pull them away from my heels. The smile on his face was barbaric and when he swung me around, pushing me hard against the railing, I issued a series of whimpers.

"I need to remind you to be a good little girl and that you belong to me and no one else."

His words were thrilling and when I felt the first hard crack of his hand against my bottom, I lifted my head, savoring the moment as the wind wafted across my face. The scent of him was exotic, filling my nostrils until I was lightheaded.

Houston smacked me several times, moving from one side to the other, the sound of his palm slapping against my skin melodic, filling me with excitement. I couldn't stop whimpering as the stings turned into pain, electricity shooting down the back of my legs.

"Oh… So mean."

"Mmmm…" he huffed. "You will learn to obey my every command no matter what I ask."

"Yes. Sir."

The words came easily, as if I'd always belonged to him. He continued the rough spanking, taking his time to cover every inch of my bottom. Heat increased, spreading to every limb. I was breathless, barely able to let off strangled moans.

And still, he refused to stop.

I clung to the railing, my hands aching and my ass cheeks now on fire. He wanted me uncomfortable during the presentation. The dark and dangerous man wanted to ensure that my cheeks remained flushed, my blood pulsing.

"Five more. Then I fuck you."

His filthy words were even more powerful than before and as he delivered the last five, each one harder than the one before, I fell into a moment of pure euphoria. Nothing existed but the two of us. There were no worries, no fears of the unknown. Just the moment that I would remember for the rest of my life.

When the round of discipline was finished, I didn't move. I couldn't move. A series of moans bubbled to the surface as I heard him unfastening his pants and when he pushed his throbbing cock against my bruised bottom, I let out a ragged scream. Another wave of colors splashed in front of my field of vision as he kicked my legs further apart, rubbing his fingers up and down my hot, wet pussy.

"I'm hungry," he murmured then pushed the tip of his cock against my swollen folds. After sliding his cockhead just inside, he moved his hands over mine, forcing our fingers to entwine.

The hard thrust forced both of us to gasp and when he growled as he pulled out, slamming into me again, I closed my eyes.

"God, yes. So good," I managed.

"So damn tight. I could fuck you for hours."

"Then do it."

He chuckled in my ear as he pounded into me, the force shoving me against the railing. I was lost to the pleasure, uncertain what day it was or if I even cared. The way his cock filled me, my muscles expanding to accept his thick shaft was raw and wonderful. Within seconds, I was shoved into utter bliss, my entire body tingling as an orgasm surfaced, taking its time to slide up the insides of my legs before shooting into my pussy.

"Oh, yes. Oh. Oh!" The climax caught me off guard, the explosion of sensations stealing what was left of my breath.

"That's it, baby girl. Come for me. Come hard." His growl was husky, the vibrations of his voice skittering into every cell and muscle. I couldn't get enough of this man. I wanted every inch of him.

His body.

His soul.

And his heart.

As the orgasm shifted into a massive wave, catapulting over every inch, I could no longer focus or even think, the ecstasy all I'd ever wanted.

His actions became more brutal, the man fucking me long and hard, driving me onto my toes. He was so powerful, so dominating. So handsome.

I could tell he was close to coming, his breathing coming in ragged pants. After biting back another cry, I squeezed my muscles, pulling him in even deeper, the throbbing now more intense.

"Fuck. You are… Beautiful," he huffed. "And mine. Mine!"

When he threw his head back and roared, all I could do was smile.

Except that a single tear slid past my lashes, trickling down my cheek slowly.

An ugly reminder.

This wasn't real.

I'd never thought I'd be with a man like Houston, but now I couldn't imagine my life without him.

Such is life. We want the things we can't really have.

Or at least shouldn't.

We'd started with a lie.

Not a fairytale.

An indecent invitation that had sparked a fury, but the fire would always remain between us. Two lost souls who'd found each other through Dark Overture.

Maybe it was time to say goodbye.

I stood quietly in the back of the room, happy to see Riley getting the accolades Houston had mentioned. There was excitement in the air. The combined press conference was a planned event, complete with a lavish party immediately afterwards. Everyone who was anyone had been invited. The dreaded press filled the room, along with several prominent members of the military. Then there were A-list corporate moguls, a few celebrities, and several politicians. This was a full-blown effort to reestablish the Powers' reputation.

Champagne was being served by a well-dressed waitstaff in crystal flutes, canapes of caviar and salmon offered in giant silver trays. Everything was gorgeous and meant for the rich and famous.

Which didn't include me.

"Ladies and gentlemen, I'm proud to announce that the contract with Powers Enterprises has been signed. Together we'll move into the next generation, protecting our beautiful country." The general shook William's hand, grinning as several photographs were taken.

The entire audience clapped, photographers snapping picture after picture.

After William shook hands with everyone involved, he moved to the podium, glancing over at Houston. "Thank you so much. I can't tell you how pleased we are to be a part of this incredible opportunity. I wanted to take the opportunity to thank my son, Riley, for his tireless work on perfecting the chip. Without his brilliant design, none of this would be possible."

Riley seemed surprised, yet I could sense a moment of eagerness for the future.

"And I'm very happy to announce that Riley will be taking the position of vice president of Powers Enterprises. In addition, I'd like to take the opportunity to let everyone know that as of next week, this old man is retiring."

There was a combination of gasps as well as applause.

William held up his hands, grinning from ear to ear. "Don't worry. I have the right man following in my footsteps. Chase Powers will provide the leadership we need moving into the future."

I found myself shifting closer, pushing through the crowd so I could clearly see Houston. This was the decision he'd been toiling over. When he caught my gaze, he smiled then winked.

"With Houston as CFO, I think it's a good time for me to work on my golf game. Now, it's time to enjoy the party."

As the laughter and congratulations flowed, Houston walked toward me, the same grin I'd seen before on his face.

"CFO, huh?"

"Well, it suits me better than day trader. Don't you think?" he asked as he wrapped his arm around me, grabbing a glass of champagne as a waiter walked by. He lifted it, waiting for me to do the same. As we both took a sip, the same wonderful feeling remained from before.

I was tingling all over.

"Mmm… A man with a title. I think that's sexy as hell."

"Oh, you do, huh?" When he tugged my panties from his pocket, I groaned, the heat on my face increasing.

"You are so bad." I scanned the people around us, praying they didn't notice.

"Yes, I am. I needed a little good luck charm. I think they worked." The man dared to pull my panties to his face, taking a deep whiff.

I closed my eyes, shaking my head. "What am I going to do with you?"

"You have plenty of time to decide. It's time to go."

"We're not staying for the party?"

"I have more important things to tend to, like keeping you in line." He took our glasses, casually placing them on one of the tables then grabbing my hand. "Besides, we're going on a short trip."

"What? Now?"

"I have a business meeting in a couple days in Palm Springs, but I thought we could take a little time and sightsee."

"You? Sightsee? Not a chance."

As he tugged me toward the door, he gave me an even more powerful explosive look.

The man was planning on ravaging me.

As soon as he pulled me to the car, he opened the trunk, allowing me to see that he'd already packed for the two of us.

"You had this planned," I said in passing, my heart skipping several beats.

"I did."

"Why didn't you tell me?"

"Because it wouldn't have been a surprise," he huffed. "Get in. Only a couple hours and we'll be there."

"What's to see in Palm Springs?" I asked coyly as he opened the door, ushering me into the car.

Leaning over, he pressed his lips against mine, barely darting his tongue inside. "You're going to have to wait to find out. But if you aren't a good and patient girl, I have no issue pulling over somewhere and reminding you."

He laughed as he closed the door and I could swear the man was whistling as he walked around to the driver's side. What the hell did he have up his sleeve?

He ceremoniously removed his jacket, ripping off his tie and unbuttoning his shirt. When he donned his sunglasses, I could swear the man looked like a movie star.

After jumping in, he found an old rock station on the satellite radio then turned his head slowly, squeezing my leg until I shivered. "Buckle up, baby. You're going for a ride."

And a ride it was. He'd purchased not only a Mercedes for me to drive, but one powerful Charger as well. Today was all about the sportscar. As he rolled up the highway, pushing not only the limits of the hemi but the speed limits as well, I'd never seen him so joyous. It was as if the weight had been yanked off his shoulders and tossed away.

He insisted we stop for lunch at a tiny Mexican restaurant. The food was delicious, the margarita incredible.

And the man someone I could fall in love with all over again.

By the time we were within the city limits, I was relaxed, singing to whatever Bon Jovi or Whitesnake song popped up on the music selection. He took his time, showing me parts of the city, even stopping at several small shops along the way.

I was floored by his actions as well as his easygoing attitude.

The heat of the day was oppressive but as the sun began to lower, he shifted onto the highway again.

Destination unknown.

Less than twenty minutes later, he made a turn and I barely had time to notice the sign.

"What? A tram? To where?"

As he cut the engine, the same devilish smile crossed his face that I'd seen countless times before. "The sunset at the top of the mountain is beautiful. There's this perfect place that allows you to see the entire city. I haven't been there in years. I thought you'd enjoy."

"Then let's go."

I was surprised that there was no one else waiting to board the tram. It was obvious he'd already paid for the ride in advance, allowing us to breeze through to the steel car without any hesitation.

"Enjoy your ride."

The employee closed the doors, leaving just the two of us inside. I moved toward the side, taking several deep breaths. My thoughts had been all over the place, but I'd honestly convinced myself it was best to move on. The jerk of the tram as it was rolled forward made me laugh nervously. "I'm afraid of heights."

He inched closer, flanking my side. "Don't worry. It's perfectly safe."

The way he remained close as the tram started its trek up the cables, the incredible mountains coming into view within seconds was heartwarming. Yet there was a stillness to him that confused the hell out of me.

"This will only take a few minutes," he whispered as he wrapped his arms around me, holding me close.

"What a crazy thing we've shared," I finally said after a few seconds.

"Yeah, I know. I didn't know what to expect."

"Did you find what you were looking for?"

"Absolutely, and much more."

When he pulled away, I felt nothing but cold inside, trying to pretend that there wasn't a continuous ache. If only this could be the perfect ending to a fairytale.

"I need to say something to you," he said quietly, tugging me around to face him. "What we've shared has been amazing."

"But?"

Chuckling, he took my hand into his, my left hand, rolling his finger around the gorgeous diamond he'd given me at the start of the adventure. "But…" He allowed the single word to trail off as he slowly removed the ring from my finger.

A rush of emotions crowded into my mind and heart and almost instantly tears slipped past my lashes. I could barely watch as he shoved the ring into his pocket.

"But what?" I struggled to say, no longer able to look him in the eyes. He knew this couldn't last. Neither one of us were fools. We'd entered into a fake relationship under false pretenses. That didn't make for a happy relationship on any level. There would always be questions.

There would likely always be lies.

"But…" he repeated before dropping to his knees.

"What are you doing?"

"You are so damn hardheaded," he huffed as he pulled a tiny black velvet box from his other pocket. He pulled my hand closer, running his fingers across my knuckles. "I've been a fool but that stops here. I'm not letting you out of my life, Bristol Winters. You are everything I've ever wanted, and I can't imagine spending a day without you by my side. The other ring wasn't about love. This one is."

As he opened the box, my entire body trembled. "I don't..."

"I wanted to do this right. Will you do the honor of becoming my wife?"

A flash of images rolled into my mind from the day we met. The quaint jazz bar. The plane ride. The horrible dinner.

And the fact he'd saved my life.

"Yes. Yes!" There was no other answer. There was no other choice.

I was desperately and madly in love with him.

The moment he slid the ring on my finger, the rush of emotions was almost too much to take. He stood, staring into my eyes, his twinkling from the gorgeous sunlight shimmering in through the bank of windows.

"I love you, Bristol. I think I have from the moment I laid eyes on you."

The tram swayed as it arrived at its destination, but I wasn't certain I gave a shit about the majestic view.

All I cared about was the man who held me in his arms.

"I can't believe you did this," I whispered.

"Mmm... I'm not finished."

Pulling away, I pressed my hand against his chest. "What have you done?"

"Do you trust me?"

I cocked my head, brushing the tip of my finger down the side of his chiseled face. "With my life."

"Remember that," he said, growling in such a deep tone that I shuddered to my core.

He took both my hands, pulling me toward the door, the same damn rebellious smile on his face. After disembarking, he eased his arm around my waist, walking us up a set of stairs.

There was no way to describe seeing his entire family waiting on the platform. The area had been decorated in ribbons and flowers, the wind tickling through them. There was even the sound of bells, the beautiful ring floating toward the heavens.

"What is this?" I managed, looking from his father's face to Ashley's. She was beaming, tears already streaming down her face.

"This is our wedding, my lovely bride to be."

"How did you manage?"

"I have my ways," Houston laughed as we walked closer.

Ashley held out her hand. "Come with me."

"Go." Houston pushed me forward.

As his family gathered around, I was struck by how close they seemed to be, their words of love and congratulations not what I would have expected.

But then again, my soon to be husband had managed to save a corporation.

Why not the entire family?

Ashley led me to a sparse restroom, the ugliness of the steel stalls and concrete floor actually making me smile.

When she held out my dress, the one I'd purchased as part of the ruse, I had no idea what to say.

"You deserve to have a special day," she said in such a revered whisper I almost burst into tears.

"You are amazing."

"Nah. I'm just a Powers girl. A friend of mine allowed me to believe in love. I thought I'd return the gesture." She winked, her smile remaining.

As she helped me into the dress, taking her time to make certain every button was in place, the small train fluffed and in position, all I could do was smile.

When she was finished fixing my makeup and hair, adding a small spray of flowers on top of my head, she squeezed my arms.

"Someday, you're going to have to tell me the real story."

I glanced into the cracked mirror, studying our combined reflection. "What story?"

"Uh-huh. I know my brother too well. But you can keep pretending." Her smile genuine, she took a step away. "I have one more surprise."

The beautiful bouquet she pulled into her hands was exactly what I would have chosen.

"They're gorgeous."

Winking again, she placed them in my arms. "Just like the bride. Welcome to the family, Bristol."

Every bride envisions their wedding day.

The music.

The flowers.

The dress.

The reception.

And the man.

On this day, as I walked onto an expansive deck overlooking a lovely city, the mountains highlighted by the warm glow of the ebbing sun, I realized that dreams were not always fantasies, but could be made real.

If we allowed them.

When I took Houston's hand, gazing into his eyes, the dark clouds finally disappeared.

We'd started this wild ride with deception.

We were ending it with a promise.

And I was happy to belong to a man who I'd thought had no soul.

The End

AFTERWORD

Stormy Night Publications would like to thank you for your interest in our books.

If you liked this book (or even if you didn't), we would really appreciate you leaving a review on the site where you purchased it. Reviews provide useful feedback for us and our authors, and this feedback (both positive comments and constructive criticism) allows us to work even harder to make sure we provide the content our customers want to read.

If you would like to check out more books from Stormy Night Publications, if you want to learn more about our company, or if you would like to join our mailing list, please visit our website at:

http://www.stormynightpublications.com

BOOKS OF THE MERCILESS KINGS SERIES

King's Captive

Emily Porter saw me kill a man who betrayed my family and she helped put me behind bars. But someone with my connections doesn't stay in prison long, and she is about to learn the hard way that there is a price to pay for crossing the boss of the King dynasty. A very, very painful price…

She's going to cry for me as I blister that beautiful bottom, then she's going to scream for me as I ravage her over and over again, taking her in the most shameful ways she can imagine. But leaving her well-punished and well-used is just the beginning of what I have in store for Emily.

I'm going to make her my bride, and then I'm going to make her mine completely.

King's Hostage

When my life was threatened, Michael King didn't just take matters into his own hands.

He took me.

When he carried me off it was partly to protect me, but mostly it was because he wanted me.

I didn't choose to go with him, but it wasn't up to me. That's why I'm naked, wet, and sore in an opulent Swiss chalet with my bottom still burning from the belt of the infuriatingly sexy mafia boss who brought me here, punished me when I fought him, and then savagely made me his.

We'll return when things are safe in New Orleans, but I won't be going back to my old home.

I belong to him now, and he plans to keep me.

King's Possession

Her father had to be taught what happens when you cross a King, but that isn't why Genevieve Rossi is sore, well-used, and waiting for me to claim her in the only way I haven't already.

She's sore because she thought she could embarrass me in public without being punished.

She's well-used because after I spanked her I wanted more, and I take what I want.

She's waiting for me in my bed because she's my bride, and tonight is our wedding night.

I'm not going to be gentle with her, but when she wakes up tomorrow morning wet and blushing her cheeks won't be crimson because of the shameful things I did to her naked, quivering body.

It will be because she begged for all of them.

King's Toy

Vincenzo King thought I knew something about a man who betrayed him, but that isn't why I'm on my way to New Orleans well-used and sore with my backside still burning from his belt.

When he bared and punished me maybe it was just business, but what came after was not.

It was savage, it was shameful, and it was very, very personal.

I'm his toy now, and not the kind you keep in its box on the shelf.

He's going to play rough with me.

He's going to get me all wet and dirty.

Then he's going to do it all again tomorrow.

King's Demands

Julieta Morales hoped to escape an unwanted marriage, but the moment she got into my car her fate was sealed. She will have a husband, but it won't be the cartel boss her father chose for her.

It will be me.

But I'm not the kind of man who takes his bride gently amid rose petals on her wedding night. She'll learn to satisfy her King's demands with her bottom burning and her hair held in my fist.

She'll promise obedience when she speaks her vows, but she'll be mastered long before then.

BOOKS OF THE MAFIA MASTERS SERIES

His as Payment

Caroline Hargrove thinks she is mine because her father owed me a debt, but that isn't why she is sitting in my car beside me with her bottom sore inside and out. She's wet, well-used, and coming with me whether she likes it or not because I decided I want her, and I take what I want.

As a senator's daughter, she probably thought no man would dare lay a hand on her, let alone spank her thoroughly and then claim her beautiful body in the most shameful ways possible.

She was wrong. Very, very wrong. She's going to be mastered, and I won't be gentle about it.

Taken as Collateral

Francesca Alessandro was just meant to be collateral, held captive as a warning to her father, but then she tried to fight me. She ended up sore and soaked as I taught her a lesson with my belt and then screaming with every savage climax as I taught her to obey in a much more shameful way.

She's mine now. Mine to keep. Mine to protect. Mine to use as hard and as often as I please.

Forced to Cooperate

Willow Church is not the first person who tried to put a bullet in me. She's just the first I let live. Now she will pay the price in the most shameful way imaginable. The stripes from my belt will teach her to obey, but what happens to her sore, red bottom after that will teach the real lesson.

She will be used mercilessly, over and over, and every brutal climax will remind her of the humiliating truth: she never even had a chance against me. Her body always knew its master.

Claimed as Revenge

Valencia Rivera became mine the moment her father broke the agreement he made with me. She thought she had a say in the matter, but my belt across her beautiful bottom taught her otherwise and a night spent screaming her surrender into the sheets left her in no doubt she belongs to me.

Using her hard and often will not be all it takes to tame her properly, but it will be a good start…

Made to Beg

Sierra Fox showed up at my door to ask for my protection, and I gave it to her… for a price. She belongs to me now, and I'm going to use her beautiful body as thoroughly as I please. The only thing for her to decide is how sore her cute little bottom will be when I'm through claiming her.

She came to me begging for help, but as her moans and screams grow louder with every brutal climax, we both know it won't be long before she begs me for something far more shameful.

MORE MAFIA ROMANCES BY PIPER STONE

Caught

If you're forced to come to an arrangement with someone as dangerous as Jagger Calduchi, it means he's about to take what he wants, and you'll give it to him... even if it's your body.

I got caught snooping where I didn't belong, and Jagger made me an offer I couldn't refuse. A week with him where his rules are the only rules, or his bought and paid for cops take me to jail.

He's going to punish me, train me, and master me completely. When he's used me so shamefully I blush just to think about it, maybe he'll let me go home... or maybe he'll decide to keep me.

Ruthless

Treating a mobster shot by a rival's goons isn't really my forte, but when a man is powerful enough to have a whole wing of a hospital cleared out for his protection, you do as you're told.

To make matters worse, this isn't first time I've met Giovanni Calduchi. It turns out my newest patient is the stern, sexy brute who all but dragged me back to his hotel room a couple of nights ago so he could use my body as he pleased, then showed up at my house the next day, stripped me bare, and spanked me until I was begging him to take me even more roughly and shamefully.

Now, with his enemies likely to be coming after me in order to get to him, all I can do is hope he's as good at keeping me safe as he is at keeping me blushing, sore, and thoroughly satisfied.

Dangerous

I knew Erik Chenault was dangerous the moment I saw him. Everything about him should have warned me away, from the scar on his face to the fact that mobsters call him Blade. But I was drawn like a moth to a flame, and I ended up burnt... and blushing, sore, and thoroughly used.

Now he's taken it upon himself to protect me from men like the ones we both tried to leave in our past. He's going to make me his whether I like it or not... but I think I'm going to like it.

Prey

Within moments of setting eyes on Sophia Waters, I was certain of two things. She was going to learn what happens to bad girls who cheat at cards, and I was going to be the one to teach her.

But there was one thing I didn't know as I reddened that cute little bottom and then took her long and hard and oh so shamefully: I wasn't the only one who didn't come here for a game of cards.

I came to kill a man. It turns out she came to protect him.

Nobody keeps me from my target, but I'm in no rush. Not when I'm enjoying this game of cat and mouse so much. I'll even let her catch me one day, and as she screams my name with each brutal climax she'll finally realize the truth. She was never the hunter. She was always the prey.

Given

Stephanie Michaelson was given to me, and she is mine. The sooner she learns that, the less often her cute little bottom will end up well-punished and sore as she is reminded of her place.

But even as she promises obedience with tears running down her cheeks, I know it isn't the sting of my belt that will truly tame her. It is what comes next that will leave her in no doubt she belongs to me. That part will be long, hard, and shameful... and I will make her beg for all of it.

Dangerous Stranger

I came to Spain hoping to start a new life away from dangerous men, but then I met Rafael Santiago. Now I'm not just caught up in the affairs of a mafia boss, I'm being forced into his car.

When I saw something I shouldn't have, Rafael took me captive, stripped me bare, and punished me until he felt certain I'd told him everything I knew about his organization… which was nothing at all. Then he offered me his protection in return for the right to use me as he pleases.

Now that I belong to him, his plans for me are more shameful than I could have ever imagined.

Indebted

After her father stole from me, I could have left Alessandra Toro in jail for a crime she didn't commit. But I have plans for her. A deal with the judge—the kind only a man like me can arrange—made her my captive, and she will pay her father's debt with her beautiful body.

She will try to run, of course, but it won't be the law that comes after her. It will be me.

The sting of my belt across her quivering bare bottom will teach Alessandra the price of defiance, but it is the far more shameful penance that follows which will truly tame her.

Taken

When Winter O'Brien was given to me, she thought she had a say in the matter. She was wrong.

She is my bride. Mine to claim, mine to punish, and mine to use as shamefully as I please. The sting of my belt on her bare bottom will teach her to obey, but obedience is just the beginning.

I will demand so much more.

Bratva's Captive

I told Chloe Kingstrom that getting close to me would be dangerous, and she should keep her distance. The moment she disobeyed and followed me into that bar, she became mine.

Now my enemies are after her, but it's not what they would do to her she should worry about.

It's what I'm going to do to her.

My belt across her bare backside will teach her obedience, but what comes after will be different.

She's going to blush, beg, and scream with every climax as she's ravaged more thoroughly than she can imagine. Then I'm going to flip her over and claim her in an even more shameful way.

If she's a good girl, I might even let her enjoy it.

BOOKS OF THE CLUB DARKNESS SERIES

Bent to His Will

Even the most powerful men in the world know better than to cross me, but Autumn Sutherland thought she could spy on me in my own club and get away with it. Now she must be punished.

She tried to expose me, so she will be exposed. Bare, bound, and helplessly on display, she'll beg for mercy as my strap lashes her quivering bottom and my crop leaves its burning welts on her most intimate spots. Then she'll scream my name as she takes every inch of me, long and hard.

When I am done with her, she won't just be sore and shamefully broken. She will be mine.

Broken by His Hand

Sophia Russo tried to keep away from me, but just thinking about what I would do to her left her panties drenched. She tried to hide it, but I didn't let her. I tore those soaked panties off, spanked her bare little bottom until she had no doubt who owns her, and then took her long and hard.

She begged and screamed as she came for me over and over, but she didn't learn her lesson…

She didn't just come back for more. She thought she could disobey me and get away with it.

This time I'm not just going to punish her. I'm going to break her.

Bound by His Command

Willow danced for the rich and powerful at the world's most exclusive club… until tonight.

Tonight I told her she belongs to me now, and no other man will touch her again.

Tonight I ripped her soaked panties from her beautiful body and taught her to obey with my belt.

Tonight I took her as mine, and I won't be giving her up.

BOOKS OF THE DANGEROUS BUSINESS SERIES

Persuasion

Her father stole something from the mob and they hired me to get it back, but that's not the real reason Giliana Worthington is locked naked in a cage with her bottom well-used and sore.

I brought her here so I could take my time punishing her, mastering her, and ravaging her helpless, quivering body over and over again as she screams and moans and begs for more.

I didn't take her as a hostage. I took her because she is mine.

Bad Men

I thought I could run away from the marriage the mafia arranged for me, but I ended up held prisoner in a foreign country by someone far more dangerous than the man I tried to escape.

Then Jack and Diego came for me.

They didn't ask if I wanted to be theirs. They just took me.

I ran, but they caught me, stripped me bare, and punished me in the most shameful way possible.

Now they're going to share me, and they're not going to be gentle about it.

BOOKS OF THE MONTANA BAD BOYS SERIES

Hawk

He's a big, angry Marine, and I'm going to be sore when he's done with me.

Hawk Travers is not a man to be trifled with. I learned that lesson in the hardest way possible, first with a painful, humiliating public spanking and then much more shamefully in private.

She came looking for trouble. She got a taste of my belt instead.

Bryce Myers pushed me too far and she ended up with her bottom welted. But as satisfying as it is to hear this feisty little reporter scream my name as I put her in her place, I get the feeling she isn't going to stop snooping around no matter how well-used and sore I leave her cute backside.

She's gotten herself in way over her head, but she's mine now, and I protect what's mine.

Scorpion

He didn't ask if I like it rough. It wasn't up to me.

I thought I could get away with pissing off a big, tough Marine. I ended up with my face planted in the sheets, my burning bottom raised high, and my hair held tightly in his fist as he took me long and hard and taught me the kind of shameful lesson only a man like Scorpion could teach.

She was begging for a taste of my belt. She got much more than that.

Getting so tipsy she thought she could be sassy with me in my own bar earned Caroline a spanking, but it was trying to make off with my truck that sealed the deal. She'll feel my belt across her bare backside, then she'll scream my name as she takes every single inch of me.

This naughty girl needs to be put in her place, and I'm going to enjoy every moment of it.

Mustang

I tried to tell him how to run his ranch. Then he took off his belt.

When I heard a rumor about his ranch, I confronted Mustang about it. I thought I could go toe to toe with the big, tough former Marine, but I ended up blushing, sore, and very thoroughly used.

I told her it was going to hurt. I meant it.

Danni Brexton is a hot little number with a sharp tongue and a chip on her shoulder. She's the kind of trouble that needs to be ridden hard and put away wet, but only after a taste of my belt.

It will take more than just a firm hand and a burning bottom to tame this sassy spitfire, but I plan to keep her safe, sound, and screaming my name in bed whether she likes it or not. By the time I'm through with her, there won't be a shadow of a doubt in her mind that she belongs to me.

Nash

When he caught me on his property, he didn't call the police. He just took off his belt.

Nash caught me breaking into his shed while on the run from the mob, and when he demanded answers and obedience I gave him neither. Then he took off his belt and taught me in the most shameful way possible what happens to naughty girls who play games with a big, rough Marine.

She's mine to protect. That doesn't mean I'm going to be gentle with her.

Michelle doesn't just need a place to hide out. She needs a man who will bare her bottom and spank her until she is sore and sobbing whenever she puts herself at risk with reckless defiance, then shove her face into the sheets and make her scream his name with every savage climax.

She'll get all of that from me, and much, much more.

Austin

I offered this brute a ride. I ended up the one being ridden.

The first time I saw Austin, he was hitchhiking. I stopped to give him a lift, but I didn't end up taking this big, rough former Marine wherever he was heading. He was far too busy taking me.

She thought she was in charge. Then I took off my belt.

When Francesca Montgomery pulled up beside me, I didn't know who she was, but I knew what she needed and I gave it to her. Long, hard, and thoroughly, until she was screaming my name as she climaxed over and over with her quivering bare bottom still sporting the marks from my belt.

But someone wants to hurt her, and when someone tries to hurt what's mine, I take it personally.

BOOKS OF THE ALPHA BEASTS SERIES

King's Mate

Her scent drew me to her, but something deeper and more powerful told me she was mine. Something that would not be denied. Something that demanded I claim her then and there.

I took her the way a beast takes his mate. Roughly. Savagely. Without mercy or remorse.

She will run, and when she does she will be punished, but it is not me that she fears. Every quivering, desperate climax reminds her that her body knows its master, and that terrifies her.

She knows I am not a gentle king, and she will scream for me as she learns her place.

Beast's Claim

Raven is not one of my kind, but the moment I caught her scent I knew she belonged to me.

She is my mate, and when I claim her it will not be gentle. She can fight me, but her pleas for mercy as she is punished will soon give way to screams of climax as she is mounted and rutted.

By the time I am finished with her, the evidence of her body's surrender will be mingled with my seed as it drips down her bare thighs. But she will be more than just sore and utterly spent.

She will be mine.

Alpha's Mate

I didn't ask Nicolina to be my mate. It was not up to her. An alpha takes what belongs to him.

She will plead for mercy as she is bared and punished for daring to run from me, but her screams as she is claimed and rutted will be those of helpless climax as her body surrenders to its master.

She is mine, and I'm going to make sure she knows it.

MORE STORMY NIGHT BOOKS BY PIPER STONE

Claimed by the Beasts

Though she has done her best to run from it, Scarlet Dumane cannot escape what is in store for her. She has known for years that she is destined to belong not just to one savage beast, but to three, and now the time has come for her to be claimed. Soon her mates will own every inch of her beautiful body, and she will be shared and used as roughly and as often as they please.

Scarlet hid from the disturbing truth about herself, her family, and her town for as long as she could, but now her grandmother's death has finally brought her back home to the bayous of Louisiana and at last she must face her fate, no matter how shameful and terrifying.

She will be a queen, but her mates will be her masters, and defiance will be thoroughly punished. Yet even when she is stripped bare and spanked until she is sobbing, her need for them only grows, and every blush, moan, and quivering climax binds her to them more tightly. But with enemies lurking in the shadows, can she trust her mates to protect her from both man and beast?

Millionaire Daddy

Dominick Asbury is not just a handsome millionaire whose deep voice makes Jenna's tummy flutter whenever they are together, nor is he merely the first man bold enough to strip her bare and spank her hard and thoroughly whenever she has been naughty. He is much more than that.

He is her daddy.

He is the one who punishes her when she's been a bad girl, and he is the one who takes her in his arms afterwards and brings her to one climax after another until she is utterly spent and satisfied.

But something shady is going on behind the scenes at Dominick's company, and when Jenna draws the wrong conclusion from a poorly written article about him and creates an embarrassing public scene, will she end up not only costing them both their jobs but losing her daddy as well?

Conquering Their Mate

For years the Cenzans have cast a menacing eye on Earth, but it still came as a shock to be captured, stripped bare, and claimed as a mate by their leader and his most trusted warriors.

It infuriates me to be punished for the slightest defiance and forced to submit to these alien brutes, but as I'm led naked through the corridors of their ship, my well-punished bare bottom and my helpless arousal both fully on display, I cannot help wondering how long it will be until I'm kneeling at the feet of my mates and begging them take me as shamefully as they please.

Captured and Kept

Since her career was knocked off track in retaliation for her efforts to expose a sinister plot by high-ranking government officials, reporter Danielle Carver has been stuck writing puff pieces in a small town in Oregon. Desperate for a serious story, she sets out to investigate the rumors she's been hearing about mysterious men living in the mountains nearby. But when she secretly follows them back to their remote cabin, the ruggedly handsome beasts don't take kindly to her snooping around, and Dani soon finds herself stripped bare for a painful, humiliating spanking.

Their rough dominance arouses her deeply, and before long she is blushing crimson as they take turns using her beautiful body as thoroughly and shamefully as they please. But when Dani uncovers the true reason for their presence in the area, will more than just her career be at risk?

Taming His Brat

It's been years since Cooper Dawson left her small Texas hometown, but after her stubborn defiance gets her fired from two jobs in a row, she knows something definitely needs to change. What she doesn't expect, however, is for her sharp tongue and arrogant attitude to land her over the knee of a stern, ruggedly sexy cowboy for a painful, embarrassing, and very public spanking.

Rex Sullivan cannot deny being smitten by Cooper, and the fact that she is in desperate need of his belt across her bare backside only makes the war-hardened ex-Marine more determined to tame the beautiful, fiery redhead. It isn't long before she's screaming his name as he shows her just how hard and roughly a cowboy can ride a headstrong filly. But Rex and Cooper both have secrets, and when the demons of their past rear their ugly heads, will their romance be torn apart?

Capturing Their Mate

I thought the Cenzan invaders could never find me here, but I was wrong. Three of the alien brutes came to take me, and before I ever set foot aboard their ship I had already been stripped bare, spanked thoroughly, and claimed more shamefully then I would have ever thought possible.

They have decided that a public example must be made of me, and I will be punished and used in the most humiliating ways imaginable as a warning to anyone who might dare to defy them. But I am no ordinary breeder, and the secrets hidden in my past could change their world… or end it.

Rogue

Tracking down cyborgs is my job, but this time I'm the one being hunted. This rogue machine has spent most of his life locked up, and now that he's on the loose he has plans for me…

He isn't just going to strip me, punish me, and use me. He will take me longer and harder than any human ever could, claiming me so thoroughly that I will be left in no doubt who owns me.

No matter how shamefully I beg and plead, my body will be ravaged again and again with pleasure so intense it terrifies me to even imagine, because that is what he was built to do.

Roughneck

When I took a job on an oil rig to escape my scheming stepfather's efforts to set me up with one of his business cronies, I knew I'd be working with rugged men. What I didn't expect is to find myself bent over a desk, my cheeks soaked with tears and my bare thighs wet for a very different reason, as my well-punished bottom is thoroughly used by a stern, infuriatingly sexy roughneck.

Even though I should have known better than to get sassy with a firm-handed cowboy, let alone a tough-as-nails former Marine, there's no denying that learning the hard way was every bit as hot as it was shameful. But a sore, welted backside is just the start of his plans for me, and no matter how much I blush to admit it, I know I'm going to take everything he gives me and beg for more.

Hunting Their Mate

As far as I'm concerned, the Cenzans will always be the enemy, and there can be no peace while they remain on our planet. I planned to make them pay for invading our world, but I was hunted down and captured by two of their warriors with the help of a battle-hardened former Marine. Now I'm the one who is going to pay, as the three of them punish me, shame me, and share me.

Though the thought of a fellow human taking the side of these alien brutes enrages me, that is far from the worst of it. With every searing stroke of the strap that lands across my bare bottom, with every savage thrust as I am claimed over and over, and with every screaming climax, it is made more clear that it is my own quivering, thoroughly used body which has truly betrayed me.

Primitive

I was sent to this world to help build a new Earth, but I was shocked by what I found here. The men of this planet are not just primitive savages. They are predators, and I am now their prey...

The government lied to all of us. Not all of the creatures who hunted and captured me are aliens. Some of them were human once, specimens transformed in labs into little more than feral beasts.

I fought, but I was thrown over a shoulder and carried off. I ran, but I was caught and punished. Now they are going to claim me, share me, and use me so roughly that when the last screaming climax has been wrung from my naked, helpless body, I wonder if I'll still know my own name.

Harvest

The Centurions conquered Earth long before I was born, but they did not come for our land or our resources. They came for mates, women deemed suitable for breeding. Women like me.

Three of the alien brutes decided to claim me, and when I defied them, they made a public example of me, punishing me so thoroughly and shamefully I might never stop blushing.

But now, as my virgin body is used in every way possible, I'm not sure I want them to stop...

Torched

I work alongside firefighters, so I know how to handle musclebound roughnecks, but Blaise Tompkins is in a league of his own. The night we met, I threw a glass of wine in his face, then ended up shoved against the wall with my panties on the floor and my arousal dripping down my thighs, screaming out climax after shameful climax with my well-punished bottom still burning.

I've got a series of arsons to get to the bottom of, and finding out that the infuriatingly sexy brute who spanked me like a naughty little girl will be helping me with the investigation seemed like the last thing I needed, until somebody hurled a rock through my window in an effort to scare me away from the case. Now having a big, strong man around doesn't seem like such a bad idea...

Fertile

The men who hunt me were always brutes, but now lust makes them barely more than beasts.

When they catch me, I know what comes next.

I will fight, but my need to be bred is just as strong as theirs is to breed. When they strip me, punish me, and use me the way I'm meant to be used, my screams will be the screams of climax.

Hostage

I knew going after one of the most powerful mafia bosses in the world would be dangerous, but I didn't anticipate being dragged from my apartment already sore, sorry, and shamefully used.

My captors don't just plan to teach me a lesson and then let me go. They plan to share me, punish me, and claim me so ruthlessly I'll be screaming my submission into the sheets long before they're through with me. They took me as a hostage, but they'll keep me as theirs.

Defiled

I was born to rule, but for her sake I am banished, forced to wander the Earth among mortals. Her virgin body will pay the price for my protection, and it will be a shameful price indeed.

Stripped, punished, and ravaged over and over, she will scream with every savage climax.

She will be defiled, but before I am done with her she will beg to be mine.

Kept

On the run from corrupt men determined to silence me, I sought refuge in his cabin. I ate his food, drank his whiskey, and slept in his bed. But then the big bad bear came home and I learned the hard way that sometimes Goldilocks ends up with her cute little bottom well-used and sore.

He stripped me, spanked me, and ravaged me in the most shameful way possible, but then this rugged brute did something no one else ever has before. He made it clear he plans to keep me...

Auctioned

Twenty years ago the Malzeons saved us when we were at the brink of self-annihilation, but there was a price for their intervention. They demanded humans as servants... and as pets.

Only criminals were supposed to be offered to the aliens for their use, but when I defied Earth's government, asking questions that no one else would dare to ask, I was sold to them at auction.

I was bought by two of their most powerful commanders, rivals who nonetheless plan to share me. I am their property now, and they intend to tame me, train me, and enjoy me thoroughly.

But I have information they need, a secret guarded so zealously that discovering it cost me my freedom, and if they do not act quickly enough both of our worlds will soon be in grave danger.

Hard Ride

When I snuck into Montana Cobalt's house, I was looking for help learning to ride like him, but what I got was his belt across my bare backside. Then with tears still running down my cheeks and arousal dripping onto my thighs, the big brute taught me a much more shameful lesson.

Montana has agreed to train me, but not just for the rodeo. He's going to break me in and put me through my paces, and then he's going to show me what it means to be ridden rough and dirty.

Carnal

For centuries my kind have hidden our feral nature, our brute strength, and our carnal instincts. But this human female is my mate, and nothing will keep me from claiming and ravaging her.

She is mine to tame and protect, and if my belt doesn't teach her to obey then she'll learn in a much more shameful fashion. Either way, her surrender will be as complete as it is inevitable.

Bounty

After I went undercover to take down a mob boss and ended up betrayed, framed, and on the run, Harper Rollins tried to bring me in. But instead of collecting a bounty, she earned herself a hard spanking and then an even rougher lesson that left her cute bottom sore in a very different way.

She's not one to give up without a fight, but that's fine by me. It just means I'll have plenty more chances to welt her beautiful backside and then make her scream her surrender into the sheets.

Beast

Primitive, irresistible need compelled him to claim me, but it was more than mere instinct that drove this alien beast to punish me for my defiance and then ravage me thoroughly and savagely. Every screaming climax was a brand marking me as his, ensuring I never forget who I belong to.

He's strong enough to take what he wants from me, but that's not why I surrendered so easily as he stripped me bare, pushed me up against the wall, and made me his so roughly and shamefully.

It wasn't fear that forced me to submit. It was need.

Gladiator

Xander didn't just win me in the arena. The alien brute claimed me there too, with my punished bottom still burning and my screams of climax almost drowned out by the roar of the crowd.

Almost…

Victory earned him freedom and the right to take me as his mate, but making me truly his will mean more than just spanking me into shameful surrender and then rutting me like a wild beast. Before he carries me off as his prize, the dark truth that brought me here must be exposed at last.

Big Rig

Alexis Harding is used to telling men exactly what she thinks, but she's never had a roughneck like me as a boss before. On my rig, I make the rules and sassy little girls get stripped bare, bent over my desk, and taught their place, first with my belt and then in a much more shameful way.

She'll be sore and sorry long before I'm done with her, but the arousal glistening on her thighs reveals the truth she would rather keep hidden. She needs it rough, and that's how she'll get it.

Warriors

I knew this was a primitive planet when I landed, but nothing could have prepared me for the rough beasts who inhabit it. The sting of their prince's firm hand on my bare bottom taught me my place in his world, but it was what came after that truly demonstrated his mastery over me.

This alien brute has granted me his protection and his help with my mission, but the price was my total submission to both his shameful demands and those of his second in command as well.

But it isn't the savage way they make use of my quivering body that terrifies me the most. What leaves me trembling is the thought that I may never leave this place… because I won't want to.

Owned

With a ruthless, corrupt billionaire after me, Crockett, Dylan, and Wade are just the men I need. Rough men who know how to keep a woman safe… and how to make her scream their names.

But the Hell's Fury MC doesn't do charity work, and their help will come at a price.

A shameful price…

They aren't just going to bare me, punish me, and then do whatever they want with me.

They're going to make me beg for it.

Seized

Delaney Archer got herself mixed up with someone who crossed us, and now she's going to find out just how roughly and shamefully three bad men like us can make use of her beautiful body.

She can plead for mercy, but it won't stop us from stripping her bare and spanking her until she's sore, sobbing, and soaking wet. Our feisty little captive is going to take everything we give her, and she'll be screaming our names with every savage climax long before we're done with her.

Cruel Masters

I thought I understood the risks of going undercover to report on billionaires flaunting their power, but these men didn't send lawyers after me. They're going to deal with me themselves.

Now I'm naked aboard their private plane, my backside already burning from one of their belts, and these three infuriatingly sexy bastards have only just gotten started teaching me my place.

I'm not just going to be punished, shamed, and shared. I'm going to be mastered.

Hard Men

My father's will left his company to me, but the three roughnecks who ran it for him have other ideas. They're owed a debt and they mean to collect on it, but it's not money these brutes want.

It's me.

In return for protection from my father's enemies, I will be theirs to share. But these are hard men, and they don't just intend to punish my defiance and use me as shamefully as they please.

They plan to master me completely.

PIPER STONE LINKS

You can keep up with Piper Stone via her newsletter, her website, her Twitter account, her Facebook page, and her Goodreads profile, using the following links:

http://eepurl.com/c2QvLz

https://darkdangerousdelicious.wordpress.com/

https://twitter.com/piperstone01

https://www.facebook.com/Piper-Stone-573573166169730/

https://www.goodreads.com/author/show/15754494.Piper_Stone

Made in the USA
Columbia, SC
09 February 2022